DRUID'S STORM

AN ALICE SKYE NOVEL

TAYLOR ASTON WHITE

DARK WOLF PUBLISHING

DISCLAIMER - Written in British English including spelling and grammar.

Edited by Rayne Dowell

ACKNOWLEDGMENTS

This is for the Gazzard's, who were far from happy at not being mentioned the first time around.

Alice Skye Series

Witch's Sorrow
Druid's Storm
Rogue's Mercy
Elemental's Curse
Knight's War

Alice Skye Short Story

Witch's Bounty

This book is written in British English, including spelling and grammar.

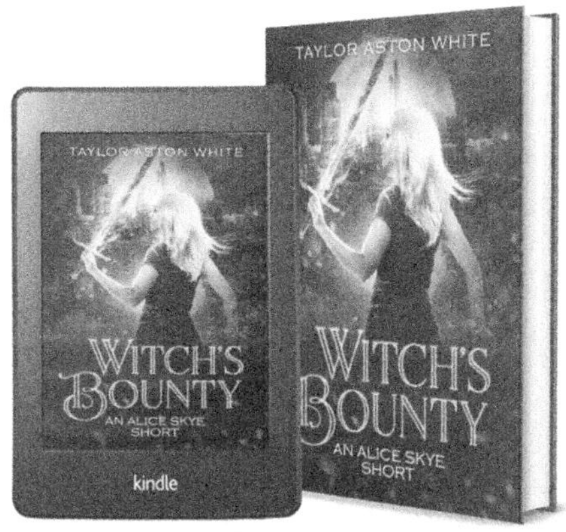
TAYLOR ASTON WHITE
WITCH'S BOUNTY
AN ALICE SKYE SHORT
kindle
TAYLOR ASTON WHITE
WITCH'S BOUNTY
AN ALICE SKYE SHORT

BOOK TWO

PROLOGUE

Dread felt like he was on trial. The box The Council made him stand in small and confined.

"So it has come to our attention…" a slight pause as Valentina, the head of The Council looked down at her notes. "Alice has come of age."

"Define 'come of age'," asked Dread, slightly anxious. He didn't get nervous, not in his thousand plus years roaming the earth. He had seen kingdoms fall, queens conquer lands and fought the Great War.

Yet, he felt nervous now.

The Council governed all Breed. It was they who made the laws, who had worked out a treaty with humans almost three centuries ago. It was they who publicly executed anyone they believed to have a difference of opinion. Dread had worked hard to keep under their radar, and had run the Supernatural Intelligence Bureau as directed, no questions asked. He'd worked even harder to keep Alice under control, to downplay her power surges as a child. He had hoped, prayed even, that her ancestry was simply an exaggeration.

How wrong he was.

The Council of Five stared, their attention on him absolute. On the left, seemingly uninterested in the situation was Xavier, his orange eyes flashing in challenge as Dread met them. His hip tilted, feet dangling off the side of his wooden throne. A slow smile crept across his thin lips, showing a row of sharp, pointy teeth as his other half, the tiger, shone through. He was very much dressed down in ripped jeans and a short- sleeved T-shirt with a bands name Dread had never heard of.

"Don't be so crass. You know exactly what we mean."

Beside Xavier sat Frederick Gallagher, one of the most powerful witches in Europe.

"Do you think her sudden power flare has gone unnoticed?" He leant forward as he spoke, his velvet green robe opening to reveal a white ruffled shirt.

"As my fellow councilman has pointed out, we know of her recent power incline. You were asked when you became her legal guardian to inform The Council when she started to show the power her heritage gifted her." Valentina pursed her lips disapprovingly. "We will do well not to allow her to succumb to the same fate as her brother."

Dread said nothing, not wanting to inform them that Kyle was believed to be alive, but missing.

The Council craved power.

The children of Dragon were power.

"This is getting –"

"– tiresome." The Fae twins sat to the far right, each sitting on an arm of their single throne. Quention and his sister Liliannia were both faeries with straight white gold hair, oversized lilac eyes and pointy ears. They were identical to the point their androgynous appearance made it exceedingly hard to tell them apart, it was only the slight curve of Liliannia's breast that gave her away. They watched Dread as if he were a bug, boring and unimportant.

"Does she even know –"

"– about her legacy?" Quention finished for his twin, their voices painfully high-pitched.

"No."

He was sure of it. She wasn't ready to understand, wasn't prepared to have that sort of responsibility.

"Do you think us fools, monsieur Grayson?" Valentina tapped her exceedingly long nails against the wooden arm, painted a blood red.

"I would never lie to The Council, Mistress."

He almost choked on the last word, a name he was forced to use out of 'respect' for the leader of his Breed.

"He's telling the truth." Mason Storm was the last member, sitting directly to Valentina's right.

He stood for the druids, completing The Council of Breeds.

"She seems to know nothing of her heritage," he said on a laugh. "Ignorant."

"Careful." Dread felt his fangs release, his eyes darkening in a warning.

"How dare you speak..."

"ENOUGH!" Valentina's voice echoed throughout the room, anger surging across her delicate features as she demanded attention.

She carefully pushed her straight black hair behind one ear, showing more of her delicate porcelain skin. Dread looked at the large ruby at her throat, not wanting to meet her dark, slitted eyes. Valentina was old, older than even him although she looked around fifteen, an undeveloped fifteen-year-old.

"You mock us."

Frederick had sat back in his seat at Valentina's outburst, a ball of pure white arcane rolling playfully through his fingers.

"It was agreed that once Alice came of age, she would be trained. I demand she immediately be turned over to my guidance."

"We had all agreed at the time, that monsieur Grayson would be the most suitable..." Valentina started.

"I did it as a favour to a friend. Not for The Council," Dread stated, watching Valentina's face tense at the blatant disregard.

"This is ridiculous." Frederick extinguished his arcane, fidgeting in his seat. "Her care should have been given to The Magicka and me. Not this vampire who hasn't even trained her in basic magic."

Dread growled, unable to stop the sound.

"I have done what is best for her, unlike you..."

"Hold your tongue," Valentina snarled, flashing her fangs. "We have not forgotten that you lied about her survival. We could have executed you on principle but decided it was better for the child to stay with you for stability."

Dread clenched his jaw. He had hidden Alice successfully for years, created a spider web of lies to keep her safe from the people who would use her for their own personal gain. Unfortunately, nothing got past The Council.

"I understand."

"Good. Now, we have been given reports that Alice is unable to control her power surges, can you confirm?" she asked, raising a dark eyebrow.

Dread wanted to hit something, his fingers crushing the edge of the wood he gripped in anger. He knew Valentina had sent a spy to work for him, knew instantly his new recruit was The Mistress' soldier and he was sure the others had sent spies too.

"She's been seeing a doctor regularly, a witch," he added before Frederick could protest, "who is helping her with control."

"You failed as her Caretaker," Xavier's deep, smoky voice said. "You need to be punished." His orange eyes flashed finally with interest, clearly the one who wanted to do the punishing.

"She should be with me," Frederick stated.

"Do you think we do not know –"

"– what you would do with her Frederick?" The twins chimed in. "It is why we decided she shouldn't be with The Magicka –"

"– until she could hold her own. We can't have you syphoning off all that power now, can we."

A chuckle as Xavier leant forward, stripes appearing then disappearing on his tanned skin as he played with his beast.

"This little witch sounds interesting." He tilted his head in a feline way. "Mason," he started, turning those unusual orange eyes towards the druid, "is it not your job to deal with Daemons?"

Mason's face flushed a deep red, his eyes hard as he adjusted his necktie.

"That situation has been dealt with."

"Your transgression almost cost us dear little Alice's life. Maybe you're the one who needs to be punished." Xavier tensed as if he was ready to pounce.

"We have called this meeting to discuss the future of Alice," Valentina said sternly, ignoring the tiger.

"Alice should be turned over to myself and The Magicka." Frederick shot to his feet aggressively. "We have the ability to train her."

"I disagree, it should be an impartial party that cannot benefit from her." Xavier smiled lazily, loving the friction he caused.

"This is just ridiculous." Frederick sat down again, his long robe floating down to rest beside him.

"We agree with the tiger." Quention settled for the twins.

"I have a suggestion." Liliannia joined in with her brother. "She should have a Warden assigned. One who should train her –"

"– in both defensive abilities as well as magic."

"Interesting." Valentina clicked her tongue. "What do you think, Commissioner?"

Dread tensed, not usually addressed with his proper title.

"If it pleases The Council then a Warden couldn't hurt."

"I will put myself forward." Mason inserted. "As a Druid, we are gifted warriors in both combat and magic."

"This is absurd," Frederick grumbled.

"This is becoming boring," Xavier dragged a claw against the wooden chair arm, leaving a long scratch. "I vote for Mason."

"A druid would be the appropriate choice considering her lineage," Liliannia added.

"I agree with my sister, we vote for Mason," Quention agreed.

"I must disagree." All eyes turned to Dread. "Councillor

Storm, you are the head of The Order, or have you forgotten? You could not possibly give Alice the attention she would need for such training."

"The Guardians then." He smirked as if he had won. "They are trained since children with discipline. It's exactly what that girl needs."

"We have voted." Valentina flicked her hand. "Councillor Storm will assign one of his Guardians as a Warden to Alice. They will be in charge of training her in the correct skills to defend herself as well as controlling her increasing power."

She quietened Frederick as he started to object.

"After an initial period, Alice will be asked to prove her skills with a test. If she shows no sign of control, she will be turned over to The Magicka. They will decide her fate." That pleased the male witch.

Dread looked over at Mason as he fought not to comment, not wanting any emotion to leak through his words. Alice was his daughter in every way but blood, and he was honoured to bring her up for his late best friend. Yet, he felt helpless as he watched the Council decide her fate.

He just hoped that one day she could forgive him.

Dawn's light woke him as a bird chirped outside the open window, the white curtain blowing gently in the breeze. Opening his eyes he stared at the ceiling, the small imperfections memorised as he checked how his pet spider was doing in the far corner.

Jumping out of bed he grabbed his clothes quickly , pulling them on methodically as he flicked his eyes to the clock above his bed, the only decoration in the stark, square room.

Ten minutes.

He began to pace, it was only a matter of time before he was due to be trained again. Due to be humiliated as the teachers beat him to a pulp.

It wasn't supposed to be this bad, his training. It was supposed to come naturally according to his father.

He was born for this.

Yet he couldn't control his beast.

So they trained him. Trained him beyond what his body could handle until his bones ached and his skin became swollen. The beast controlled him, not the other way round. His beast was better, stronger.

His spirit animal.

The other half of his soul.

Five minutes.

Letting out a puff he sat on the bed, the only piece of furniture in the room beside a clothes rack, which held three identical black outfits. There wasn't even a mirror, strange considering vanity was an asset according to the teacher. Which was crazy. The prey he was being trained to hunt, to extinguish, wouldn't care about his looks.

One minute.

He stood up, making sure his tight black shirt was wrinkle free and that his arms were folded behind his back as he waited for the bedroom door to be opened, for his training to begin.

It was only another four years, two months and twenty days before he would be back home where he belonged. Not that he was counting.

CHAPTER 1

The black, floor-length dress was modest, high in the neck but low in the back as she posed in front of the mirror. Alice knew as she walked that flashes of her legs would be seen through the almost indecent slits down each side. Not necessarily appropriate for a charity Gala, but perfect for being able to access the twin daggers strapped high on her thighs.

She hated shopping, which was why Sam was the one who went and purchased the dress specifically for the Gala.

He would make a great wife, she mused to herself.

A flash of light caught her eye, her favoured sword sitting where she left it a few months back.

According to Dread, it had been her mother's, a traditional blade passed down through the family. It was still bittersweet that she never received it from her parents, that they would never be able to see her use it. That she would never get to ask why the blade flashed with twinkly lights now every time she touched it, glowing runes that only appeared when she either stroked the steel or held the hilt. Writings she couldn't understand.

It had never happened before. Not to her at least.

Not wanting to think about it, or the man who could also make the steel glow, she faced the mirror once again, glancing at the elegant lines of the dress as she applied a dark lipstick.

Struggling with the zip she strode down the stairs into the living room, surprised to see Sam stretched out on the sofa half asleep in a way only a feline could. He let out a little sneeze, his eyes opening a slit as he appraised her outfit with a knowing smile. He really enjoyed shopping.

"Come here baby girl..." He motioned for her to stand before him, his movements lazy as he reached for the hidden side zipper. "You look delish, all those rich snobs won't know what hit them."

"You know this is a work thing," she said with a grin.

This was her first contract in months. Well, technically it wasn't a formal contract, but that couldn't ruin her mood. She was joining a team of Paladins as security for the charity 'Children of the Moon,' an organisation that helped young children who suffered from life-threatening illnesses caused by the vampira virus.

The Gala was held yearly in the Grande Hotel, a sizeable, flashy event that allowed a handful of celebrities and the local wealthy elite who used the limelight generated to showcase their own personal wealth.

"Does that mean they have cleared you from medical leave?" Sam asked as he started to play with her hair, curling it around his finger before pining it artfully into a bun.

"I've been cleared for weeks."

Her doctor had declared her healthy and strong enough to get back to work.

Dread, on the other hand, had disagreed.

She had asked daily to get back to the hunt, almost squealed in delight when he had said he needed her for that night.

"That's it, you go have fun with the uber-rich while I stay home with Mr Shorty over there," Sam sighed, stepping back to admire his work. "Bloody thing is back, almost gave me a heart attack."

"What?" She looked at him like he was crazy. "Oh, you mean Jordan?"

"Aye," he nodded towards the space beneath the stairs.

Following his gaze, she searched beside the cardboard boxes that still held some stuff they were yet to unpack. At this point, she had no idea what was in them, clearly something unimportant if they hadn't noticed anything missing.

Beside one large box stood Jordan the gnome, his fists clutched tightly around a fishing rod, face frozen into a smile. With his blue coat, green belt and red-capped hat, they had no idea know how he had ended up there. He had just appeared one day and hadn't left since.

She had tried to return Jordan to Al, his rightful owner, on numerous occasions but the happy fisherman somehow always made his way back. Whether it was sitting by the tree in the garden, hiding in a cupboard in the kitchen or lying on the bottom of the bed, the gnome never left for long. They had no idea how it moved, just knew it could when no one was watching.

They tried not to think too much about it.

"What do you think, Jordan?" She twirled for the gnome. "Don't I look sophisticated?"

Of course the gnome didn't reply, just continued to smile wide.

"That good, huh?"

"Stop playing with it, we're trying to get it to go home," Sam scolded. "If you keep acknowledging it, it might never want to leave."

"Don't be so silly. It's an inanimate object."

Just one that liked to move around on its own.

Sam snorted as he tilted his head to the side, his ear twitching.

"Your ride's here."

Sam moved towards the front door, opening it as Dread approached in a full black tux. Alice had been best friends with Sam for years, knew shifters' mannerisms well but their heightened senses still amazed her. Something she wished she had.

Not that she disliked being a witch, but being able to see in the dark and hear over great distances always seemed pretty cool, especially when she was on a contract.

Definitely could have used those skills a time or two.

Although, the whole shifting into an animal whose instinctual personality could take over seemed too much of an effort.

"Sam," greeted Dread before turning his dark gaze towards Alice. "You look appropriate."

"Wow, thanks," she replied, deadpan.

"Now, young man," Sam began in his poshest fake voice. "You will have her home by midnight?"

"Or what? She turns back into a hag?" Dread replied, his face unimpressed.

"A hag?" Alice cried. *That's bloody rude.*

"How dare you insult her," Sam responded, fighting to

keep his face stern. "I'll have you know she will turn back into a pumpkin."

Alice noticed Dread's mouth twitch, his dark eyes narrowing.

"Duly noted."

She scowled between them. "We ready to go?"

"Yes, follow me."

Dread walked towards the black BMW where a man dressed in a chauffeur's outfit stood beside an open door.

"Take a seat, and I will brief you."

Deciding not to comment on his abruptness, she slid in beside him, thanking the driver quietly as he closed the door behind her.

"Take this."

Dread handed her an earpiece, a small flesh-coloured ball that fit inside her ear. She adjusted her hair to hide it.

"It has an inbuilt microphone. Once we get to the event, it will be turned on, and you will be able to communicate both ways with Rose, Danton and a few security personnel."

"Okay."

She sat there, fidgeting with excitement.

There had been several months of hospital appointments, physiotherapy and boredom. She knew if she didn't get back to work she was going to combust. Sam had taken some time off to spend with her, for which she was grateful, but he never left her alone. While she had appreciated everything he did to help her while she was recovering, he hadn't given her any alone time to figure out what was next. Even now, she wasn't sure.

"You're squirming," Dread said, frowning. "What's wrong?"

Oh, I'm just trying to figure out what the fuck I am.

She looked away, hoping he didn't catch her internal dilemma from her expression. "It's been a while since I've been useful."

"You weren't ready," he stated, which was his usual response.

Weren't ready, my arse, she hissed inside her own head.

Dread had always taught her to get on with life, regardless of what happened, and a lot had happened. Yet he had stopped her from returning to work, wanting her to 'take time to recover.' As if sitting at home with an overbearing leopard would have helped.

"So what's the plan for tonight?"

"The plan is for you to be my plus one."

He double-checked his silver cufflinks.

"We are to clap at the appropriate moments and pretend to be interested in what everyone has to say."

"Sounds thrilling."

He turned to stare at her, his heavy eyebrows dominating his aristocratic features. His face was slightly flushed, the result of a recent feed that gave him an almost human look. It made him dangerous, even with the obsidian ovals he called eyes, ones so dark she couldn't tell where the irises started, and pupils began.

"A threat has been made against the charity patron Markus Luera, as well as some other members of the board. As a precaution Mistress Valentina has asked for some Paladins to be present."

"Valentina? As in Councilman Valentina?"

"Stay away from her Alice, she's mean and powerful. You would likely upset her."

"Upset her?" Alice questioned before she noticed his slight smile.

Upset her my arse.

"You are to pretend to be interested in the event as a guest, not security. You are to keep your eyes and ears open and communicate with the others without giving yourself away."

The car jolted as it was driven across the cobblestones, getting closer to the red carpet Alice knew would be presented.

"As much of a pain as you are with following orders you have a great eye for detail, which is why I have chosen you to act the part of a rich, charitable woman rather than staff."

Alice fought not to beam at the compliment, had to chew the inside of her cheek to stop from grinning like a maniac. She didn't usually need vocal recognition of her ability, she knew she was good. At least, good enough to have not allowed herself to be killed. But Dread didn't do compliments.

"Tell me more about this threat."

A proud smile curled Dread's lips.

"The threat was received anonymously a few days ago, no signature or prints. A typed warning stating that Mr Luera is the intended target."

"Target of what?"

"That is what we're here to figure out." A friendly voice spoke gently into her ear.

Alice felt herself smile.

"Hey, Rose."

"How come you get to be all prim and proper?"

"Just lucky, I guess."

Alice felt the car slow.

"Bonsoir, ma petite sorcière. I see we are no longer slacking, non?""

"D, nice to hear from you too. You guys found anything yet?"

Lights flashed beyond the darkened window, silhouettes moving behind the glass.

"No, the guests have only started to arrive."

"Radio silence please," Dread said as the car came to a complete stop. "Alice, remember to smile."

The red carpet was already full of tuxedos and evening gowns, paparazzi trying to syphon through the guests to the celebrities.

Walking slowly down the carpet on Dread's arm she stopped and smiled at the reporters asking him questions, her gaze sweeping across the crowd.

Faerie lights had been draped between the street-lamps, creating a fallen star's effect that was eerily beautiful against the darkness of the sky. The red carpet was a darker red than she anticipated, the fine fabric a flutter of activity from the flashes of the photographers.

Gently escaping from Dread's grasp she made her way towards the entrance of the hotel, not wanting to take attention away from anyone else.

The interior was just as beautifully decorated as the outside, a selection of large round tables having been placed around the edges of the grand room, all draped in white linen with silver candelabras. Located at the centre was a large wooden floor placed in front of a pop-up stage. A podium was set up between two display stands, displaying the Children of The Moon's logo as well as a selection of photographs.

Accepting a glass of champagne from a member of the wait staff Alice placed herself with her back against the wall, able to see the entrance as well as all the guests already walking around.

People chatted amongst themselves, ball gowns and tuxedos mingling as each person tried to compare their wealth of diamonds and expensive watches. Alice recognised a few familiar faces from television, a well-known architect as well as a famous movie actress. The Mayor of London was chatting happily to someone beside the stage, his big gut bursting at the seams of his tuxedo.

"You must be the infamous Alice Skye."

Alice spun towards the woman who spoke, her dark hair blending into the black ball gown she wore on her tiny frame.

Standing at barely five feet, Valentina looked nothing like Alice thought she would, her black boatneck dress emphasising her flawless pale skin with a fitted bodice flowing into a floor-length silk skirt. She looked almost like a child playing dress up.

"Councilman," Alice greeted, nodding her head gently.

"Dread has told me so much about you." Valentina smiled, her ruby red lips tipped at the corner. Alice fought her instincts not to step back from the predator's smile.

This woman is powerful.

"All good things I hope." Alice met her eyes, her own smile wavering as she saw the sombre depths. She thought Dread was old, but this was...

"Alice, it is time to take a seat," Dread interrupted, grasping her arm and pulling her toward a table.

"Mistress Valentina, I hope you make time for me later, we have much to discuss about your trip to London."

"Bonsoir Commissioner Grayson, I was just speaking to your Alice." Her smile was full this time, fangs peaking as white tips against her lips. "It is rude to interrupt us women, non?" A gentle laugh. "How is my youngling doing? He only has praise for you and the organisation."

"Your watchdog is doing well."

"As expected," Valentina nodded. "My Danton has been with me for centuries, I do miss him back in Paris."

Watchdog? Alice thought, sipping her champagne. *Danton's her watchdog?*

"If you trust me to do my job, then you should be able to remove your mole from my Tower." Dread forced a smile.

Valentina let out a laugh.

"Mon ami, we wouldn't have put you in such a prestigious position if we didn't trust you," she said, dark eyes narrowed.

"Alice, be careful of the Mistress," Danton spoke quietly in her ear, careful for the other vampires not to overhear. *"Do not underestimate her."*

She fought not to reply in anger, only remembering at the last minute he wasn't actually in the conversation. How long has he answered to Valentina? Where were his loyalties?

Saving the thoughts for later she did a quick sweep of the room, trying to find him amongst the staff.

"Please, take your seats," a mechanical voice asked.

"Ah." Valentina reached out to touch Alice's hand, her palm cold as she gave it a little squeeze. "It looks like we are almost ready mademoiselle, please find me later. I would love to chat more." She let go slowly, her fingertips lingering on the pulse on Alice's wrist before she wandered off towards her seat.

"Alice, we're over here." Dread guided her with a hand to her back, pulling her seat out for her when they got to their designated table.

Questions bubbled up her throat, her mouth opening to ask before she quickly closed it. It was the wrong time and place, there were too many ears. She needed to get her head back in the game, she could interrogate Dread and Danton later.

"*Something smells off,*" her earpiece rattled.

Alice tipped the champagne flute to her mouth, pretending to drink so she could reply. "What do you mean?"

"*I smell something acidic, but can't tell where it's coming from,*" Rose replied. "*I'm in the kitchen.*"

Alice thought about that for a second. Rose's nose was closer to her panther than human, could smell scents everybody else didn't even know existed.

"D?" Alice whispered quietly, making sure her head was down. "Go see if you notice anything unusual." Vampires had sensitive noses too, albeit not as good as a shifter.

The reply came swiftly.

"*Oui.*"

A waiter dressed in black slacks and a neat white shirt came up to the table, a blood red napkin draped over his right arm.

"Could I get anybody some drinks?"

"Order me a glass of the Chateau du Sang," Dread replied before anyone else could get a say in. "My companion will just have a glass of water." He quickly added before Alice could order herself. Scowling, she clutched her champagne closer.

You're working, remember. His eyes glared.

Yeah, well technically, so are you. Her own eyes replied before he turned into a conversation with the man beside him. *Fuck sake.* She savoured a small sip of her champagne, enjoying the bubbles as they burst on her taste buds.

There were only two people she could have a wordless

conversation with, have a strong enough bond to be able to read their expression. Dread had brought her up, had been her parental guardian since the death of her parents.

"Are you sure you would not like some fresh blood, sir?" The waiter asked Dread.

"Anybody holding a red napkin is available," he said as he tipped his throat, holes marking the lightly stubbled flesh.

"I would like fresh," a man opposite interrupted, his grey hair slicked back in a modern style, a complete contrast to the Victorian style suit he was wearing. His fangs were long and pearl white, a shade similar to his pale, yet withered skin.

The thing with vampires is that you couldn't really tell their age at a glance, he could be ten years undead or one hundred, his aged skin unusual amongst most Vamps. The majority of humans applied to be changed before they became thirty, the wrinkles that the vampira virus couldn't remove were fixed before his turn. From the number of wrinkles, Alice guessed he had been turned before The Change, where vampires, as well as all Breeds, hid among the humans. From the state of his skin, his life before wasn't a prosperous one.

His lady friend, on the other hand, was clearly new, her pupils dilating every time somebody came close, her tongue licking the inside of her lips. She would have been around twenty-five when she turned, as per the law stating all candidates must be in prime health and between the ages of eighteen and thirty-nine.

Before the laws, the death rate of the newly turned was around eighty per cent, the virus temperamental, which was one of the reasons why The Council created the candidate process. The second reason was an agreement with the humans back when they were negotiating Breed citizenship that vampires – who were the only Breeds that were originally human – could only be turned under a strict process. This gave the Norms a false sense of control so they didn't have to worry that they would be overrun with the living dead.

"So do you let your date order for you every time?" a male voice beside her asked.

"Excuse me?" Alice spun toward the dark-haired man. "He isn't my date," she replied before thinking. *Bollocks, yes he was.*

"Well, that's going to make flirting a hell of a lot easier." The stranger's mouth erupted into a full smile, highlighting a single dimple in his left cheek. "The name's Nate Blackwell." He held out his hand, flaring his chi in greeting.

"As in Blackwell Casino?" She felt his chi brush against hers, fuzzy in its sensation.

Blackwell Casino was one of the newer skyscrapers built in the southern district, a beast of a building that stuck out like a sore thumb against the protected Victorian structures that surrounded the expensive area.

"That's the one."

"Alice." She clasped his hand, allowing some of her own chi to reciprocate, just enough to seem polite, but not enough to encourage.

"Alice." He seemed to taste her name on his tongue. "Pretty name. Haven't seen you in these circles before."

"I don't normally get invited," she replied with a genuine smile.

"Well, I hope you get invited to many more."

"One, two. One, two." A man started to tap the microphone on the stage, testing the sound.

"Looks like it's about to start."

Alice continued to sip her champagne, ignoring the water the waiter had placed beside her.

"Then I guess I will be chatting with you a little bit later," Nate said with a wink.

"Welcome everybody to the tenth consecutive charity gala and the first for 'Children of the Moon.' If you could please put your hands together for the charity patron, Markus Luera."

The speaker on the stage clapped, stepping down as another man took his place.

Markus Luera was dressed in a tailored dark blue suit with black bow tie, his white beard was a shock compared to his jet black hair that was spiked up at every angle possible. Holding a cane against his tanned left arm he held his hand over his breast pocket, smiling to the crowd before turning towards the central table.

"Mistress Valentina, it is a pleasure you could join us."

He gracefully bowed, dipping his head before standing straight.

"It is an honour that you would grace us with your presence for a charity so close to home."

Mistress?

Alice studied Markus Luera carefully, noticed the nervous gesture of his hand as he tugged at his cane. Mistress was Valentina's title from other vampires, as a member of The Council she stood for all the Vamps, was essentially their leader, their voice. 'Mistress' was supposed to be a label of respect. Or fear. Which meant Markus Luera was a vampire, one with a tan.

Vampires don't tan.

Valentina smiled at the attention, waving elegantly from her seated position.

"Monsieur Luera, I'm interested to hear from the guest speaker, I hear he has been exceedingly generous."

"Then I will keep this short and sweet, Mistress."

He turned to address the crowd.

"Friends, I have gathered you here today to highlight the great work 'Children of the Moon' have been doing for the local children affected by their horrible inflictions. The actions of my fellow board members have helped over one hundred younglings with their life-changing conditions, building moon rooms for the children to live out their final days safely. As it stands, we are closer than ever to a cure, every donation counts towards a future where children who are born with the vampira virus will be able to live to an age where they can survive the transition."

The room was quiet, everybody listening intently as Markus passionately spoke about the condition that had affected around five per cent of children. They still didn't understand the disease, couldn't comprehend how the virus could attack a child while still in the womb of a parent who wasn't a vampire.

"As you have all paid the £10,000 entrance fee you are all greatly thanked by the children who are still going strong, and by the children who are yet to be born."

Holy shit, this cost £10,000 each?

"But my next guest has gone far and beyond to help out the children. He and his family have donated a total of one million pounds over the last year to help build a research facility here in London. Please welcome with open arms, our guest speaker, Mason Storm."

Alice choked on the final bit of champagne, the bubbles bursting in her throat as she tried to control her breathing. Eyes around the table shot to her in annoyance, sniffing and tutting in displeasure at the disruption. Dread silently handed her a napkin, his attention not wavering from the stage. Coughing into the linen, Alice watched as Mason smiled to the audience, their applause loud and over the top.

Her heart skipped a beat once she noticed the other man who joined him on stage. Anger, embarrassment, and, weirdly, excitement all flowed across her brain too fast for her to really decipher. Her emotions were chaotic as she watched Riley stand beside his father, a beautiful redhead clinging to his arm.

You have got to be shitting me.

CHAPTER 2

Alice clapped along with everyone else, her ears unable to pick up the speech Mason delivered as her senses concentrated on Riley. She didn't understand why she had this reaction to him, a man who was there when she was at her worst, someone who pretended to care and then vanished. It had been months since she last spoke to him, last saw him, last thought of him.

The man who saved her life.

She still felt the attraction, his black tuxedo blending in with the tattoos that danced across his throat every time he swallowed. She knew his eyes were grey, like a storm that his name represented, that he had a faint, barely visible scar that started high on his cheekbone and finished at the top of his upper lip, the same lips that were once electric against her own.

Yet he had still left, not giving her a reason.

Staring at him now she knew it wasn't him she missed, it was the answers he possessed. She still couldn't recall with any certainty what had happened, her memory of the night she received the Daemon's bite blurred and disjointed. She had hoped he would tell her.

Riley saw her then, his eyes flashing in surprise as his smile wavered. The redhead on his arm pushed her breasts into his arm, speaking gently into his ear as she battled for his attention. Riley responded, his mouth moving silently as he replied, but his eyes never left hers. The redhead was tall, almost as tall as Riley in her red heels and dark pink, exceedingly low cut dress.

"Alice, I think you need to come see this."

Alice blinked, welcoming the distraction from Rose. Quietly excusing herself from the table, she made her way towards the back of the room, following the waiters through a set of double doors. The kitchen was large, full of gleaming stainless steel cabinets. Chefs wearing white aprons worked frantically to prepare the five-course meal that was to be served sometime in the next few hours. A waitress leant against a wall beside the ovens, a colleague holding a white sheet against her throat as red seeped through the cloth.

"Excuse me, no guests are allowed back here." The waiter holding the cloth exclaimed as he applied more pressure. "You need to leave."

"Over here."

Danton's head poked through another door, his eyes a warning as he ushered her though.

"Please, don't," he whispered to her. "I'll explain everything."

Alice gently nodded, understanding. They had been friends since her first day as a Paladin, so she would allow him time to explain.

"We found this." D moved to stand beside Rose, her nose scrunched up as she gripped a white shirt in one fist.

Her panther prowled behind her eyes, Rose channelling her beast's instincts.

"What is it?" Alice accepted the shirt when it was held out, not understanding. "It's just a shirt." The same one all the waiters wore, including D and Rose.

"It smells acidic," Rose said, her voice deeper than usual. "We found it in the alley."

Alice couldn't smell anything.

"D, what about you?"

"It smells sweet," he shrugged. "The blood on the wrist smells the strongest, étrange."

Alice glanced at the small mark on the sleeve even as she made her way to the emergency exit. The alley behind the hotel was surprisingly nice, considering it was full of dustbins. The cobbled stones, that were the same as the front pathway, shone as if they had been polished to a high shine. Lights flooded the small area, mostly from the many windows of the guest rooms high above.

"The smell is strong back here," Rose said, her eyes flashing as she took a step forward.

"Wait." Alice held up her hand, making sure they stood by the door as Alice slowly walked forward, following the barely visible droplets of blood.

"Morte," D muttered under his breath.

"There's a body slouched against the brick."

Alice bent at the knee, making sure her dress didn't dip into the pool of blood embellishing the cobblestones, the lights from above making it look like a giant jewel glistening in the night. Rose and Danton wouldn't have been able to see the body from the door, the man hunched enough to be hidden behind the furthest bin.

"He smells acidic," Rose whispered, turning her nose away.

"He smells sweet," D frowned, crossing his arms across his chest.

"He smells dead," Alice added, recognising his uniform as a waiter from the Gala, one without a shirt. Blood stained the front of his bare chest, a sea of red wet against his skin. "It's his neck."

She turned his head, having to use some strength when his muscles resisted.

"He hasn't been dead long." He wasn't stiff enough to be in full rigor mortis. "He must have been killed just as the guests were arriving."

Alice studied the few small holes in his flesh, neat, not what she was expecting considering the amount of blood. "He was a blood donor." She released his head, cringing when it didn't immediately drop back to its original position. "He shouldn't have bled out this much."

"I'll call The Tower, we need to get someone down here," Rose said as she got out her phone.

"He's a Norm, you'll have to call the Met too," D added.

"Do you think I don't know that?"

Alice left them to bicker, not wanting to be away from the party for too long.

Slipping back into the main hall she spotted Dread standing at their table. The speeches had finished, so the guests were mingling amongst themselves as soft music filled the room from the pianist in the corner. A small crowd had appeared on the dance floor, their bodies slowly swaying.

"Commissioner..." She began politely before she felt someone jerk her shoulder.

"Alice." A hand encircled her wrist, pulling her away from the table and into the array of the dancers.

"Riley?" She tugged against him, his grip like iron.

"What are you doing here?" he asked as he pulled her toward him, clasping their hands together until he moved her into a gentle dance matching the rhythm of the piano. She allowed him to lead, not wanting to make a scene as she tried to catch Dread's attention. She didn't have time for this.

"I was invited." Well, technically, she was still a guest.

Riley narrowed his eyes, it was obvious he could not imagine how she could afford a ticket. She tried not to scowl in response.

"What is S.I. doing here?"

He controlled their dance, moving seamlessly between the other dancers. She was lucky he could lead so well, she had no idea what she was doing. His hands started to crush into her hips, his fingers finding their way up the high slits of her skirt.

"You're working, I can feel your knives."

She yanked his hands away, trying not to draw attention to herself.

"Maybe I like always to be armed." She caught a look behind his shoulder, Mason staring at them from beside the stage, his face like granite as he followed them across the dance floor. "Your dad doesn't seem impressed with our dance."

"Wouldn't take it personally, he doesn't like anyone," Riley said as Alice tried to hide her laugh, the noise escaping in a snort. "You look... good, your aura is much better than the last time I saw you."

"Yeah well, growing back most of your aura isn't a fun experience, I wouldn't recommend it," she quipped. "Not that you would know."

"Look, I haven't come here to upset you. I just need to talk..."

"You've had several months to talk. I'm not interested."

She had searched for him, wanting to know what happened with the Daemon. Yet she couldn't find him. He had left her at the hospital once her aura was stable enough and disappeared, left her to figure it all out for herself.

She turned her head away, not wanting to look at his face. Her eyes immediately wandered back to Mason, Riley's father talking to the redhead with pillow breasts. The woman abruptly turned to stare, her eyes shooting daggers as she puckered her cosmetically enhanced lips. Alice couldn't tell from this distance whether it was a permanent enhancer or just a charm.

"Well, this was a nice dance. But if you mind..."

"I'm trying to talk." He gripped her harder. "I've been assigned as your Warden."

"My what?" Rose buzzed in her ear, the noise a hum she couldn't concentrate on.

"Look, this wasn't my decision. The..."

"May I interrupt?" a voice interjected. "I would like this dance."

Riley pulled her against his chest, his arms enclosing her as he spun them away from Nate. "Fuck off Blackwell," Riley snarled, his eyes flashing silver in a warning.

"The lady clearly wants to leave. Go be with your bimbo over there." Nate nodded towards the redhead. "Didn't think you were into forcing women, Storm."

"Excuse me, gentlemen." Alice slipped beneath Riley's arm.

"Enjoy dancing together."

What the hell was a Warden? Her mood darker than before she finally made her way back to the table, her ear still buzzing as Rose and Danton argued.

"For goodness sake just call it through," Rose moaned.

"I thought that was your job?"

"Can't you see I'm a little busy here?"

"His heart stopped a few minutes ago, you can stop holding his throat now."

"Guys," Alice tried to break into their dispute. "What's happening?"

"Another waiter has died, bled out." Rose quickly replied, breathing heavily.

"We need to talk to all the staff," Danton added.

"We need to shut this thing down," she murmured to herself, reaching out for Dread. The man opposite her started to choke, the Victorian clutching his throat as he began to convulse, blood spluttering from his mouth to cover his shirt.

Alice raced towards him, catching him as he fell to the floor while his date screeched beside them.

"Help me!" she shouted at the hysterical woman as she struggled to hold his weight.

Another guest reached over to help, laying the Victorian onto the floor safely away from the table. He suddenly shouted, throwing himself forward as a fountain of black poured out of his mouth. The violent movement pushed Alice away, the black liquid barely missing her as she watched his spine twist at an impossible angle.

"What's happening?"

"Can someone call 999!"

"Alice, we have a problem," Danton said into her ear.

"Yeah, well I have a problem of my own," she muttered into the microphone, scanning the crowd for Dread. He stood with his back towards the wall, his eyes razor- sharp as he took in the chaos surrounding them. A feminine scream brought her head around, another guest convulsing as her eyes bled down her porcelain skin.

Dread began to bark orders, people running in panic as they tried to escape. Among the confusion, Alice noticed a single waiter wearing a smirk. He watched everything unfold while he held a cloth against his throat, the fabric turning a pale pink.

She caught his eye, his own flashing in panic before he turned and ran towards the back of the hotel, towards the lifts. Without thinking she followed, her dress wrapping around her legs as she ran through the crowd.

"HEY!" she shouted after him. "Fuck sake." She kicked off her heels before unclipping one of her knives. Within a few seconds she had sliced off the bottom of the dress just above her knees, leaving the remaining fabric behind as she followed the blood trail quickly up the carpeted stairs.

The hotel's décor was minimalistic, pale grey carpet with white walls and wood panelling, helpful when tracking the blood. Trailing the droplets, she walked down the hallway lined with closed doors, her back to the wall as she listened intently. She had already noted the map by the elevator, knew there was no exit this direction other than the way she had already come.

"Hey, what's happening down there?" a man asked as he opened his hotel door, his face angry as he stepped into the hall in just a towel.

"Get back into your room please, sir."

"What, you a stripper or something?" he said before he spotted her knife she still had in her hand, his face becoming ashen before he ran back into his room. She couldn't really comment, she could feel the breeze on her bare legs.

Red smeared against the wall, leading around a corner.

A woman shrieked, running past her from the direction

of one of the bedrooms. The door was ajar, showing the minimalist design flowing elegantly throughout.

The waiter was half crouched, half collapsed beside the bed, the sheets soaked through with blood as if he had tried to stem the flow.

"Are you okay?" Alice asked as she quickly checked the room for threats.

The bathroom door was open, the oversized mirror allowing her to see it was empty from her position. The room itself was large but bare, giving her confidence there wasn't anybody there other than the two of them. She sheathed the knife.

"Why did you run?" she asked as she knelt beside him, watching his eyes glass over as blood seeped from between his fingers. "Let me help you."

With a last burst of energy, he jumped to his feet. "You can't help me." He pushed past her towards the balcony. Unable to stop him in time she watched him disappear several floors below.

CHAPTER 3

The bus screeched as it pulled up at the end of the road. Alice tried to step off with as much dignity as she could muster, ignoring the open stares from the other passengers.

She looked deranged, wearing a dirty evening gown with the hem badly ripped. Her hair was no longer in its bun, the blonde strands tickling her bare neck and shoulders. She wasn't even wearing shoes, the heels having been lost in the commotion.

Dread had been forced to leave the event early, leaving Alice the option of walking home or public transport. Luckily she lived in London where night buses were a thing, although apparently that was when the weirdos liked to ride. Which proved how unstable she must have looked, as no one would sit next to her, preferring the crazy cat lady or even the man who had chatted happily to himself.

Curtains twitched, letting light leak into front gardens as the curiosity got the better of her neighbours. She's sure she'd hear about her unsocial behaviour from Mr Jenkins a few doors down as soon as dawn broke.

He had candidly introduced himself as the head of the Neighbourhood Watch, one who expected complete decorum from his street. He had almost had a heart attack when he once found Sam as a leopard sleeping in the windowsill, soaking up the sun. The fact Sam was a shifter didn't bother him, it was the fact he decided to shift in full window view to give him a wave.

It was unfortunate that clothes didn't reappear magically once shifters changed back into their human form.

Alice personally thought it was funny, but she was used to shifters aversion to clothing. They liked to touch too, their animalistic personalities finding it comforting while everybody else thought it was invasive.

Mr Jenkins liked to remind her repeatedly he had lived on the street for over fifty years, meaning he had probably known her parents. She had decided not to ask him if he remembered, it didn't matter. She had accepted their deaths, was no longer haunted by them. So she allowed him to moan at her for Sam's indecent behaviour, their loud music and her late nights. He meant no harm, just an old man who needed to fill in the loneliness since his wife passed away.

Alice stopped cautiously by her front door, her eyes scanning the darkness before settling back on the medium-sized box that was sitting in the middle of her welcome mat. Warily she approached, wishing the Neighbourhood Watch that Mr Jenkins gloated about so often actually worked.

"What's that?" a voice asked from directly behind her.

Jumping she turned, not having heard anyone sneak up behind.

"You almost gave me a heart attack!" she glared as Riley

stepped out from the darkness. "What are you doing here?" She didn't want to talk with him right now, she had a strange box to deal with.

"I thought you might have needed your shoes back?" he smirked as he held her heels on the ends of two fingers. "I also wanted to compliment you on the lovely legs."

His eyes travelled down past the poorly cut dress, his smile telling her he was messing around.

"What do you want Riley? It's late."

She glanced at the box again, wondering what it was. She wasn't a shifter, so couldn't smell its contents and she didn't know any spells that could check whether it had a curse on it or not.

She didn't have many options, one: kick it, run away and hope for the best. *I'm sure that would amuse Riley.* Or two: pour salt water over the box, ruining the curse and possibly the contents. That's if it even was cursed, which was entirely possible knowing her luck.

"We need to talk," he said as he swung her heels gently. "I'm also pretty interested in why you have something dead in a box on your doorstep?"

"Dead?" Surely he was joking.

Riley stepped forward, bending down to open the cardboard before she could stop him.

"Wait, it could be a trap..."

"What the fuck Alice?" Riley looked at her, mouth agape as the lid of the box flapped open.

"Keep your voice down," she hissed as she peeked inside.

She could barely make out the shape, her crap porch light barely illuminating the dark object. She had only just got rid of the latest ravens that had nested there. They returned every time she cleaned them out, breaking the bulbs every time. It was getting to the point that she might just let them be.

"Why do you have a severed head in a box?"

"A head?" It came out a squeak.

Unlocking her front door she ushered him through, pushing the box past the threshold with her foot. The house was dark, Sam had left for work a while earlier.

"Did you say a head?" she asked in disbelief as she turned on a light.

"You're clearly making friends," he commented as he looked around the living room, his eyes stopping on the gnome that was sitting on the sofa. "A friend who likes to send decapitated heads."

Alice didn't respond, instead looking into the cardboard box at the thick head of black hair. She didn't want to touch it but found herself needing to know who it was. Gently lifting it by the scalp she scrunched her nose, trying not to make eye contact with the pallid white eyes. The head had been neatly sliced off, the skin almost perfect other than some slight third degree burns along the edges.

"Holy shit," Alice dropped the head, cringing at the noise it made when it hit the wooden floor before rolling away.

"Who is it?" Riley picked it back up, studying the face in detail before turning to her. His nostrils flared, an eyebrow coming down as he stared.

How can he hold it so comfortably?

"No one, I don't know her," she replied too quickly, not wanting to tell him it was the Necromancer who had been finding candidates for The Becoming, the same witch that burned away her aura.

"You're lying to me."

He placed the head back in the box, folding his arms

across his chest. She had only just realised he was still in his tux, the bow tie slack against his lapels.

"Am I?" She didn't owe him anything.

She knew as soon as she recognised the head who had left her the present. Would do anything to protect him. It was why she would never tell, never want Riley to look in his direction.

She had only seen fleeting glimpses of her brother in the last few months, a shadow that wore dark jeans and black hoodies. She hadn't even told Dread, not wanting to draw attention. Her brother was broken, the slave bands that encompassed his neck and wrists bonded to him on a level she couldn't comprehend, so she couldn't tell anyone, not until she knew for sure he wasn't a danger, to himself or others.

At least, not a danger to people who didn't deserve it.

"Why are you here?" *Please fuck off.*

"We should discuss this Warden thing." His eyes flickered to the box. "And I'm still interested in the head."

"Firstly, that isn't happening," she dismissed him, turning to climb the stairs towards her bedroom. "Secondly," she shouted down from the top, "it's my head, not yours. Now thank you for my shoes, but you can leave."

She wasn't going to be forced into something she didn't want to do, especially with a man who seemed to bring the worst out in her. She could feel it even now, her chi energised as it felt his own unconsciously caress hers. Could feel her fire grow within, desperate to get out, stronger in his presence. It was as if he was a battery, her personal charging cell, a catalyst that she didn't understand.

She didn't have time for him, not when she was searching for her brother, was searching for answers to her ancestry. She didn't need a Warden, a babysitter. He would just get in the way.

She angrily stripped off the remaining fabric of her dress, tossing it on her bed as she unclipped her knives.

Bloody stupid druid.

"Alice, we need to discuss this." She heard his deep voice through her bedroom door.

"I asked you to leave."

"Look, this wasn't my choice," he said through the wood, the door rattling as if he leant against it. "I don't want to do this..."

"Of course, you don't. You have such issues that you couldn't answer my questions before you..."

The door crashed open.

"You need to calm down." His eyes were pure silver.

Fire choked her throat, could taste smoke on her tongue as sparks crackled between her fingertips.

"Alice." Her name came out a growl as his hand clamped down on her forearm, his palm warm on her skin even as the intense heat dissipated. "Calm down." Riley's tattoos gently glowed, the patterns hypnotic. "Don't tell me about issues. You know nothing."

"Exactly. You told me nothing."

She calmed her breath, flame receding as she fought it back down. She hadn't had a flare up in weeks, had thought she had it under control.

"How can you do that?"

She broke the connection, stepping back. He had syphoned her excess magic, taken it into himself. Something he had done before, but something she didn't think she needed. For weeks she had been training, practicing bringing herself to the peak of her power then back again without a flare out. Something that would have taken her a few minutes to calm down had taken him seconds.

He wiggled his fingers, his eyes slowly returning to their usual grey.

"Magic."

"What are you?" she asked, a question that had haunted her for almost as long as she had known him. She always wondered if that's why he had never come to see her, she saw more of him than he wanted to show. "You're not just simply a druid."

She would know, her father was one. Technically her brother was one too, only males inherited the genes to harness ley lines.

His eyes became guarded.

It seemed everyone had secrets, some just more interesting than others.

"Shouldn't I be asking you the same question?"

Alice started to laugh, the sound on the edge of hysteria before she noticed her reflection in the mirror.

"Why am I always naked around you?" She quickly grabbed the closest shirt, the black fabric covering enough to pass for modesty.

Riley's eyebrows shot up before his face crumbled, a smile breaking through.

Her shirt read *'I hope you like animals because I'm a BEAST in the bedroom.'* She tugged the hem down.

"It's one of Sam's," she said in its defence.

"Sure." He didn't seem to believe her. "Cute bedroom."

"It's a place to sleep."

It was her old room, the walls the same baby pink covered in glittery stars from her childhood. She had decided to leave the painting until the summer, just adding accents of creams and greys to help it resemble more of an adult's room. She couldn't think of anything worse than staying in the master, so had allowed Sam to have it.

"Why are you even here?" she asked.

"You invited me."

The fuck I did.

"I vividly remember asking you to leave."

She was getting tired, knew there were only a few hours left before she had to be at The Tower. She had wanted to speak to him months ago, now she couldn't get him to leave.

He ignored her, instead wandering across to her chest of drawers where he picked up a trophy she'd won when she was five before his eyes settled on a photograph.

"Your family?" he asked as he handed it to her.

"Yes." She stroked the glass of the frame before putting it down.

"You look like your mum."

"Why does my dad not have as many tattoos as you?" she said, a lump in her throat.

That had always confused her, she had initially recognised what Riley was from those runes tattooed onto his skin, her father having had similar around his wrists. Yet she had never seen another druid with as many as Riley. She knew they held spells, but wasn't sure exactly what.

"You have something against tattoos now?" He crossed his arms, leaning back against the doorjamb. "That your brother?" His eyes moved back to the photograph.

She nodded, not adding anything further.

"You've never mentioned him."

She didn't say anything, instead her eyes traced the photograph.

"I don't have any siblings genetically, but I have a group of friends who I consider my brothers."

Alice looked at him then, surprised he told her something so personal. He had always been business, prioritising his job as a Guardian for The Order over everything else. Not that she had any idea what that was as, unsurprisingly, he never explained. The only fact she knew were what she was told as a child, that it was an organisation strictly of druids.

"We trained at school together," he continued.

"School?" she echoed. "I could never see you as a schoolboy." No, she could only ever imagine him as he was now. Never a defenceless child.

"It's our childhood that defines us."

"Maybe," she quietly said, undecided whether she agreed or not. "Why are you telling me this?"

"I don't know." He seemed confused himself. "But you need my help..."

He stopped her when she began to interrupt.

"The Council have decided you need to be trained in both self-defence and magic."

"Why a Warden? Why you?"

Why couldn't it be anyone else?

"I don't need any help." She moved into the hallway, forcing Riley to follow her back down the stairs.

"I don't know why me. I was told, not asked."

"So you're The Council's puppet?" Alice said as she played with a flame along her fingertips.

She felt her anger renewing, needed something to help control it. She had never had problems with her temper before.

"Leave."

She began to open the front door, Riley's palm slamming it closed.

"You really aggravate me sometimes, Alice. Stop cutting off your nose to spite your face."

"I'm not." She wasn't. Was she?

"The Council can go fuck themselves. I have no interest in their petty politics."

He watched the flame carefully, his jaw clenched as he towered above her.

"You're an adult, a fucking Guardian. You could have said no."

She extinguished the blue sparks with a light pop, instantly missing the small heat.

"There aren't many people who can do what I do."

"I don't need any help," she repeated, the words sounding less convincing even to herself.

"Really? What was that earlier then?"

He stepped impossibly closer, crowding her against the wood.

"Why do I feel it when you're about to lose control. It's like this intense heat against my chi." He lifted his hand, almost as if he was physically feeling her aura.

"I know what I'm doing."

She didn't want him to touch her, her pulse erratic in his presence. It was overwhelming, especially as she fought for the control she desperately argued she had. She was tired of it, tired of men having an overpowering effect on her. It made her reactions feel forced, unnatural, as they were with Rex.

"Sure you do sweetheart."

"I need you to leave."

Riley tensed as Alice stood her ground, his jaw tight as he looked down his nose at her. This was all her patience had left.

"We're not finished."

"Tonight we are."

Riley growled, his breath close enough to brush her face.

"Stop being a brat. You need my help whether you want it or not. I'm not going to let you combust because of your bloody stubbornness."

Riley let go of the door, allowing her to open it a sliver.

The winter air tangled with her shirt, the coldness separating them, allowing her a second to calm down.

"I guess I will be seeing you around."

She stared at the door, not wanting to know his expression. She didn't want to ask for help but understood she needed it.

It wasn't really Riley she was furious at, it was everything else. The feeling that her life wasn't in her control, that she was helpless in the hands of the universe that laughed at her tragedies.

She refused to fail.

Her eyes landed on the cardboard box that was still where Riley had left it, wondering why Jordan the gnome was curiously peeking inside.

When life gives you lemons.

You squeeze them in the bastard's eyes.

CHAPTER 4

Alice exited the lift on the forty-second floor of the Supernatural Intelligence Bureau – also known to the locals as The Tower. The usual drab grey cubicles were a welcoming sight as she made her way to the space she had occupied for the last five years.

She broke into a grin at all the cards and notes welcoming her back, enough to hide the cat-themed knick-knacks she kept on her desk. An unopened bakery box had been left beside her computer, Alice's smile changing to a smirk once she saw the note scrawled on the inside.

'About time you got your lazy arse back.'

From the handwriting, she knew it was Rose.

"Oh, I didn't realise you were back," Michael sneered as he wandered over. "I heard you were still hospitalised."

Alice plastered on a fake smile, hiding her grimace from the coffee stench Michael always seemed to emit. It was like he bathed in it, or used it as fuel. She couldn't stand Michael since she had trained with him at the academy. She wasn't sure why, but had decided long ago it must simply be a character flaw that he was such an arsehole.

"Nice to see you too, Mickey," she said, smiling at his scowl. "How has it been?"

"Oh, you know, the usual. Don't worry though, I've taken up your slack," he said in an ostentatiously pompous tone. He flicked his head back, moving his shoulder-length ginger hair away from his eyes.

She had always thought it was a beautiful colour, but would never tell him that to his face.

"Been working with the big guys recently. There's a lot of change comin' you know." He sniggered, flicking at his hair again. "Ya betta watch out."

"Hey Michael," a squeaky voice said from behind them. "Your latest assignment has landed on your desk. Oh, doughnuts."

Barbara, Dread's assistant, grabbed a jam filled doughnut from the bakery box, biting into it aggressively.

"Don't mind if I do."

"Help yourself."

Alice quickly closed the lid on the box, saving them for later before Barbara – also known as Barbie due to the likeness to the doll, could devour anymore. Alice smiled, waiting patiently for Barbie to finish the treat, which included sucking her fingers clean of the excess sugar.

It had only been a few months since Alice last saw her, but Barbie seemed to have aged, her nickname not as apparent. The once platinum blonde hair had darkened a few shades, especially at the roots and the baby pink nails that were usually well- manicured were chipped, partially bitten. Even her charm, the magically infused necklace that helped to hide her wrinkles seemed to be expiring, her wrinkles blurry but visible against her unusually pale complexion.

"Nice to see you Barbara." Mickey grinned, winking at her blush. "I guess I'll be speaking to you girls later."

"Hope you enjoyed your holiday Alice, it's been so stressful around here recently," Barbie said once Mickey moved back to his own desk, her eyes following his departure for longer than necessary.

"It wasn't a holiday," Alice sighed, shaking her head. "I was on medical leave."

Barbie continued as if Alice hadn't spoken.

"It's been a nightmare," she whispered, her attention becoming distracted with Michael before returning to Alice. "New rules are being implemented, and The Council keep making surprise visits." She seemed flustered at just explaining.

Maybe that's why she looked so unkempt.

"The Council have decided they want a more hands-on approach with the organisation."

Barb opened the box of doughnuts back up, selecting an iced one before closing the lid again.

"It's become unbearable. Those council suits keep commenting on my job. Bloody bastards if you ask me..." Her eyes darted to Alice, shocked at her own comment. "Please don't tell Commissioner Grayson I said that."

Alice just smiled. "Is there anything I can help you with?" *Like more doughnuts?* "I need to get to work."

"Oh." Barbie brushed the crumbs from her fingers onto the floor. "The Commissioner wants to see you."

"Dread?" Alice frowned. She had only just got there, surely he couldn't find an excuse to check on her already?

"Oh Alice, you really should call him Commissioner. It makes you look tacky and unprofessional when you call him by his forename," Barbie said with an absent wave of her hand. "It's called work etiquette."

Alice was about to reply with a snarky comment but kept it back. It was a habit Alice couldn't break, she had always called him his given name since she was a child. Their relationship wasn't known in The Tower, Dread never mentioning it and neither did Alice. It kept accusations of favouritism to a minimum, not that he ever gave her an easy time because of his parental guardian status. Probably the opposite.

"Thanks, Barb, I'll keep that in mind." Alice grabbed her satchel, tossing the strap over her shoulder as she made her way to the back of the floor.

"Alice, welcome back."

Dread's office was dark, the window that hid one of the most beautiful views of London hidden beneath a specialised blackout blind. He seemed to reflect his mood with the blind, wanting to sit in the dark when he was angry or indifferent. The majority of the time the blind was down.

"Take a seat."

Alice sat down heavily , a frown pinching her eyebrows.

"What's this about? I spoke to you yesterday."

"I have your assignment, I wanted to hand it over personally."

"Why?" she asked, apprehensive. Dread didn't hand out contracts personally. The last assignment he administered directly ended with her being hospitalised.

It wasn't a good omen.

"Fine, I wanted to talk to you before you return to active duty."

He studied her, his gaze creating a chill on the back of her neck. He was angry, but she wasn't sure why.

"I want to make it clear that it wasn't me who signed off on your return. I still don't believe you're ready..."

"How can you not think I'm ready?" She surged onto her feet, Dread's eyes eerily following her outburst. "I have done..."

He didn't give her the chance to finish. "We haven't discussed your recovery."

"I'm healed, what else is there to discuss?"

"You haven't spoken to anybody about it, not even Samion. That's unhealthy, you might be suffering from PTSD..."

"I'm not, and I'm fine."

She truly was. She no longer gave it much thought, had gone past it almost instantly. It wasn't the actual incident that frustrated her, it was who had put her in that position in the first place. She no longer thought of him anymore either, not wanting to waste competent brain cells. Besides, it wasn't like she hadn't suffered accidents while at work before. She had been bitten on numerous occasions by both Vamps and shifters, nearly sliced in half by an irate leprechaun and now almost sacrificed by a Daemon.

"Alice, I'm not going to give you a choice." Dread scowled as his eyes turned dark with impatience. "If you will not discuss it with either myself or Sam, you will talk to your doctor. Otherwise, I will remove your Paladin status."

"You can't do that!" *Fuck. He can do that.*

She watched the warning flash across his face, knew he wasn't messing around. Biting the inside of her cheek she sat back down, tapping his desk with her fingertips.

"I don't want to go back to the doctor."

She had been forced to go weekly for months to become a lab rat.

She had agreed at first, just as interested in what her

power could do. It was what kept her up at night, her magic and ancestry an enigma she wanted to understand. She knew nothing of her heritage, had hoped learning about her magic would bring her a step closer to knowing.

But not at the expense of herself, her sanity. Because they weren't helping her, forcing her to do test after test while explaining nothing. She figured out pretty quickly they were only interested in the effects her fire could create, as if she was a weapon they were figuring out how to harness. So instead of reacting, she had kept calm, controlled her chi, much to the frustration of the doctors. Then she stopped going entirely.

She hadn't had a flare up in weeks.

Until Riley.

"Alice, listen to me. It is paramount you keep going. We don't have a choice."

"*We* don't have a choice?" Alice felt irritation flicker.

"Please." That one word broke her. Dread didn't beg. "Keep attending until I say so."

Alice thought about it for a moment.

"It's The Council, isn't it?"

Dread smiled, a slight tug at his lip.

"You were always an observant child. Yes, it's why you have been assigned a Warden. The Council have decided your power flares are unpredictable. They do not like unpredictable."

"Do they know why?" She had never told Dread the names she had been called, wanting to figure them out on her own. Dragon. War. Now she wondered if he actually knew all along, as The Council seemed to.

Dread took a moment to reply, the vein in his forehead pulsating.

"They suspect you're a descendant of one of the Elemental families, a Draco to be exact."

"And what do you think?" she quietly asked, her heart in her throat.

"I think that I have kept that information secret for as long as I could, for your own safety."

Alice closed her eyes, taking a second.

"You shouldn't have kept these sort of secrets from me." Her voice was hoarse when she spoke, her lips trembling. He had known all along.

"No, I shouldn't," he agreed, which shocked Alice. "For that, I apologise. I kept this knowledge from you because The Elementals aren't revered, they're feared for their power. But, after your recent incident, I trust it would be wise for you to understand your ancestry. There's an exhibition on The Elementals in the National Museum, I believe it would be wise for you to visit."

Alice nodded, not sure what to say. Dread wasn't a traditional father, but he had brought her up to the best of his ability, and she loved him for it. She understood the sacrifices he had made to look after her, even more so now. She couldn't be angry at him for that.

"Have you had any reports on Kyle?"

Kyle had visited her a few times over the last couple of months, barely letting her catch a glimpse. She wasn't going to mention the head in the box, she hadn't really thought up an appropriate excuse.

"Short sightings over the city. I have decided to let him be for the time being. He will come home when he is ready."

She wanted to protest, demand he come home straight away. She was becoming impatient, not wanting to leave him to wallow in his own self-pity. She knew first-hand the consequences.

"You going to show me this contract yet?"

"It's an assignment, not a contract."

Dread handed over a manila envelope full of documents and photographs. Flipping it open Alice scanned the front page.

"What you have is all the witness statements and photographs of the recent genocide where a total of eight vampires were poisoned."

"The Gala?" Alice scanned the images, noticing how all the dead looked eerily similar.

Bodies that slumped at abnormal angles as if the spines couldn't support their weight, their skin shrunken, dehydrated with black veins visible through the paleness. Blood covered the majority of the areas surrounding them, the red turning to black.

"I thought this would be handled by The Met?"

The Metropolitan Police handled everything to do with homicides for both the Norms and Breed. They called Paladins – the official name for her role within S.I. glorified bloodhounds as their jobs were to hunt down and track the Breeds The Met weren't trained to deal with. After the Breed was detained, they would be handed back.

"It is. However, new protocols have come into place. The Council believe there is still a divide between humans and Breed, to help close that divide they have implemented a programme where detectives in The Met can ask for Tower assistance. This has been in the works for a while now."

"What does that mean?"

"It means you are on retainer until further notice. You will be working with a team chosen to investigate these murders. The lead detective on the case will be in contact sometime today."

Alice clutched the manila folder to her chest, a grin creasing her cheeks.

"I won't let you down."

CHAPTER 5

Checking the motel name, Alice parked next to an unmarked police car, ignoring the disgruntled looks from the men in uniform as her car spluttered to a stop.

She loved her Beetle, the first and only car she had ever bought. Unfortunately, no amount of oil changes or services would save it from the inevitable. It was a miracle the old rust bucket had survived as long as it had, it was old even when she bought it five years ago from a dodgy looking selkie.

It had been cheap, which is what she had wanted at the time. To be fair, that's what she wanted now. Alice loved her job as a Paladin, enjoyed the investigative hunt, the thrill of the chase. She did not, however, enjoy the high mortality rate for a crap wage. Hazard pay was a curse word when brought up to the board of directors directly above Dread. They believed the honour of serving justice was payment enough. There was a reason Paladin enrolment was declining rapidly.

"Excuse me, ma'am, you can't park here," a uniform said from beside the yellow police tape. "Can't you see the area is closed off to civilians?"

"I was invited." She had received a phone call minutes after leaving Dread's office asking her to attend. "I'm the liaison from S.I."

He didn't seem to believe her, even when she showed him her badge.

"I'll handle it from here officer."

A man she recognised as Detective Sullivan O'Neil stepped forward.

"Agent Skye, a pleasure to see you again." He wore a long black trench coat over a white shirt and tie, a packet of cigarettes sticking out of his breast pocket.

"Detective O'Neil," she nodded in greeting. "I'm surprised to be here in all honesty."

Over three centuries of peace between humans and Breed and there was still prejudice. Alice never took it personally, always wondered if it was a subconscious instinct that the majority of Norms tried to limit their interaction with people who could eat, maim or kill them by accident or otherwise. The Met was no different.

"Aren't we all?" He adjusted the single cigarette that was tucked behind his ear before shaking her hand. "I assume you've been briefed?"

"Not really."

She shrugged at his displeased look.

"Well, the basics are you have been selected to be part of a team specialising in the more... abnormal crime cases."

"Abnormal?" she asked. "What do you mean abnormal?"

"You will see." He nudged her to follow him through the car park. "As it stands, the statistics of a human on human homicide is around a sixty-eight per cent charge rate. However, add any Breed to that mix, and the percentage drops dramatically to around twenty-five per cent."

"Why do you think it's so low?" Alice asked as she followed.

The motel was just off the motorway, a large building with around five floors as well as a separate one-storey structure that faced the road. O'Neil guided her past the main building towards the other side of the carpark.

"My superiors believe it's human ignorance."

He shrugged, stroking his goatee in thought as they approached the crime scene, third door from the left.

"I can't say I completely disagree."

"What do we have?" Alice said as she stepped past the threshold, careful to not disturb the blood that had soaked into the carpet.

"Is this our Breed consultant?" A man the size of a wrestler, asked from beside the bed. He wore an identical trench coat to O'Neil, his expression less than friendly. "She's smaller than I imagined."

"Agent Skye, this is my partner Detective Michael Brady." O'Neil shot his partner a warning look. "You'll get used to him."

"Fuck you, Shelly." Detective Brady scowled, turning his dark eyes, almost as dark as the ebony of his skin, towards Alice. "What are you? We haven't been briefed other than we are expecting somebody from S.I."

"I'm a witch," she said as politely as she could. "Are we going to have a problem?" How was she expected to work with someone who was that instantly hostile?

The distrust seemed to disappear, replaced with caution.

"I didn't mean to cause offence. Now let's finish here so I can go home to my wife."

He seemed to take a long look at the body before moving to stand by the open door.

"You should stop calling your hand your wife, it's creepy man." A short skinny man stepped inside the room. He was wearing a full body white plastic sheet, including the hood. "You must be the new member of Spook Squad, the names Jones. Pleased to meet ya."

He went to shake her hand before he pulled back, noticing the red smear across his glove.

"Oh, sorry," he grinned, his brown eyes flashing in mischief.

"Spook Squad?" Alice asked, looking between the three men.

"Ignore it," Brady said. "Stupid uniforms think it's funny," he huffed as if he wasn't pleased with the name, or being a part of the 'Spook Squad.'

"Is this the whole team?" she asked, her gaze sweeping across the room before settling on the body spread-eagled on the bed.

"No, Officer Peyton is dealing with the manager." One of the men replied, from the deep tone of voice, she guessed it was Brady.

"This is a strange situation to meet everyone," she murmured as she carefully moved towards the bed, trying to get a closer look.

The motel room itself was budget, the front mainly glass with a door covered by an ugly green brocade curtain. A woman lay splayed naked across the duvet, her arm at an awkward angle hanging off the side of the mattress. The bed sheets, Alice guessed, would have matched the brocade curtain, the pattern the same but the colour darker, almost black as it soaked the blood.

A syringe had fallen through her fingertips, track marks consistent with the size of the needle decorating the inside of her arms. Blood had seeped from the tiny holes, red and shiny as if it was fresh. Bite marks bruised the inside of her thighs, the bites neat compared to the jagged horizontal scars along both her arms.

"There's too much blood." Almost her entire lifeblood. "She didn't clot."

"We haven't confirmed, but it seems so, the whole of the bed as well as a good circumference of the carpet is soaked through," Jones said. "The wounds suggest feeding."

"A blood junkie?" Alice turned back to the door, noticing how only Detective O'Neil and Jones remained.

A nod from O'Neil. "One of the boys also recognised her from the strip."

"Looks to be dead around twelve hours guessing from the state of the body," Jones chimed in, his suit crinkling as he fidgeted.

"There's no bag." Alice checked the bathroom, careful not to touch anything.

"Bag? Why would she need a bag?"

"She would at least have a bag with spare clothes, maybe even a small suitcase."

Alice searched around the room, bending down to check underneath the bed. The frame was too low to be able to fit a suitcase beneath, and the wardrobe was completely open. Someone had smashed the door from its frame, leaving only the hinges.

"There isn't any makeup. Surely if she were a professional, she would have everything within easy reach?"

"What are you saying?"

"I'm saying she never planned to stay here long." There wasn't even a spare pair of underwear, only the one lace thong that was just outside the blood's radius.

"So she's just passing through?"

"I can't say for sure, I don't have much experience in the field. But if you were a sex worker, surely you would want to freshen up between clients?" Or at least have a packet of condoms to hand.

"It's an interesting thought. Officer Peyton might know more."

"Okay." Alice took one last look at the blood, the previous night's conversation with Danton and Rose giving her an idea. "We need a Vamp."

"A vampire?" O'Neil looked surprised. "Why would we need a vampire? You're the Breed expert."

"Firstly, I'm not technically a Breed expert. Just because I'm a witch doesn't mean I know everything. Secondly, this condition looks similar to an event that happened last night."

"You talking about the Gala? You should have received information regarding the genocide from the Commissioner, but it's the Norms involved we're interested in right this moment."

Detective O'Neil touched his cigarette, almost reassuring himself it was still there.

"Several human waiting staff died of blood loss last night, surprising considering their wounds were considered minor."

"It's called exsanguination," Jones added. "Although an official coroner report hasn't yet been published."

"Why would a team specialising in abnormal Breed cases be called in for blood loss?"

"It isn't the waiters we were originally called in for."

O'Neil opened a breast pocket on his jacket, flipping open a black book and reading his notes.

"Eight vampires died within a small time frame of consuming, what we are assuming, was blood from the blood-waiters. All those affected had severe reactions to an unknown substance found in the blood. The five waiters who were affected all bled out from the bites, wounds that wouldn't normally be fatal."

He snapped the book shut.

"So they bled to death." Alice nodded, confirming her suspicions. "What can stop your body's natural healing mechanism?"

"We're waiting on the lab to confirm, but we're suspecting it's some sort of poison. If it is, it will help explain what happened to the vampires."

"You think they're both related?"

"Why do you think we're here?" Jones smiled cheerfully. "Exsanguination is a pretty common C.O.D. but not like this. It's interesting that we have found another body in the space of twelve hours that has also bled out in suspicious circumstances. So until we prove this otherwise the case is also ours."

Alice looked at the fang marks decorating the dead woman's thighs.

"That would mean we're looking for another body."

"We have uniforms patrolling. The suspected poison was safe long enough in the blood-waiters for a few hours, at least. The vampires that ingested it had symptoms roughly thirty to sixty minutes after."

He seemed to frown to himself before locking eyes with Alice.

"You asked for a vampire, why?"

"One of my colleagues smelled something unusual

about the blood of a blood-waiter we found in the alley. It could help to confirm if it is, in fact, the same substance."

"Interesting." O'Neil passed a look to Jones.

"On it," Jones said quickly as he scurried out the door, his white plastic overall creaking as he moved.

"Fascinating team," Alice said as she waited by the door.

"You could say that." O'Neil sniffed as if displeased before allowing a police officer in uniform to pass into the room.

"Detective, how may I be of assistance?" the newcomer asked.

"Officer Dunton, could you please see if you can smell anything unusual about the deceased."

"Sir." Officer Dunton looked surprised but nodded before entering the crime scene carefully.

"You have a vampire on the force?" Alice questioned, shocked. Breed didn't get hired into human law enforcement.

"He's new. Good guy, keen to learn."

O'Neil turned back to the officer as he approached.

"Sir, I'm not quite sure what you need, but the room smells sweet."

"Sweet?" O'Neil turned to Alice, an eyebrow raised.

"Officer Dunton, what does blood normally smell like to you?"

"It usually smells like copper, sir."

Alice stepped outside, allowing the clean air to remove the smell of death from her nose. She nodded as Dunton left the crime scene, his face puzzled as he went back to his post by the small crowd that had gathered.

"You think you can handle this?" O'Neil asked when he joined her, a lit cigarette between his lips. "I know Paladins don't usually deal with this side. You will need a strong stomach."

"I can handle It."

Paladins were usually behind the chase, not the investigative side. Her standard contracts consisted of finding an unruly shifter who pissed in the wrong garden or tracking down a black charms dealer. Not investigating a gruesome murder.

"We heading to the manager's office?"

"Hmmm." He took a drag of his cigarette, savouring before blowing out the smoke. "What made you think of a Vamp?"

"My vampire colleague stated the blood smelled sweet. Yet a shifter who has a stronger nose couldn't smell anything but death."

"That indicates they are targeting vampires."

"That's what I'm thinking."

Alice stepped into the small, stuffy reception. Who she assumed was the manager sat behind an old desk, his eyes wide in panic as he flashed a look to Alice and Detective O'Neil.

The walls were covered in plastic that looked like wood and the window was partially covered by an off-white lace curtain. A thin key cupboard was beside him, covered in cobwebs. The room stank of tobacco, strong enough Alice desperately wanted to open the window to allow some fresh air in.

"I told you I don't know anything." The older man was dangerously thin with pure white hair. "I just found her there," he said as he nervously patted the sweat from his brow.

"Mr Johnson, my name is Detective O'Neil, and this is

my colleague Agent Skye. You have already met Officer Peyton."

Alice glanced at Officer Peyton, his face blank as he appraised her. He was tall yet slim, his height dwarfing O'Neil, who was already four inches taller than her five foot five. His hair was white blonde, the strands just covering his ears while his eyes were crystal blue.

She kept her face blank as she assessed him back.

He isn't human, she thought to herself. Not that she could be sure, just a gut instinct. Fighting her reflex to touch his chi with her own she turned to Mr Johnson with a friendly smile as he paled.

"Why have you brought a witch? What is she going to do?" Mr Johnson licked his dry lips, his hands gripping the edge of his desk to the point his knuckles were white.

"How did you know I was a witch?" Alice asked, stepping back to give the man some breathing space before he started to hyperventilate. You couldn't tell at a glance what Breed someone was generally, especially a witch who just looked human.

"I feel you," he whispered, as if it was a secret.

"So you're a mage?" It was the only explanation she could think of. Mages were humans with witch ancestors. They had the ability to harness magic but generally weren't powerful. He probably felt her aura when she entered the room, hers would feel slightly electric compared to the others unless she concealed it.

"Can you confirm you're the manager here?" O'Neil asked before Mr Johnson could answer her question.

"Yes, sir." He visibly swallowed, his eyes darting back and forth to Alice.

Stepping even further back, she made herself as unthreatening as possible. Considering she was wearing jeans, a fluffy dark purple jumper and leather jacket she didn't think it was too hard. Luckily he couldn't see her Paladin blade strapped to her back beneath.

"How long has the victim been using one of your rooms as an... office, shall we say?" Officer Peyton said with just a touch of an accent she couldn't place.

"I have already told you this. I wasn't aware she was even a..." A cough, Mr Johnson collecting himself. "A lady of the night."

Bullshit.

You didn't have to be trained to see he was lying. His eyes were constantly moving when he wasn't checking to see if Alice moved. Every time he lied, he looked down, even when being directly spoken to.

"When did she hire the room?"

He licked his lips once again. "Yesterday, around three or four? I can't be sure."

"Did she sign anything? Leave credit card details?"

"No, she paid in cash up front," he seemed to sniffle. "She signed the guest book." He opened a drawer on his desk, pulling out a large plastic folder. "Look, here she is. Room three, Stacey Cartman."

"Stacey Cartman." O'Neil wrote in his little black book. "Anything else you can tell us? Did she have any visitors?"

"Surely CCTV would have caught something," Alice added.

"No," he squeaked. "We don't have CCTV here. She was the only visitor in the outbuilding. All my other guests are here, in the main building." He looked around as if he could see through the walls.

Alice froze, her head automatically turning towards the door as she felt something brush against her chi. Frowning she glanced at Johnson, then O'Neil, wondering if they felt something too. When they didn't react, she allowed some of her own chi to release, to explore around the room.

O'Neil was definitely human, his aura bland and unused. When her chi touched Peyton, he shot her a cautionary look. His chi felt human too, yet he knew when she touched it, which was impossible if he wasn't a magic user.

"What are you doing?!" Mr Johnson leapt from his chair, the hairs on his arms standing on edge.

"Sorry." She reigned herself back, giving him an apologetic smile.

Something brushed across her chi again, something hot. Her gaze shot straight to a shadow standing beside a lamppost on the other side of the motorway.

"Excuse me," she said as she felt herself walking past the police tape, almost without thought.

The shadow stood leaning against the street lamp, a black hoodie covering the face as the light flickered ominously overhead.

"Kyle?"

It had been weeks since he had allowed her to catch a glimpse of him and now he was only across the road.

Her brother stepped away, walking down the street in the opposite direction.

"Wait!" she called as she started to panic. "Kyle!"

"Agent Skye, are you okay?" Detective Brady came to stand beside her, his eyes scanning the road. "You almost stepped into traffic."

Catching her breath, she composed herself.

"Sorry, I thought I saw someone I knew." She stretched her chi as far as it could reach, unable to sense her brother who had disappeared into the darkness. She had never been able to feel him, only be able to see him as shadows.

Was he finally reaching out for her?

Or was he starting to lose control?

"We have a lead on Stacey Cartman. She's on parole for drug trafficking so we have a current address. According to the system, it was her husband that originally paid her bail so we're hoping he will be available for an interview."

Alice had one last look down the street.

"Okay, let's go."

CHAPTER 6

Alice pulled up beside Detective Brady, his expression bored as he leant against his black BMW.

Out of all the members of her new team, Detective Brady seemed the most zealous, as if he took everything personally. O'Neil seemed indifferent, like he didn't care whether or not he was a part of the team while Jones was happy to be anywhere. Peyton, on the other hand, was just... other. She wasn't sure what to think of him just yet.

"Did you get lost or something?" Brady asked as he bent at his waist, close enough his breath misted up the window. "You getting out the car?"

Alice sighed, stepping out of her Beetle, eyes scanning the cheap housing estate. They were still in London, as far out as the Breed district could go before turning into the countryside. The small building was covered in scaffolding, making the entrance to the flats dreary and unwelcoming. The surrounding streets seemed to be deserted, in the way bad neighbourhoods did when they noticed someone from law enforcement.

"What do you expect to find?" Alice said as she allowed him to take the lead. The security door was broken, allowing them to enter into the hallway without being buzzed. The air stank of damp, the carpet squidgy beneath her boots as Brady looked around.

"Hopefully the husband can give us a timeframe," Brady grunted as he knocked on the first ground floor flat on the right.

After a few seconds he knocked again, harder.

"Hello? It's the police, open up." Another knock, this one hard enough to rattle the door, the cheap wood crashing open with a bang.

"Shit." Alice and Brady said at the same time, both drawing their weapons, Alice with her sword and Brady with his gun.

The room inside was covered in darkness, the curtains drawn and the lights off. An intense smell of decaying flesh assaulted their noses as they took a step forward, her blade giving little light as her runes glistened. Brady's eyes flicked to her sword, his lashes covering his expression before he quickly looked away.

"Hello?" he called, his deep voice echoing through the room. "Is anyone in here?"

Alice came to stand beside the overturned sofa, noticing a body half- draped across one of the cushions. The man's eyes were wide and lifeless, a single bullet hole in the middle of his forehead.

"It's clear," Brady said as he came to stand opposite. He reached up to pull at one curtain, illuminating the room in as much sunlight as the scaffolding across the window would allow.

"Bloody hell!"

What was once a standard living room had been covered in a green fluffy film. Almost every available surface surrounding the body had vegetation growing, grass, flowers and even toadstools. A table had been overturned, what remained of a copper spelling pot and crushed herbs scattered across the floor. Glancing back at the body, she noticed the green substance partially covered his flesh too.

"What is all this?" Brady opened the remaining curtain.

"He's been executed," Alice said gently, as if she could still upset the dead, which was debatable depending on who exactly had died.

"What makes you say that?" Brady knelt, taking a closer look.

"Just a hunch." She shrugged, unable to explain her gut feeling. "Can you touch his necklace?" It was costume jewellery, a red jewel encased in gold. She could see from where she was standing it wasn't real, the ruby plastic.

"Excuse me?"

"I can't reach it from here." She made eye contact with Brady, making it almost a challenge. She saw how he looked at her sword, wasn't sure of what it was until just now.

He didn't trust her.

His jaw clenched as he slowly reached for the necklace, hesitant as if it was going to bite him. As soon as his flesh touched the stone the glamour broke, the magic dissipating in a burst of sandalwood.

"Shit!" He snapped his hand back, eyes accusing.

"He's Fae."

Alice pointed to the body's new look, the one he was born with before he wore the charm that altered his appearance. Made him appear more 'normal.'

"Or at least half-Breed." The body looked more human

than usual Fae, his skin a pastel green with eyes only slightly on the larger size. His hair – which was sacred to many Fae – was cut short, showing off his pointy ears. "Maybe even a dryad." It would explain the greenery.

"A tree nymph?" Brady looked sceptical. "Why was he executed?"

"Fae can't lie," she said before correcting herself. "Well, high caste Fae can't lie. I'm not sure about the lower caste."

It wasn't known whether they were unable to lie, or had simply been forbidden by the High Lords. It has made the majority of the higher Fae master manipulators, twisting words into half-truths. Just as The Council reigned over all Breeds, each Breed had their own ruler. For the Fae, it was the High Lords, the oldest and most powerful amongst their kind.

"He may have known too much information." Or just a small pawn in a bigger game, they would never know.

"They may be incapable of lying, but they can be perfectly dishonest with the truth," Brady said deadpan, almost as if he were quoting.

"That sounds like something the Church of the Light would say."

The Church of the Light came into existence around the same time Breed became recognised citizens. It was a place humans went to worship a god and condemn everyone that disagreed or was different.

All Breed were classed as different.

"My father was a minister," he said without any emotion. "I was brought up in the church."

"Is that why you don't trust me?" she asked before she even realised she spoke. "If your religion believes all Breed are inferior, then why are you on this team?"

She wasn't angry, just interested. Many different religions were strictly human, The Church of the Light was just the one that craved media attention the most. She didn't see Brady as someone who would follow such a strict faith.

"I never said I followed my father's beliefs." His face was stern, his body language closed off.

Alice decided not to comment further. Instead, she turned her attention back to the fake ruby.

"He's wearing the colours of the Unseelie court." The Dark Fae were a genuinely cruel race compared to their lighter brethren. Although being part of the Seelie Court, also known as Light Fae, didn't necessarily mean they were good.

"Fucking faeries," Brady grunted.

"Fae, not faerie. He isn't a faerie." That she thought, anyway.

"It's the same thing," Brady said as he glanced around the room.

She just shook her head.

"There's been a struggle." He pointed out a dent in the wall, shaped like a fist.

Leaving him to study the wrecked living room, Alice walked down the hallway, her eyes catching on a photograph beside the bed. A young man stood alongside a woman she recognised as Stacey, the woman found in the motel. His arm crushed her against his chest as they both smiled to the camera. Around his neck she could make out the gold chain, the fake ruby hidden beneath his shirt. They were beautiful, tanned skin with bright clear eyes, Stacey's hair was cut at the shoulders, several inches shorter than it was now. They looked like a genuine, kind and happy couple, their smiles not showing the poor choices they were yet to make.

The room was reasonably clean if a bit messy. The duvet cover wasn't made, pillows were tossed across the sheets while a large amount of lace and silk underwear scattered beside the pillows. A cardboard box was half open by the dresser, unopened boxes of condoms and sex toys tossed messily inside.

The moss, Alice noticed, hadn't reached the bedroom apart from a few toadstools that had started to grow beside the door. The greenery seemed to be growing in a controlled area around the circumference of the body. Fae died in strange ways, their bodies not decaying as others did.

This one was turning back to the earth.

Alice began to walk back to the living room when she spotted more spelling pots on the kitchen counters. Hesitating at the threshold, she looked back to see Detective Brady on his phone, his back to her.

Not wanting to interrupt she stepped toward the counter, frowning at the contents thrown across the countertop. Stacey's Breed hadn't yet been classified, the examiner had yet to do a series of tests to determine her true Breed. Even then it was not always accurate. From the herbs, she would have guessed a witch, the spelling pots and utensils not usually used by Fae, their magic much different. Dandelion, galangal and feverfew lay partially crushed as if she was interrupted while she was making a potion. Or she was just messy.

One copper pot was half filled with a dark liquid, and a few leaves Alice couldn't identify floating on the top. A small opaque tube connected the pot to a smaller one placed beside it on a high pedestal. Every thirty seconds or so the unknown liquid would drip from the top pot into the bottom via the tube. The drop broke the surface of the dark water, creating a ripple effect that smelt of sulphur.

Scrunching up her nose Alice leant forward, trying to guess what she could have been making that would create a sulphur smelling concoction.

Only dark magic...

"What do you think you're doing?" A deep voice growled from directly behind her.

With a jump Alice turned, her arm knocking into the larger of the two pots, making the water slosh down one side. Instantly the countertop started to bubble, the plastic overlay warping as if it was in contact with intense heat. Within a few seconds the liquid evaporated, leaving a fine layer of crystal.

"Fuck sake Brady, why did you sneak up on me like that?"

He narrowed his eyes, his face stern as he looked around the small kitchen.

"What do you think you're doing?" he repeated.

"I wanted to know what it was." She gestured to the setup. "I wanted to see..."

The words escaped her, lungs tightening as she noticed the carvings on the counter. When she had accidentally moved the pot she exposed the pentagram that has been scraped into the plastic.

"Agent Skye?"

"There's a pentagram here."

She moved the rest of the pots gently to the side, exposing the whole pentagram.

"It's inverted." *Fuck. Fuck. Fuck,* Alice chanted silently to herself.

The chances of meeting a Daemon was one in a million, their Breed beyond rare.

The first time she met one, she was barely six.

The second time she almost died.

The chances of meeting one again...

"What does that mean? Don't you all use those stars?"

"It's inverted," she said as if that was explanation enough.

His face said differently.

"It's a sign of Daemonic worship."

Witches pentagrams consisted of a five-pointed star within a circle. An inverted pentagram was identical except it was flipped, the twin bottom points at the top, symbolic of Baphomet, the devil's ram.

"She could just be a fanatic."

"Maybe." She needed to talk to Riley.

"Guys I'm just finishing up!" A voice called from down the hallway.

Alice looked at Brady, his face thoughtful before he turned and left. Following she noticed a man was standing by the body, a large DSLR camera in one hand.

"Oh, hey, Jones."

"Who else would it be?" he said with a grin. "You find anything?"

She told him about her theory with the moss.

"That's fascinating. I don't get to work with many Fae, they don't seem to ever die," he said cheerily as he photographed the room from different angles.

"Agent Skye, you're our resident Breed expert." Brady started with a raised brow. "Aren't Fae immortal?"

"Tell that to the dead." She nodded to the body.

"Seriously though, in my line of work we see many dead bodies. In my fifteen years this is the first Fae." Jones finished his photography, his face screwed up in concentration as he measured something with his hand.

"Yes and no." Alice thought about her answer, her knowledge on Fae far from perfect. "Fae is an umbrella term, a faerie is very different from a troll yet are both are classed as Fae. The majority have longevity, they don't age in the same way as us, and they can't catch diseases."

She looked back down at the body.

"Although, clearly a bullet works."

"You said us. You're not one of us," Brady said nonchalantly.

Alice's response was instinctive. "My DNA would disagree."

It was how the majority of Breed remained undetected before the war. Scientifically her DNA matched that of a human, they didn't understand why witches were born with the ability to manipulate magic. Nor did they understand why shifters had human DNA when human and animal DNA when shifted. Scientists were still trying to figure that particular question out.

"Brady man, careful," Jones warned.

"I didn't mean anything by it." He seemed genuinely confused. "I don't care what you are, or where you're from. I care whether you can do the job or not."

"Ah, there's the usual grumpy old Brady," Jones laughed. "Alice, as you're new you get his extra offensive side."

Brady replied with his middle finger.

"Don't worry about it." For someone who supposedly didn't follow the Church of the Light, he sure thought like one. "You see something we don't, Jones?"

"The blood spatter on the wall behind indicates that the gunman was standing." Jones made a hand gesture of a gun, pointing it at the wall before frowning. Looking around, he opened the front door, stretching his legs to make himself taller.

"Right here. The victim would have been standing a foot from the door. The bullet entered straight through the frontal bone resulting in instant death. The momentum threw him back into the sofa, which overturned and landed him there."

"So are you suggesting the gunman didn't even enter the room?"

"Doubtful. The bullet hole implies it was a small calibre weapon, but it still would have been loud enough to force the shooter to leave immediately. The only other explanation would be if a silencer were used, even though they're not as silent as the name suggests but still quieter than a normal shot. There's no residue around the wound that I could see, however, to really know I would have to analyse the bullet and see if there are any deviations along the metal."

"Then who trashed the room?" Alice asked.

"Well the deceased wouldn't have been able to defend himself, so the abrasions along his right fist suggests he hit something solid..."

"Like a wall." Brady finished for him.

"Maybe there was an argument?" Alice shrugged, it was the only idea they had.

"Entirely possible." Brady got out a little black book from a pocket, identical to O'Neil's. "It would explain why Stacey used the motel to entertain her clients, rather than here."

"That's saying she brought her clients home, which is unusual but isn't unheard of. It might be worth talking to the neighbours." Alice said, moving towards the front door.

"O'Neil already has that covered, although I doubt anything will come from it." He scribbled something down.

"What makes you say that?"

"I find with estates like these all the neighbours have selective hearing."

He tucked away his book, his dark eyes appraising the room once more before settling on her.

"Agent Skye, it seems we're finished here." He gestured for her to follow him out the door.

Saying goodbye to Jones she exited the flat, noticing how O'Neil was questioning a neighbour a few doors down, his sighs audible as the neighbour repeatedly expressed they didn't know and hadn't heard anything.

Selective hearing. Alice would smile if their blatant uncooperativeness weren't helping someone get away with murder.

"So you gonna tell me why your face went white as a sheet when you saw that pentagram?" Brady asked as he walked her to her car. "We're not going to have an issue, are we?"

"What exactly are you suggesting Detective?" Alice stopped at her car door, turning so she was full on facing the Detective.

He didn't reply, his face like granite. If it was an interrogation technique, it was pretty good.

"Daemons haven't been recorded since the late nineteenth century." She opened her car door, throwing in her bag.

"That didn't answer my question." Brady placed his hand on the top of her door, his dark eyes barely blinking. She could tell he used his sheer size to intimidate and manipulate. Luckily she wasn't easily intimidated.

"Thank you for your help today, Detective." Alice

smiled, showing teeth. "Now if you would excuse me." She pointedly looked at his hand. "I have somewhere to be."

With an irritated twitch, Detective Brady let go.

"You were right before. I don't trust you, and it isn't because you're a witch." He turned to his car. "Have a good evening, Agent Skye."

"Arsehole," she whispered beneath her breath, her eyes tracking him until his headlights had disappeared down the road.

Darkness had started to fall as they analysed the crime scene, winter creeping in as autumn gave way. She was going to have to be wary of him.

Alice was about to get in her car when she noticed a woman hiding behind an overgrown tree directly opposite the crime scene. She watched for a few minutes, deciding whether to approach. She could hear the woman's hollow cry, her eyes shiny as she watched unblinking from her hiding spot.

Unable to leave Alice cautiously approached, making sure her smile was friendly. "Hello, are you okay?"

The woman, pale as a ghost turned almost mechanically as if she was too petrified to move.

"Do you know what's going on?" She started to scratch her elbows, her nails broken and bit to the quick.

Alice debated on what to tell her, only now noticing how her pupils were huge, not reacting to the lights flashing from the emergency vehicles.

"They found someone in one of the flats." She decided on not enough information for details but enough to gain a reaction.

"Stacey?!" Her voice was a high squeak, her throat scratchy as she started to sob. "Was it Stacey?"

"No, a man." Alice wanted to comfort the woman who

had wrapped her arms around herself, almost as if to control the tremble as her cries stormed through her body. "It was a man."

"Steve?" The woman sniffled. "I told her it wasn't worth it. I said we would find something else, try chemo again..."

The woman started to murmur to herself, forgetting Alice was there.

"Chemo?" Alice gently pushed, understanding this woman was not stable. "Was Stacey sick?"

The woman sniffed again as snot dripped down her nose before she wiped it off with a dirty sleeve. In fact, her whole outfit was dirty, mud and grass stains patterning the oversized coat and jeans. The woman's hair was dark and greasy, what was left of her cheap lipstick smeared across her face from the sleeve.

"Cancer." She choked out the word. "Doc's said there's nothing more to do, said they couldn't do anything else. I think they fucking stopped because we're working girls. Didn't want to infect their stupid clean hospitals with the likes of us," she snarled, anger breaking through the tears. "She was desperate, no money to go private. Couldn't figure out dark magic. Even got Steve to start dealing but it still wasn't enough."

She stood staring at the entrance to the flats, almost mesmerised.

"Santa offered her a lifeboat."

"Santa?" Alice stepped forward, trying to read her reactions without startling her.

The woman's head twisted around slowly, her face oddly blank.

"He looked like Santa. Old, chubby with a white beard. Said he could give her a special drink. Make her better again." She started to laugh, the tone on the edge of hysteria. "Santa can do that, you know? He's magic."

Another chuckle.

"Let the light guide you."

Let the light guide you? Alice repeated to herself.

"What's your name?"

"Name?" The woman asked, her eyes now wholly vacant. She had no idea where she was, either the drugs taking their toll or the grief.

"Can I take you anywhere?" *Like a woman's shelter.* "Can I get you some food? A nice warm place to stay the night?" *Anything.*

"Mia, my names Mia."

She started to sob again, the cries racking her body violently as she scratched at her hair, knotting the strands.

"I need to... I need to... go, yeah, go." With that she bolted away, leaving Alice to stare after her.

He groaned as he held his ribs, the wind knocked out of him as he knelt on the black mat. They were trying to make him angry. Make him release his beast.

But he couldn't, he knew his beast was pure rage. Would destroy all of them, kill them as they had beat him.

They didn't understand. Couldn't comprehend the uncontrollable anger his spirit beast held. He understood, the boy. He no longer showed the anger that still made his blood hotter at the thought. No longer wept openly with grief.

Accepted what he could not change.

His beast could not.

Could not accept the death of their mother, the woman as peaceful as Goddess Gaia herself. The woman who taught him the old ways, of using the earth itself, using the ley lines. Not the way he's being taught now, with darkness and blood. Marking his flesh with permanent glyphs, making him stronger, faster.

Under their control.

They didn't know he didn't need them, he was already stronger, faster.

Choking out a breath he felt his ribs crunch. The teacher had broken them, again.

His beast would kill them.

CHAPTER 7

Puffing out a breath, Alice scowled at the illegible writing scrawled along the edges of the page.

She didn't realise there would be so much waiting around while the investigation progressed. She wasn't used to following The Met's rules and regulations, she wanted to track down the perpetrator immediately, not wait around for the autopsy report.

She knew she was being unreasonable, but weeks of sitting around doing nothing was taking its toll.

So she had spent the majority of the last several days trying to figure out what her mother had written, the notes doodled beside instructions in the leather-bound grimoire.

Each page, Alice had discovered, held different spells, potions and wards the majority of which she had never heard of before, all scripted by hand.

Her success rate was precisely zero per cent. Two days and half a dozen potions later and not one had gone right. So Alice glowered at the writings, wondering if she was just a terrible witch or her mother's recipes were wrong. She had followed the instructions, as much as she understood, exactly. Yet all she had to show for it was one unhappy roommate, a half dead and overgrown garden, a hole in the wall and a smashed copper pot.A pot that, somehow, had exploded into several shards that were still embedded into the kitchen wall and would stay that way for the foreseeable future. Or until she bought a step ladder.

Sleeping Potion

INGREDIENTS:
20 Lavender Stems
100 grams Valerian root
50 grams Hawthorn
50 grams Magnolia Bark
500ml goat milk
Handful of Straw

METHOD:
Bring the milk to a boil then add the valerian root and hawthorn. Meanwhile, burn the bark into fine ash and sift into the mixture. Continuously stirring with a copper spoon add the lavender. Cover and leave to boil for a further two minutes. Once the timing is up, carefully pour the milk into a bottle, making sure to sift out all the remaining lumps using the straw.

Alice re-read the instructions for the eighth time, memorising them before she attempted it.

'*Great defensive strike. Pour over the opponent for them to instantly fall into a deep sleep. Chance of death 0%,*' was messily written beside the directions, making her wonder why her mum would need to know defensive spells considering she was just a simple gardener before her death. That's what she had always been told anyway. She doubted it now, wondering what her mother or even her father did to be targeted by Daemons.

It was why she was carefully studying the grimoire, looking for answers.

Since finding the inverted pentagram Alice felt a sense of urgency that her house was unprotected. She wanted to set a ward, a spell that helped to discourage evil influences and deflect misfortune. Human superstition believed good luck charms or even hand gestures did the same thing. Unfortunately for Alice, she felt a four-leaf clover or crossing her fingers wasn't going to be enough for her. But before she attempted something as complicated as a protection ward, she needed to master at least one potion.

Sitting back on her heels Alice adjusted her copper pot, making sure it was correctly positioned over the hot coals. This time – unlike the others, she had decided to create the potion within a circle she had carved into the tiled floor, salt teased into the grooves to act as an extra barrier. Big enough she could sit comfortably inside along with her instruments. The five-pointed star within a circle was ready, the candles in place at every anchor point. Lighting them in sequence, first earth, then fire, water, air and lastly spirit, Alice felt the circle materialise with an audible pop.

It always amazed her when she saw her aura reflected on the shimmery surface, the green and blue moving across the opaque surface, the same colours as her flame. Bringing her hand to barely a centimetre away from the barrier, she felt a gentle tingling along her fingertips, the colours swirling to concentrate on the almost connection before she moved away.

Auras were thought to represent you as a person, the colours reflecting your very soul and thoughts.

She wondered what hers said.

Reaching forward she grabbed a mouthful of her katsu curry, nibbling the chicken from the bowl in her lap. Sam was the chef in the house, so when he was home he would cook. When he was out Alice survived on leftovers, sandwiches and takeaway. Baking, on the other hand, she was quite good at but only if you preferred the taste to the look.

Setting down her fork Alice started the potion, waiting for the milk to boil before she added any of the ingredients.

"*Adolebtique.*" She flicked her wrist towards the coals, helping them burn faster so she could begin. Before she added the first herb, Alice checked the instructions, holding her breath as she mixed in the final lavender, happy the concoction didn't explode in her face.

She sifted the milk through the straw, smiling as the liquid settled into the small bottle, even if the colour was slightly purple. *It's supposed to be purple, right?* Popping a cork into the top she tilted it, watching the milk swirl with a gentle glisten. She had no idea if it worked, wasn't sure how she could test it.

BZZZZZ

Alice jumped at the distraction, frowning as she looked around for the noise, wondering if she had set off the fire alarm, again.

BZZZZZ

Her phone beeped from the table, the handset lighting up from the table.

"Shit. Shit. Shit." She scrambled to her feet, careful not to break the bottle that she clutched in her palm.

"Hello, this is Agent Skye," she said as she placed the potion onto the table.

There was a pause at the end of the phone.

"Hello, is this Alice?"

Alice checked the number, realising too late it wasn't any of the team, but an unknown number.

"Ah, yes, that's me. Can I help you?"

"This is the reception at Club X. I've been asked to call you regarding one of our employee's Ranger..."

"Ranger?"

"I apologise, I meant to call him Samion."

"Oh, Sam isn't available at the moment," she said, most of her attention on the bottle. "He's at work."

"Yes," the voice said dryly. *"He works here, that's why I called."*

Alice took longer than it should to understand what was said. Sam had only recently returned to work after taking time off to spend with her while she healed. He was supposed to be working at the Blood Bar.

"You're his emergency contact. The manager has asked for you to come speak to him immediately regarding syringes found in his locker as well as a bag of what we expect is Brimstone."

"You must be mistaken. Sam doesn't do drugs." She didn't believe it. He had promised, that of all his vices, he would never turn to drugs, even though his personality was that of an addict. They were each other's rock, had been since they first bonded as children in their trauma support group.

"Well, be that as it may, he was still found with narcotics. If you do not attend, we will..."

"No, no. I'm coming." Alice felt her pulse race, her nerves on edge at the very thought of Sam using any drugs.

"What's the name of this place again?"

The bouncer looked shocked when he noticed Alice standing before him, her hair messy and curry staining part of her basic grey T-shirt. In her defence, she had been in a hurry to leave, barely giving herself time to squeeze into some jeans and trainers. He was lucky she hadn't turned up in her pink unicorn lounge bottoms and rabbit slippers.

"Hello," she said a little breathlessly. "I'm here to pick up Sam."

She had pretty much run from the car, the traffic light at this time of night, or as light as traffic in a central city could be.

"You the new girl?" He looked her up and down, seemingly unimpressed. "You're not dressed appropriately."

"I'm sorry, I didn't realise there was a dress code for a nightclub," she replied tensely. What would he have preferred, her pyjamas?

He looked confused.

"Well, we technically don't have a dress code, but all the girls dress... erm..." He shrugged as he struggled to find the right word. "You're pretty, but not like we normally hire."

"I'm not a hire," she said sternly, "I'm here to pick up Sam." *What is he on about?*

"What?" he frowned, the fat of his face creasing. "Excuse me."

His hand went to the side of his face, pressing the small headpiece further into his ear.

"Oh, you're here to pick up Ranger. Why didn't you say so?"

Alice felt her mouth open, then thought better of it.

"You sure you don't want to change? You're going to stick out like a sore thumb in there," he chuckled to himself.

"I'm sure it will be fine," she murmured as he escorted her through the reception area. "Oh fuck sake, you've got to be kidding me."

"Have fun," the bouncer sniggered as he left her amongst the throngs of patrons and dancers.

Well, it could have been worse.

Alice had never felt overdressed before, but that's definitely what she was. It wasn't a night club like she had initially thought, but a strip club. The dancers were wearing barely any clothes and neither were the customers.

From what she could see in the dark, the room was all centred around one large stage with oversized speakers and flashing lights standing beside it. Dark wooden tables were strategically placed facing the stage, almost every single seat occupied with people drinking and squealing at the woman dancing provocatively in a latex suit, money hanging out of zips along the sides.

A few private booths were placed against the back wall, each with a metal pole speared through a circular table. Both male and female dancers stood on the tables, dressed in either leather or latex.

"Excuse me, ma'am, you need to find a seat," a soft voice said from beside her. "The show has already started."

Alice turned, her gaze taking in the short, dark-haired man with the most beautiful lavender eyes she had ever seen.

"Huh?" She could barely hear as the music pounded and the audience cheered.

"You. Need. To. Find. A. Seat," he shouted at her, his grip hard as he grabbed her forearm and leant forward.

Without thinking, she twisted his arm, dislodging him as he screeched in pain. "Ow! Ow! Ow!"

"Don't touch me," she hissed as she let go. "I'm here to speak to the manager."

Mr lavender eyes seemed to groan, his face contorted in pain.

"Do that again," he moaned.

"What? Hurt you?" Alice asked, horrified. *Where the fuck am I?*

"Ladies and gentleman..." A voice purred over the microphone. "May I introduce to you the man you have all been waiting for... Ranger!"

Alice automatically turned to the stage as a man dressed in full body leather walked out barefoot. White blonde hair blanketed around his shoulders, long enough to reach the small of his back. Alice felt her face burn as soon as she recognised Sam, his body like liquid as he danced to the music.

The audience went wild, men and women throwing money, underwear and other things onto the stage. As she watched, he started to remove parts of the leather, starting with the corset, allowing the golden flesh of his chest to show through.

Alice wanted to look away, her gaze locked as she watched her friend of seventeen years dance. She had never seen him in any other way than her best friend, their relationship a strong bond that had nothing to do with sex. Yet, even as her cheeks burned, she didn't look away, able to appreciate his beauty, his inner leopard giving him grace in his movements.

As more leather was removed the scars started to appear, getting a loud reaction from the audience, as if they were excited by the history of his abuse.

She watched as Sam's nostrils flared, his fingers curling to the point his claws threatened to break his skin. His ambers eyes scanned the crowd.

"Oh god, he's choosing."

"Pick me, pick me!"

"He's so amazing." People hopped up from their tables, arms raised.

Sam caught her eye, his own confused as he hopped down from the stage. She felt stuck in place as he stalked toward her, people's hands brushing against him as he approached.

"What the fuck are you doing here baby girl?" he whispered, his breath tickling her ear as she stood like a statue. He started to move around her, the crowd going wild behind.

"I got a call," she explained. "What the fuck do you think you're doing?"

"Just go with it," he said as he danced around her. Quickly, he bent her backwards, a hand at the small of her back as he leant towards Mr lavender eyes, their lips locking in a clash of tongue above her. The crowd erupted into a cacophony of noise, each shout barely distinguishable.

"That's it, I'm done." She pushed him away, conscious of touching his naked chest. She had never had any issues with his nudity, had accepted it was part of him being a shifter. But she couldn't handle it right now.

"Alice," he hissed as she started to walk away. "Come here."

His hand shot forward, grabbing her wrist in an iron grip.

"Take a bow." He pulled her down, a fake smile plastered on his face. "Follow me." He guided her behind a velvet curtain behind the stage, releasing her once they were out of view of the audience.

"What the hell was that?" She shouted as quietly as she could, anger bubbling. "What's going on?"

Sam shrugged. "This place was hiring, so I went for it." He crossed his arms, closing himself off.

"No, you don't get to do that." She pulled at his arms. "I don't care that you're a stripper, it's your life to do with it as you choose. I'm angry because of the drugs Sam!"

She felt her heart start to race, a warmth beside her face as her little blue ball of fire burst into a happy existence.

"Fuck sake." She tried to swat the light away, but it happily danced out of reach. Her 'Tinkerbell' as Sam liked to call it was an annoyance, appearing as a physical manifestation of her anger. No one knew what it was or how she did it. All she knew it was one of the most irritating things in the universe.

"Drugs? What are you on about?" He stepped back as Tinkerbell shot towards him. It never used to do that, actually attack people who she was angry with. It was more unpredictable since her power surge but also appeared less often. It took a lot of intense anger for it to appear, unlike before, when stubbing her toe would be enough.

"Someone called me, asking me to come here because they found Brimstone!"

"That's not mine!" He looked worried. "I took it from a friend. You know me, I don't touch that stuff!"

"Ah, you must be Miss Skye. You were down as an emergency contact on Ranger's documents." A man dressed in a dark suit approached, his gaze hard as he looked her up and down.

"Hello." Alice grasped his outstretched hand, her face frowning as she struggled to recognise him.

I've seen him before.

"I'm Mr Donald, but you may call me Mac. Shall we?" He urged them to follow him. "I appreciate you coming down so quickly, Miss Skye."

"It's Alice," she interjected as she closed the door behind her. Mr Donald sat down behind his desk, allowing them to either stand or take the two seats in front of him. She chose to stand as Sam leant against the door. "Why am I here, Mr Donald? I've spoken to Sam, and he has explained the drugs aren't his."

"It's Mac. I know they're not his..."

"Then why have you called me? This isn't school, I'm not his mum."

Mac looked irritated but continued. "I apologise with how we phrased the call, but I was hoping you would help me get the answers from Ranger. He isn't talking, he might see some sense if a friend were here."

"Still seems a bit ridiculous."

Sam smirked in agreement.

"We get the dancers regularly tested. We have a zero tolerance on drugs, recreational or otherwise. We need to know who they belong to."

"They will be gone immediately and will not be brought back on the property, what does it matter who brought them?" Sam said.

A bang, a heavy fist hitting the table.

"It matters because this is my fucking business and I will not let anybody who works under my name fuck that up!"

"I thought you said the dancers were regularly tested?" Alice asked.

"They are. However, I allow some people who aren't

hired directly through the club to offer their... own product."

"He allows prostitutes to work with his patrons, he takes a cut of their earnings." Sam stepped towards the desk, anger vibrating his shoulders. His leopard prowled behind his eyelashes, wary.

"It isn't illegal. I give them a safe place to work in exchange for a cut of their profit." Mac started to stand, his eyes changing from a deep brown to a pale blue as he glared at Sam.

Fuck sake, another shifter.

"Calm down, both of you." She carefully stood between them, ignoring Sam's warning growl.

"Your roommate hasn't been helpful in finding out who has been dealing on my property."

"They weren't dealing." A snarl.

Mac went to his drawer, pulling out a large plastic bag full of red powder and a single syringe.

"This looks like a fucking lot of gear for one person." The words came out slightly garbled, his animal reacting to the aggression in the room.

That's when it clicked, she recognised him, had seen him around.

"You're one of Rex's wolves."

"Theo's wolves. Rex has gone AWOL. I was hoping you wouldn't have recognised me considering I'm not a pup, I don't have to do the dirty work." Meaning he was dominant. "I don't tangle in pack politics."

"He wasn't involved. Otherwise, I wouldn't be working here," Sam said as his palm came down on her shoulder, reassuring her.

"If you are so dominant, why did you let him get away with what he did?"

"I wasn't aware." He relaxed back into his seat. "Rex's actions do not reflect the integrity of the pack." He smiled charmingly, completely changing his otherwise hard face. "I hope there aren't any bad feelings?"

"My problem isn't with the pack." Not really, it was with their former Alpha.

"It's..." A set of lights were along the wall behind Mac's head, seven in total, each with their own gold number. The number seven flashed violently.

"I'm sorry, what is that for?" she asked curiously, pointing to the light.

"Fuck." Mac leapt up from his desk just as a woman crashed through the door, throwing Sam out of the way.

"Sir, there's been an accident." The woman said, swallowing tears. "In the Pride room."

"Ah, if you would excuse me." He patted his pocket nervously.

"I smell death," Sam stated as he moved down a corridor, letting Alice run behind.

"RANGER STOP!" Mac shouted.

"It isn't one of our girls." Sam physically relaxed once he peered into room seven. "It's a customer." His eyes were serious when he glared at Mac.

"Fuck." Mac stood in the threshold, his eyes wide. "One of our best fucking clients too."

"You have seven rooms, what are they for?"

Each door, other than the seventh, were closed. Red lights were above each one, some lit and some not.

"What do you think are everyone's most carnal desires?"

"You named your rooms after the seven deadly sins?" Alice tried not to smirk as she read the small inscriptions on each door. Lust, Gluttony, Greed, Sloth, Wrath, Envy and finally Pride.

"Mac named them. They're for clients with money, ones who like to pay for extras with the women he doesn't technically hire."

Sam crossed his arms, face angry. He clearly had some negative opinions about the rooms.

"It smells like a fang face."

"Vampire?" Alice tried to peek in the room, unable to see anything in the dark.

"Please step back, Miss Skye. We need to wait for the authorities to arrive."

"Now that you mention it..."

CHAPTER 8

Alice stood against the wall as Jones eagerly photographed inside the small room, the squeak of his plastic overall setting her teeth on edge. She had been waiting patiently for the forensics to finish while Sam stood beside her uncharacteristically quiet, his leopard analysing the situation with pure focus. She allowed him to stay for the time being, his animal instincts reacting at seeing the dead body. His leopard was always protective of her, regardless if she needed it or not.

"How was your date?" Sam asked as he carefully watched everyone who came in and out the corridor

"Date?" she replied, frowning.

"With Alistair?" He smirked down at her, his amber eyes amused.

He enjoyed telling everybody who asked about his eyes that he was born with them, in truth, they were a constant reminder of his harsh childhood. His leopard protected him the only way it knew how, but in doing so left him with permanent eyes of a predator.

"Al or whatever you want to call him." He brushed his shoulder against hers in affection.

Alice sighed, playing with the hem of her T-shirt before looking up at him. Thankfully Sam no longer wore his leather stage outfit, he had changed into a simple shirt and jeans once the authorities had turned up. His hair was in a high ponytail, keeping the blonde strands off his face. She had always been jealous of his hair, how it was completely straight compared to her natural wave. She had never told him so, didn't think his already enormous ego could handle it.

"Oh, that." She had no interest in going on a date with Al, her local magic shop owner and friend. He was a nice guy, even attractive but she wasn't interested in dating anyone. Unfortunately, Al didn't understand body language and wouldn't stop asking, so eventually, she had agreed, much to Sam's delight.

"That's tomorrow." She checked the time on her phone, the digital clock showing she had been there for hours already. "I have to meet him at Circle Plaza at six."

"The Circle, huh?" Sam whistled. "Fancy."

"Agent Skye, I didn't know you date." Detective O'Neil smiled as he walked over, a small curve of his lip. "I'll have to tell the other guys."

"Is that a joke, Detective?" She honestly wasn't sure, didn't know him well enough.

"Could be." He coughed, his small smile disappearing as he flipped open his black pad to study his notes. "According to Mr Donald, you were here before they found the dead body?" He looked at her over the paper, eyes questioning.

"I was here to pick up my roommate." She nudged Sam, who was staring into the room, arms folded.

"Aye, hello." Sam nodded towards the detective but didn't offer his hand.

"Irish?" Detective O'Neil asked.

"Aye, Galway. Not many people can tell." Sam looked surprised. He had only the slightest Irish twang, his accent having diluted from the amount of time he has lived in England. The only time it really came out was when he was angry, his accent and language changing back to that of his childhood.

"Father's from Dublin." Was all O'Neil said in explanation. "We will have to interview you once we have looked at the crime scene, please remain on the property."

"Aye." Sam waved absently before turning to Alice, his fingers brushing through the loose strands of her hair. "You okay?" *Should I stay?* His face asked.

Alice gently smiled, allowing him to continue touching her. He was calming his leopard, reassuring himself she was okay even though death was thick in his nose.

"I'll catch up with you."

He reluctantly released her. "Meet me after my late shift tomorrow? You can tell me all about your date."

"And you can tell me about your secret career change," she countered, unimpressed.

Sam smirked before disappearing down the corridor.

That boy has way too much interest in my love life. She shook her head.

The 'Pride' room was bright with artificial lighting, the glow harsh as it highlighted every little detail. Jones was thoughtful when Alice and O'Neil entered the small room, his eyes never straying from the deceased on the bed.

"What do we have?" O'Neil asked.

"Looks like we've found our vampire friend," Jones said when he finally acknowledged them.

A male was positioned on his back on the bed, half hidden beneath red furs that were draped across his body. White foam and bile had dripped from the side of his mouth onto the black sheet.

"You think this is him?" Alice asked as she watched Jones touch the thin skin, his fingers almost going through the flesh. "He doesn't even look like a Vamp."

"Yes, pretty confident in the way his body has started to degrade. As you can see..." Jones pointed to the body. "The deceased is suffering from severe dehydration as well as deterioration to muscle tone. He is almost mimicking mummification, which could explain the lack of stench." Jones studied the body closer.

Unlike faerie tales, vampires didn't turn to dust once dead. Instead, they decayed just like everyone else. The older the Vamp, the worse the smell and rot, almost as if their corpse reflected their real age.

The square room itself was floor to ceiling black latex with a drain in the corner. Alice didn't want to know what the cleaners hosed down after a client.

Mirrors covered every wall apart from the one behind the bed, that held shelves with an impressive selection of sex toys, varying from ordinary to ridiculous and dangerous.

"Mirrors for a room called Pride, funny." Alice moved closer to one, checking out the handprints along the glass. The main door caught her attention in the reflection, the light glinting off the solid metal with a single handle only accessible from the inside.

"How long has he been here?" O'Neil asked.

"It's hard to say." Jones shrugged. "An educated guess would be at least eight to twelve hours, maybe more. I would have to check in on the autopsy to make sure, wait for the blood works to match the others."

"Is there CCTV in this room?" O'Neil asked as he scanned along the ceiling.

"No, we do not record or monitor anything that goes on in the private rooms," Mac Donald said from the doorway.

"You must be Mr Mackenzie Donald?" O'Neil politely shook his hand. "Can you please explain to me what exactly happens in this room?"

O'Neil raised an eyebrow, pen poised on his notepad.

"These rooms can be rented privately by the hour. It is up to the clients what they do in here." Mac crossed his arms, closing off his body language.

"What time did he rent the room?" Alice asked, watching his iris flash a quick blue once she made eye contact. If he was getting annoyed at their questions already, he wasn't in for much fun.

"Around two."

"Is that not an unusual time for someone to hire this type of room?" O'Neil looked around, gesturing to the sex toys.

"My establishment is usually only open from eight to six. However, I make compromises for certain clients. Mr Little was a regular and big spender."

"Mr Little as in the Mayor's assistant?" Alice didn't recognise the man but definitely recognised the name, having been in the press several times in the last week alone. Mr Little was the current right-hand man to Mayor Claw ford, a mage and spokesperson for 'Breed is Us.' Highlighting equal rights to the lower scale Breeds, such as mages.

"That's correct. We take client confidentially seriously, which is why he frequented so much."

"Tell me, Mr Donald, how did Mr Little seem when you saw him?" Alice questioned, watching him flinch.

"It's Mac," he growled, "and that's confidential. What we do here isn't illegal." He started to get defensive, his shoulder tense as he leant forward. "We don't encourage the women to solicit themselves. However, we give them a safe place to do it."

"We're not judging, but this man has been dead around eight hours, and nobody thought to check on him?" She watched his face flush red. "The door is solid steel and several inches thick. The handle is on the inside with no way to open from the outside once the door is locked. You have no CCTV to act as a deterrent and have named the rooms after the seven deadly sins."

Alice stepped closer, watching how he automatically stepped back. He noticed too, the anger apparent in his expression.

"Rooms that you have named after behaviours deemed as cardinal vices, that have been tainted into excessive passions. In what way do you think people aren't going to take advantage of that?"

His eyes glowed pale blue, his wolf taking over. She didn't take much notice, shifters generally were quick to anger, especially dominant predators.

"We choose our customers carefully. They're fully vetted before they even step foot in any of our rooms."

"You still haven't answered my original question." Alice stifled her anger to maintain professionalism. She was trying to remain polite, do her job. Yet his aggressive reaction was grating on her nerves.

Predatory shifters were a pain in her arse.

"I didn't see Mr Little when he came in so cannot say how he was. He always books in advance without any assistance from us. The women or men he has chosen meet him in there."

"Who had he planned to meet?"

"All you need to know is that she's safe. Mr Little always booked a full twelve-hour slot. We've always assumed that he enjoyed relaxing on his own afterwards, so never disturbed him."

"What's her name? We would like to speak to her," O'Neil asked.

"Unless you have a warrant I will not speak to you about confidential details. I protect all my staff."

"If that's the way you wish to take it, Mr Donald..." O'Neil left the threat in the air. "I would like you to answer one more question. Do you recognise this woman?"

O'Neil produced a photograph of Stacey, the woman found in the motel. Alice recognised the picture from the bedroom, one that was on the nightstand.

Mac stared at the photograph for a few seconds, his jaw rigid. "No comment."

"Her name is Stacey," Alice said, watching his reaction. "She was found dead. We have reason to believe both the deceased knew each other."

"Stacey's dead?" Mac looked genuinely torn, it made her step back, allow him some space. "Yes, I know her. Knew her." He coughed to clear his throat. "She was a regular with Mr Little, but we let her go over a year ago." His eyes shot to Alice. "We have a zero tolerance on drugs. I wouldn't be able to tell you if they were still seeing each other outside my establishment."

"Do you know if Mr Little liked to use blood whores?" O'Neil asked. Blood whore was the term used for women who got high then allowed vampires to feed off them in exchange for money. Vampires metabolism was too fast, they couldn't even get drunk unless they drank the whole bar. The only thing that seemed to affect them was drinking contaminated blood.

Mac scowled. "So beautifully put. All I know is he asked one of my girls once to do it. When she refused, he never asked again."

"Thank you for your time, Mr Donald." Alice gave him a short nod.

He went to leave, hesitating before looking back.

"Miss Skye..." She caught his eye, was interested in how much control he allowed his wolf to have. "Get whoever did this. Stacey was a good girl who got in with a bad crowd. She wouldn't have hurt a fly."

Mac left the room, his office door slamming shut a moment later.

CHAPTER 9

T*his is just my luck.*

Alice sulked as she trudged through the busy underground, following the mass towards the vague direction of the exit. Her tyre had blown out earlier in the day, luckily relatively close to her house. She had abandoned it to Sam, hoping he would be able to sort it after his shift.

She huffed out a breath, the air freezing cold in the middle of December. Happy music flowed across the over-crowded tunnel, a mixture of acoustic guitar and violin that fought with the general noise of the crowd. As she walked the music got louder, until she was able to see buskers playing beside the mouth of the exit.

In full winter coats, scarfs and fingerless gloves they played, smiling and tapping their feet as they got into the rhythm of their tune.

Alice stopped by a train map, adjusting her scarf while enjoying the music as it flowed into a well- known musical number. As she watched, the guitarist began to mumble beneath his breath, inaudible against the instruments. Within seconds light erupted around them, little balls swirling and dancing in time with the music as the guitarist continued his silent chant. Alice couldn't help but smile as the children sang and danced along in delight.

"Stupid fucking faeries," someone spat.

"Go back to where you came from." Came another slur.

"Dirtybloods."

Alice turned to the three men, noticing their joint snigger as they kicked debris towards the musicians. They were all dressed in long black overcoats, open to show dark business suits with expensive gold watches.

"You're polluting with all that fucking sparkle."

"Humans rule this city."

"You're not wanted here, bloody faeries."

Alice felt herself get angry even as the musicians ignored the disruption. 'Faeries' was supposed to be a derogative term towards anyone of magic origin, whether they were a faerie or not. She had never met anyone who was actually offended by it, except faeries themselves of course.

"I think that's enough, boys." A tall man approached them, dressed in his own expensive suit. "You're making a scene."

"Who the fuck are..." One of the men began before he quickly stepped back, looking at the floor.

"I think you should all continue on your way now." The man's voice dropped. "Unless you would like to answer to me."

All three men quickly made their way through the exit, barely giving a backwards glance. The tall man started to turn, his eyes a bright gold before settling into a warm brown.

His face shimmered gently, the glamour he wore to

make himself look more human reactivating. Alice said nothing as she watched him adjust his coat, brushing imaginary hairs from the lapel.

His eyes shot to hers, the warm brown narrowed as he looked her up and down. Death. That's what she saw in his eyes, endless death.

Deciding she wasn't a threat he gave her a gentle nod before he walked away, heading further into the underground. Alice couldn't help but stare after him, almost as if he was a bug she needed to examine. He must have been a High Lord, the oldest amongst the Fae. Someone she knew not to mess with.

"Thank you for listening." A cheer as the musicians finished their set.

The sudden applause made her jump, shocking her out of the stasis. Laughing to herself, she followed the crowd into the cold night, happy it was only a short walk to the restaurant where she was meeting Al.

The Circle Plaza was an opulent glass conservatory situated on top of a tall, thin tower. A receptionist and doorman greeted her at the entrance to the golden lift, the metal shiny enough to reflect her image back at her.

"Do you have a reservation?" The receptionist asked, her ice blue eyes silently judging Alice's red scarf and worn leather jacket.

"I'm meeting Alistair Medlock."

"Ah, Mr Medlock. He hasn't arrived yet, you may make your way up and wait at the bar. Once your partner has arrived a member of staff will show you to your seat."

"Thank you," Alice said as the lift door closed behind her. Taking off her jacket and scarf, she held them on her arm, studying her reflection in the metal.

If it were up to her, she would have worn a dark pair of

jeans and a nice shirt. It was Sam who loudly protested what she should wear, to the point he had the dress already picked out for her. So she ended up wearing a mid-length spaghetti strapped red dress, with her hair lightly styled into waves that draped gently across her shoulders. She didn't know why she was here, why she even agreed to come on the date. It wasn't as if she had any luck with this sort of thing. Besides, Sam had enough sex for the both of them.

"Fuck sake," she mumbled beneath her breath, nerves a flutter in her stomach.

Why do I let people guilt trip me into shit?

She would happily take on a raging blood-lust vampire than a first date.

The lift dinged on the top floor, the doors opening to show a large open floor plan with the bar situated in the middle, surrounding the kitchen. The whole room was made of glass, giving a magnificent view of London in lights. Allowing a waiter to take her coat and scarf Alice settled herself onto a bar stool, ordering the first cocktail she saw on the menu.

Holy shit! Alice accepted the drink from the bartender, staring it as if it was made from gold. *Who pays this much for a drink?*

"Beautiful." A masculine voice said from behind her.

Turning her head, she gave a genuine smile, recognising the friendly face.

"The view? It's amazing, isn't it."

"I wasn't talking about the view." Nate Blackwell smiled charmingly before sitting beside her. His dark hair was shorter than the other day, the dark strands gelled into messy points. "Impressive performance at the gala by the way, I have never seen someone throw off their heels so fast while running." He chuckled, sipping his whisky.

"It's a talent." She smiled, tipping her glass.

"You never mentioned you were an agent, although I should have guessed considering you were chummy with the Commissioner." He tapped a finger against his glass, leaning forward to whisper into her ear. "You here on business, or pleasure?"

"Pleasure," she said with a small shrug. "Yourself?"

"Alas, it is business." He held his palm flat against his white shirt, feigning disappointment. "But I wish it was not."

"Mr Blackwell, how nice of you to make it on such short notice."

A man with long, pure white hair and black wrap-around glasses approached. He wore a turtle neck black jumper with leather straps across his shoulders, holding two pistols.

"Mr Storm is waiting for you." The man turned, his mouth a grimace as he noticed Alice.

Alice recognised him but wasn't sure where from, his look unusual enough to stick in her memory. He clearly recognised her, his blatant disregard obvious. She fought not to turn, trying not to give in to her curiosity of which Storm it was. Not that it mattered.

"Ma'am, Mr Medlock has just arrived, if you could follow me..." A waiter happily interrupted the awkward moment.

"It was nice to see you again Nate, I hope your business isn't too boring."

She stood up, grabbing her cocktail.

"It's business Alice, it's always boring." A chuckle.

"This way, ma'am." The waiter guided her to a table beside the window, Alistair already sitting down in his seat.

"Hello," she greeted as he stood up, kissing her on the

cheek. She tried not to show her reaction at the seating arrangement, not wanting to create a scene. She hated sitting with her back to the room, especially when she wasn't armed with anything other than a single knife strapped to her thigh, her clutch too small for a gun. Al only had his back to the kitchen with one door, compared to a restaurant full of people.

"I'm sorry I was late," he mumbled, "I had problems closing the shop."

He nervously touched his wine glass, brushing his fingertips across the surface before settling them into his lap.

"It's fine, my car decided to die today, so I had to take the tube." She allowed the waiter to set the napkin across her lap, nodding in thanks.

"Why didn't you contact me? I would have picked you up?" His smile turned to a frown.

"I didn't mind." She did, but it was either that or have no exit strategy if the date went to shit. "This view is amazing," she said, changing the subject. The view really was remarkable, a great vantage point of the city. Festive lights added to the magic, creating a serene scene as the sky threatened to snow.

"I'm glad you like it, one of my regulars mentioned this was one of the best places." His eyes twinkled. "You look, ah, wow."

"Thanks," she grinned, happy she went with Sam's idea and not her jeans and a nice shirt.

Al had dressed in a black suit with algae green tie that matched his eyes, his usual lank brown hair brushed from his face, framing his high cheekbones. She studied his skin for a second, wondering where his freckles had disappeared to until she noticed him nervously turning a black ring around his finger, the onyx glittering.

Complexion amulet, one that hid his freckles underneath a magic shroud.

"You look great too," she awkwardly complimented him back.

I'm so crap at this.

Al grinned in return, tugging his green tie. "I picked it out myself."

He held back a laugh as the waiter arrived and took their orders.

"How's Jordan? He still up to no good?"

"He keeps scaring Sam." She sipped her cocktail, enjoying the fruity flavour. "You ever going to take him back?"

"He's welcome back if he wishes, but I doubt we have any choice in the matter." He shrugged, blasé as if they weren't talking about an inanimate object that moved on its own. "Erm, Alice, do you know that guy?"

"Huh?"

"The man over there keeps staring in this direction."

Alice automatically turned, her eyes scanning the crowd until she settled on the table he was talking about. Mason Storm was charming the waiter as he ordered, Nate's dark head sitting beside him. Business meeting, he had said.

I wonder what type of business it was.

"I don't know him." She turned back to Al.

"Isn't that Councilman Storm? He just bought out one of my biggest competitors." He settled back in his chair, crossing his arms. "Bastards are putting me out of business."

"Yep, bastards," she agreed.

"I appreciate you accepting my dinner date, once Sam mentioned you were..."

"Wait, wait, wait. Hold up." She held up her hand. "You spoke to Sam?"

That weasel, he had put Al up to this.

"Guilty." He held up his palms, smiling before his eyes darted down. "Oh," Al reached forward before she could react, grabbing the crystal she wore tight to her neck. "You still wear it?"

The lapis lazuli was tied to a leather strap, the crystal singing at the sudden attention. Once Al had released it the stone went back to the hollow of her throat, settling down as it retouched her skin. He was the one who helped her unlock her crystals potential, able to create a physical barrier with a single incantation. That crystal had saved her life on more than one occasion.

"Yes," she stroked the cold surface. "I always wear it." Al caught her eye, his genuine happiness shining through.

He really is a nice guy, she thought, continuing to play with her necklace.

"Thanks for the..." She began before a distracting buzz vibrated the table. "I'm so sorry." She grabbed her clutch, unzipping to check her phone that continued to vibrate. "I thought I turned it off." She tried desperately to cancel the call, hitting any button she could in panic.

"That's okay, I know you work for the Supernatural Intelligence Bureau, if you need to answer it, go ahead, I don't mind."

"You sure?" she asked even as the phone started to vibrate once more, noticing it was Detective O'Neil.

"I'll be here once you get back," he winked.

"Thanks, I won't be long."

She left the table in a flurry, politely smiling at the people looking as she made her way towards the large balcony. Opening the door, she stepped into the cold, quickly getting herself under one of the warm heaters.

"Bloody phone," she mumbled as she flicked through her contacts.

"You shouldn't be outside without a coat. You could catch your death," a deep voice sniggered.

"Excuse me?" She glared at the man standing on the other side of the balcony, face hidden in shadow. An orange cigarette briefly glowed, highlighting his hair. "Oh, it's you."

The white- haired man who had a preference for sunglasses, even outside in the darkness of night.

"Seriously, have I done something to offend you?"

"No." Came the slow response.

"Then what reason do you have to dislike me?" she asked, not understanding why.

She didn't care if he liked her or not.

"I neither like you nor dislike you."

"How lovely," she murmured, turning her back. "Where do I even know you from?"

"Xander, what are you doing? I asked you to..." Mason stormed through the glass door. "Oh, I didn't realise you were outside," he sneered at her.

"Oh look, another fan of mine. What a lovely evening, isn't it Mason?"

"It's Councilman Storm." He glared at her before turning his frosty eyes towards the white- haired man. "Xander, get inside."

"I don't answer to you."

Another puff as he held the smoke in before releasing it out his nose.

"So fuck off."

"I'm the Arch..."

"I. Don't. Answer. To. You." Xander took off his glasses, his eyes so pale they were almost white.

Mason's face flushed red in irritation, even deeper once he caught Alice staring.

"Careful boy…" Anger apparent in every line of his body, his usual air of sophistication shattering. "Final warning."

Xander bowed sarcastically at the waist, his guns glinting from the light of the heater. Putting back on his sunglasses, he slowly walked into the restaurant, not acknowledging Alice.

"It's rude to watch another man's argument." Mason turned his impatience on Alice. "Did your parents not teach you better manners?" he sniggered.

Alice saw red, her hand crushing the phone even as the plastic groaned.

"I'm sorry, I didn't realise this wasn't a public place."

"Pathetic, let's hope my son doesn't beat you too badly into submission."

Alice ignored the threat.

"Why have The Council assigned me a Warden?"

"Because you're a liability," he replied as he grabbed the door handle, turning his back to her. "And you are a time bomb waiting to go off. We shall see if your fate matches the rest of your family."

He closed the door behind him, leaving her staring after him through the glass, up until he joined Nate back at the table with his fake smile once again in place.

What did he just say?

The phone vibrated in her hand.

CHAPTER 10

The sky had begun to glow white as Al drove her across the city, snow starting to fall as the temperature plummeted. Alice hated winter, didn't understand the joy of snow. It was cold and wet, two of the most miserable things. She touched her palm to the car window, feeling the frostbite through the glass.

"Here we are," Al said, putting the car into neutral.

"I'm sorry our date was cut short," she said, turning to face him, her hands freezing as she grabbed her bag.

"Your job is important," he shrugged. "At least we got some fancy drinks." He shot her a side smile.

She felt guilty. Not guilty because the date was cut short, but because she was glad for the excuse to leave early. The call had been O'Neil letting her know about a meeting, something she couldn't miss.

"It was a nice evening." Her eyes darted to the digital clock by the steering wheel, only 6:56 p.m. She hadn't even been at the restaurant for an hour before they had to leave. She really sucked at dates. "I'll make it up to you."

"I have an idea," he said as she turned to face him, his lips stroking across her own before she could even react. She automatically kissed him back, his tongue teasing her bottom lip as she pressed forward.

She felt nothing. No excitement. No attraction.

Nothing.

After a minute Al slowly moved back, his eyes sad as he sighed dramatically.

"You didn't feel anything either, did you?"

Alice awkwardly laughed, shaking her head gently. "I'm sorry."

"Don't be, that's what first dates are for." He rested back in his seat, closing his eyes. "Friends?"

"Of course," she gripped his shoulder, squeezing it gently before opening the door. "It really was a nice night."

"We will do it again sometime," he smiled. "But as friends."

"Friends."

Waving her goodbye, she stepped through the revolving door. She quickly took in the grand atrium, studying the white tiles, high ceiling and large opaque glass behind the front desk.

"Hello..." she started as she approached.

"Just a moment ma'am," the woman said, her attention on the paperwork scattered in front of her.

Alice waited even as she felt eyes prickle her skin. Officers milled around, some leaning against a few desks to the side of the room, their eyes tracking her every movement.

"I'm here to see Detective O'Neil," she said when her patience ran out. "I'm Agent Skye, he should be expecting me."

That caught the woman's attention, her eyes appraising Alice slowly before she frowned. "You the witch?"

"Spook squad." Someone quietly murmured from beside her, followed by a few chuckles.

Alice shot them an irritated look, watching the men's faces turn sober before she gave her attention back to the woman.

What's their problem?

Alice scrambled in her clutch for her badge, holding it to the glass so the officer could see.

"That would be me."

"What's a witch doing in our department?" Another of the men said from behind.

"She doesn't look like a witch, more like a hooker."

"Pretty though..."

Alice felt her ears burn.

"Hey guys," she said with a fake smile, moving so she had all the male officers in her sight. "Do we have a problem?"

"Do we have a problem?"

There were three men in total, one at his desk with paperwork stacked high and two who sat on the edge. The five other desks were empty.

"No, ma'am," one of them chuckled. "You going to play with our wands?"

Alice felt a blush burn her cheeks.

"What do you call a clairvoyant leprechaun who escaped from prison?"

The men looked at her as if she was crazy. Which honestly, was debatable.

"A small medium at large," she finished.

One officer broke into a grin with the other two continued to stare at her as if she had lost it.

"No?" She dramatically rolled her eyes. "What about this one. What did the policeman say to his belly button?"

"You're under a-vest," replied a deep, gravelly voice. "Agent Skye, is there a reason you're aggravating my officers?" Detective Brady frowned, crossing his arms across his chest as he glared at her.

"They invited me to play with their wands," she said, her eyes narrowed. "I was just starting with some foreplay."

Brady's' eyes shot to the men, who quickly made themselves busy. "Very funny Agent Skye. You're late, please follow me."

He turned towards a keypad and entered the passcode, consciously making sure she couldn't see. Holding the door, he waited for her to follow, his face impatient.

"I was told to get here for seven." She followed him through the corridor, meeting every set of eyes who uneasily stared her way.

This place seems welcoming.

"Through here." He opened another door with a key card, allowing her to enter before him. Quietly thanking him she passed through, greeting O'Neil, Jones and Peyton. The room smelled of fresh coffee as all three men sat quietly around a circular table, the reason for the smell evident in the centre. Behind O'Neil was a large felt board, photographs of each deceased connected with the case showcased in vivid detail.

"What are you wearing?" Jones chuckled. "You look hot."

"I was on a date." She smiled before sitting down, besides Brady.

"Did any of the boys give you any hassle?" O'Neil raised his eyebrows.

"She tried to bore them with bad jokes." Brady leant back in his chair, a small smile on his lips.

"They weren't bad, they're just a bad audience," she muttered.

"Apologies about cutting your date short Alice, but we needed this meeting sooner rather than later. Jones, as you're the one with the most information, why don't you start?"

"Right-o." Jones leapt up from his chair, his T-shirt crinkled to the point it was entirely possible that it had never seen an iron. "As you can see from the photographs, deterioration amongst the bodies is pretty consistent, with the end results including severe dehydration and muscle loss. Bones become brittle and in some cases have even disintegrated under only a small amount of pressure." Jones pointed to one photograph showing bone fragments, the once white shards now a dull grey.

"Is that in both the deceased vampires and humans?" Brady asked, leaning forward in his seat as he studied the gruesome details.

"Yes. The main difference is the process is much faster in the vampire targets. They start to degenerate within thirty to ninety minutes while the human carriers don't show deterioration until a few hours after exsanguination. We believe the carriers are ingesting the substance rather than injecting as there seems to be a more concentrated amount at the back of their throats. Other than Stacey Cartman, not one of our carriers had evidence of intravenous injection."

"Any luck on I.D.'ing the substance?"

"Yes and no."

Jones reached across the table and opened a black folder, handing out identical sheets with various numbers on.

"So as of yet, we have not been able to positively identify it completely, however, from the concentrated amount found, I have been able to cross match the results with a recent analysis." He pointed to the numbers as if anybody else could understand it. "It's blood."

"Blood?" All three of them said in unison.

"Yes. In fact, it's almost identical to that of a John Doe found in an abandoned warehouse a few months back. It's on record that he has been classified as a Daemon transition."

"What?"

"You have got to be shitting me!"

Alice felt herself go still, her full attention on Jones as he explained the similarities in the blood works.

Daemon. Fuck sake.

"Okay, so for now we will accept that it's Daemon blood until we find any evidence otherwise. What do we know of Daemons?" O'Neil asked, looking expectantly at Alice.

Alice blinked stupidly until Brady gently nudged her.

"What can I tell you about Daemons..." She hesitated, deciding carefully how much she could say. "From the limited information out there, the impression is that Daemons are well equipped with black magic. They're not technically classified as Breed as they haven't been recorded since the early nineteenth century. There is no known data regarding their origin."

"What about the significance of drinking their blood?"

Alice shook her head. "It depends on how you look at it. Vampires exchange blood when they are transitioned. So it's a possibility that drinking Daemon blood is part of the initial ritual, although this is all speculation."

"We need to know more. What's their feature characteristics? How could we identify one?"

"You would know." Alice laughed, the sound empty.

"They were named Daemons because of their physical similarities to various religions depictions. Full-fledged Daemons would have to be under glamour if they were walking among the general population."

"What about only part Daemons? Like the ones in transition?" Jones asked.

"There isn't really anything. They could look like you or me." She moved her attention to Brady. "Did you get anything more on those markings we found in Miss Cartman's kitchen?"

"I have them here." Brady shuffled through his stack of notes until he produced some photographs. "I couldn't find anything on the markings other than confirming what Agent Skye said at the scene." He pointed to the top of the pentagram, explaining the significance to the other guys.

"May I have a look?" Peyton asked, his blue eyes serious as he held his hand out for the images. "These look like Brimstone. Some manufacturers like to protect their batch as they cook, she was probably dealing."

"Actually it was her husband who was dealing," O'Neil added, squinting at his notepad. "Steven Cartman. Charged with possession, intent to supply, GBH and ABH."

"That brings me to my next point: Mr Cartman." Jones went to stand by the grey felt, pointing at the right photograph. "I've included him on the board even though he isn't a direct victim. Steven Lewis Cartman, age unknown. Breed has been confirmed as Fae, however, neither of the Courts have come forward with anymore details on specifics. He had a minute amount of the substance in his system but not enough to be deadly, it's likely his wife transferred it through a kiss."

"Bleeding gums?" Brady suggested.

"Actually that's a possibility, she was suffering from

stage four lung cancer. Bleeding gums, as well as coughing blood are common symptoms."

"What about the recent vampire?" Brady asked. "How is he connected?"

"Mr Chris Little was confirmed to have known Stacey intimately for at least a year. Forensics also found his name and details in a little black book hidden beneath her mattress with dates of their meetings."

"So are we suggesting this was a targeted kill?" Alice asked.

"It would be a great coincidence if not."

"Let's hope no other high ranking Vamp likes to sleep with the ladies of the night then, shall we," Peyton mumbled.

"So do we have any other leads?" O'Neil looked around the room. "Surely that can't be it? We can't just sit here until we have another victim to add to that fucking board." His lip twitched, his hand touching his breast pocket as if searching for something.

"Sick, she was sick." Alice stood up, walking over to the photograph of Stacey, naked on the bed. "I was approached the other night by a woman claiming to be their friend. She explained Stacey was sick and the hospital couldn't do anymore for her. Apparently, she had tried every option she could think of, including black magic."

"What's this friends name? She could be our next lead."

Alice had to think. "Mia."

Peyton searched through the paperwork before stopping at one sheet.

"Is this her?" He handed Alice the paper.

Office of the medical examiner
London

Report of examination

Decedent: *Mia Simpson*
Case Number: RF 14466-882036
Cause of death: *Fxsanguination*
Identified by: *Fingerprints *available from database*
Age: 25 *years*
Sex: *Female* ***Race:*** *Caucasian* ***Breed:*** *Human*
Date of death: (*Found*) 18/12/2017 (*Estimate*) 18/12/2017

....

Date of Examination: 19th *December* 2017 *through to* 20th *December* 2017
Examination and summary analysis performed by: *Dr Lewis Fisher*
Cause of death: *Exsanguination* (*Loss of blood to a degree sufficient enough to cause death*)

....

Findings

() *Sharp object used to cut with an upwards stroke*
() *Angle of laceration consistent with self-administration*

() *Other than throat, no other open wounds*
() *Blade matched wound*
() *Scars consistent with self-harm*
() *Brimstone found in blood sample,* 15%

....

Conclusion:
The subject fatally wounded herself by slicing her jugular in one clean movement. The manner of death is suicide.

Alice read the paper silently, the feeling of guilt crushing.

"Agent, you okay?" Jones cautiously approached her, both hands palm up as if she was a wild animal, one that could attack.

Her Tinkerbell floated around her wrist, sparking each time it approached the autopsy report.

"I'm sorry." She fluffed the ball of fire away. "Yes, this is her."

She handed the paper back, trying to ignore the stunned looks.

"Apologies for my reaction..." She couldn't finish.

"Would this put us in any danger?" Brady asked deadpan, his face serious as he cautiously watched her light.

"Sometimes, this happens. I'm sure you understand premature ejaculation Detective?" She tried to smile at her joke, her lips trembling at the effort.

"Do you remember anything else about your conversation with Miss Simpson," O'Neil asked before Brady could reply.

Alice thought back.

"Santa offered her a lifeline." She frowned even as she said it out loud.

"Santa? Are we serious right now?" Brady grumbled, her ejaculation joke having not gone down well.

"Santa had offered to protect her soul. I didn't take much notice because this woman was high and delirious."

"This is nonsense from a woman high on Brimstone, surely we can't take anything she said seriously..." Brady stood up, frustrated. "Fucking Santa for goodness sake."

"Let the light guide you," Alice whispered, finally remembering the phrase the woman muttered beneath her breath.

"What did you say?" Brady stood beside her, his mouth agape.

"Brady, do you recognise that phrase?" O'Neil asked.

"It's a saying from the Church of the Light," Peyton spoke up, his eyes darting to Brady, who had taken on a grey sheen.

"They have nothing to do with this, they're controversial but peaceful," Brady stuttered.

"Is this a conflict of interest?" O'Neil asked. "I have to know if you need to be reassigned."

"No conflict of interest," he glared, nostrils flaring. "I'm just surprised. I doubt we can take anything Miss Simpson said seriously while in her state."

"Either way it's a lead."

O'Neil wrote something down in his little black book.

"Do we know how many churches they have in London?"

"Just the one," Brady confirmed.

"What's our best approach?"

Brady took a second to think. "Undercover would be my guess. I doubt they would talk to the police, never mind a witch."

"Don't worry Detective, they won't know I'm a witch."

CHAPTER 11

"What are you wearing?" Sam asked as he took a seat opposite her in the small coffee shop. "Please tell me you didn't wear that to your date?" he glared.

"What? No!" Alice started to laugh, gaining her some odd glances from the other late-night customers.

She simply wore a vest with black workout leggings. Sam's eyebrows rose when he read the typography across the fabrics, his initial shock turning into a smirk. The words *'I don't run!'* was printed large across her breasts with *'but If I am, you probably should too as something is chasing me'* written underneath. She thought it was comical. The other customers didn't seem to agree.

The coffee shop was quiet, which wasn't a surprise considering how late it was.

She would never have known the shop existed if it wasn't for Sam's weird career change. The aromatic scents of coffee beans and homemade fruit scones were comforting as she cuddled around her caramel latte.

The place itself was cute, with a varied selection of freshly made pastries and cakes on display plus a chalkboard with over one hundred different coffee and tea blends. Babies, puppies and kittens that were dressed as fruit decorated the walls, which Alice thought was a bit strange but not totally unamusing.

"Then why are you wearing your gym gear?" he asked while he waved his hand for the employee's attention. "You don't normally work out this late."

"Because if I don't hit something soon, I might explode," she sighed, sipping her coffee.

"Was the date that bad?" he asked as he ordered a black Americano from the barista.

"It wasn't awful." *It wasn't exactly good either,* she wanted to add.

But Sam could read her eyes, his own replying, *you're obviously too good for him.*

She couldn't hide her smile. There were only two people she could have a word-less conversation with, able to understand each other's expressions. It took knowing someone better than yourself to understand.

"There was no spark," she explained out loud. "Maybe I'm just destined to be alone forever."

"So sad, baby girl," Sam laughed. "Maybe you could become one of those crazy women with a ton of cats?"

"Well, I technically already have one," she grinned.

"Very funny," he said as his eyes danced mischievously.

"So are we going to talk about the elephant in the room?"

An eyebrow shot up, a smile playing across his lips. "What elephant?"

"What happened to being a bartender at The Blood Bar?"

Sam smiled at the barista when he brought over his coffee, winking charmingly.

"I don't know really," he shrugged. "Saw it advertised and thought why not?"

Alice shook her head. Sam was the most impulsive person she knew.

"I love to dance and enjoy people's reactions when I do. So what that I slowly take my clothes off?"

"I don't care that you strip for a living, I care because you didn't tell me."

Alice looked down at her coffee, staring at the caramel liquid. They told each other everything; it was what they did. A mutual dependency on each other's crap. She knew the reason he never told her wasn't that he was embarrassed, Sam didn't get embarrassed. So why didn't he tell her?

"I wanted to tell you, but you were still healing. You didn't need the added stress of knowing I was working for one of the pack."

"I'm not angry at the pack!" She raised her voice, causing eyes to shoot in their direction. "I don't blame the pack," she said quieter. At least, she didn't anymore. She knew how hierarchy worked, knew that the low-level dominants, as well as the submissive, were compelled to follow their Alpha's orders.

"Good, because we had an unwanted guest this morning while you were out."

"Guest?" she frowned. "Who?"

"Theo Wild."

Alice sat back in her seat, staring at Sam as she thought it through. Why would the new Alpha of White Dawn want to speak to her? She had already told him what she thought, wanted nothing to do with him or his twin.

"What the hell does he want?"

"Apparently he had petitioned for you through The Tower. Dread refused the contract and he wanted to personally ask you for your help."

"Dread refused?"

Dread never refused work, the man would accept the last blood covered penny from a dying old woman.

"Wait, what does he need help with?"

"Theo wants to find Rex. Apparently, he's disappeared, refusing any calls or summons. I know there's something Theo didn't say, he seemed worried, desperate even."

"Desperate?"

"Something bad is happening. An Alpha doesn't show weakness, at least, not a proper Alpha. Yet he begged me to ask you." Sam shook his head.

Alphas didn't beg.

"I wouldn't have accepted it anyway," she quietly said, finishing off her drink.

"You sure about that?" Sam asked, his amber eyes seeing through her.

No, she wasn't sure.

"You need to..." Sam stopped mid-sentence.

"Sam? What are you..." she felt it then, the familiar current across her chi. She whipped her head around, mouth open as her brother stood in the threshold.

Kyle stared between them, his movements agitated as if he was ready to flee. He wore all black, his face slightly obscured by the oversized dirty black hoody. She didn't notice Sam move until he was already beside Kyle, he spoke softly, his voice not carrying across the short distance. He waved goodbye before he left, but Alice couldn't look away from her brother.

Kyle warily took a seat opposite her, pushing off his hood. He had cut his hair, darker than she remembered, almost black compared to the mousy brown of his childhood.

"Your cat threatened me at the door," Kyle said, a shadow of a smile creeping across his lips. "I like him."

Alice burst into laughter, feeling a tear burn down her cheek. "Yeah, he's overprotective."

Kyle hesitantly reached over, his hand shaking as he brushed the tear away. His sleeve pulled up at the movement, revealing the silver band that encircled his wrist. Her eyes shot to it before he quickly covered the band back up.

Slave bands, once controlled by a Daemon before Riley destroyed him. She knew he had another on his other wrist, as well as a choker around his neck.

"Why haven't you come home?" she said, feeling desperation grow.

"I can't." His voice broke, making her heart ache. "How can you live there, knowing what happened? How can you survive the memories?"

"You have to learn to accept your past. Accept the things you can't change."

"We shouldn't have to accept them," he growled. His pupils grew, encasing the majority of his eyes before he closed them, breathing heavy.

No, I guess not.

"It doesn't hurt as bad."

Kyle's jaw clenched and his cheekbones grew sharp, his hands clawed as he silently struggled. She longed to reach out and comfort him but knew that would only push him away.

The barista started to make his way over, a friendly smile plastered on his face until Alice caught his attention, silently begging him not to approach.

Relaxing back into her seat once he nodded she cupped

her drink, patiently waiting. Kyle had put on weight since she last saw him properly, his face not as gaunt. But he was still too skinny. Too pale.

Alice hitched in a breath, pain resonating through her left palm, her crescent scar pulsating. Frowning, she clenched her fist to try to stop the ache. It had never done that before, not since the bite had healed. She opened her hand, tracing the darkened skin that started in the middle of her palm, curling down to just below her wrist.

"I'm sorry," Kyle said, eerily soft. His eyes were once again green, the same as hers, the same as their mothers.

"It was never..."

"It hurts, doesn't it?" he interrupted as he stared at her palm. "Where he bit you."

"It's fine." She clenched her hand again, hiding it in her lap beneath the table. "None of it was your fault."

"You don't know that," he snapped, his eyes darkening with his anger. He started to shake, his control splintering. "I can't... I need..." His chair crashed to the ground as he abruptly stood. "I'm sorry."

"Kyle, wait..." She reached for him, only grasping air as he left the coffee shop, forcing people out his way.

"KYLE!" She ran after him, stumbling to a halt on the street.

He was gone.

Fuck.

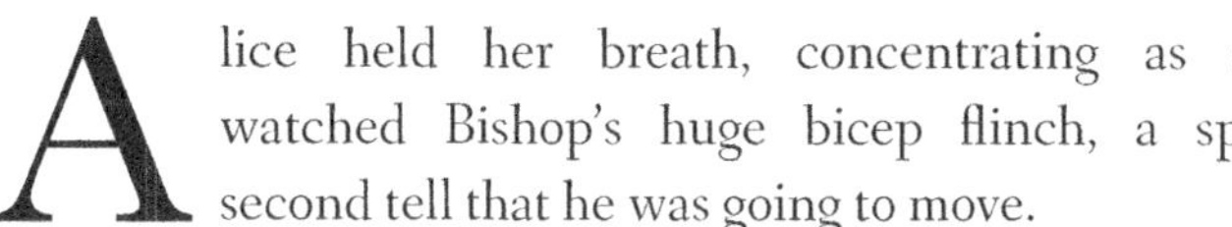

Alice held her breath, concentrating as she watched Bishop's huge bicep flinch, a split-second tell that he was going to move.

She jumped back just in time, barely missing the head-sized fist as she kicked out, catching his knee with her foot which gained her a satisfying grunt.

She was too wound up, needed to vent her excess energy.

The talk with Sam hadn't helped the violent turmoil in her gut, it just added to it.

She should have helped that woman, instead she was dead. Now she had the option to help a man she never wanted to see again, his brother begging for her assistance. Then there was Kyle...

Alice needed to hit something, to process through her emotions just as the doctors had advised. She was grateful she lived in a city, a place where it wasn't uncommon for a gym to be open late.

"Stupid bitch, that fucking hurt," Bishop snarled, spit jumping from his swollen lips.

She ignored the jibe, instead ducking as he launched at her once more.

"Stay the fuck still."

Alice knew she was pissing him off, was watching his face turn a dark shade of red as she kept evading him.

"Take your time, Bishop," she goaded, enjoying his angry grunts.

Bishop was over six foot, double her weight with a face only a mother could love. She knew that one hit from a meaty fist could end her, so she had to wear him down first. As a workout, it was average. Her heart rate was barely up, and she hadn't broken into a sweat. But as a distraction, it was perfect. It forced her to concentrate, slowing down her rage until it was a quiet simmer that she could think past.

Dodging yet another move she kicked out, showing him off balance and into the mat.

"Alice, stop playing with him," Sensei scolded. "You

should have had him pinned by now, but you're too busy toying."

He shook his head in disappointment before moving onto the next couple.

"She can't fucking pin me!" Bishop roared, teeth bared as veins pulsated down his thick neck. He was panting at the edge of the mat, elbows rested on his knees.

Alice rolled her eyes, bouncing on the balls of her feet when she felt something tickle across her aura.

She frowned, wondering what it was as she quickly glanced around, unable to find the source. Checking to make sure Bishop was still panting in his corner she turned around, finally spotting the man dressed in dark jeans and a black top, a leather jacket draped across his arm.

He leant against the wall, arms folded across his chest as his razor-sharp gaze watched unwavering. She had no idea how long he had been standing there.

"Fuck sake," she moaned beneath her breath.

She gestured to him, a smile curving his cheek before his eyes hardened to something behind her.

Abruptly she was airborne, the wind rushing out her body in one startled exhale when she hit the mat hard, her lungs struggling to recover as a heavy weight settled on her torso. She twisted, trying to dislodge the pressure to no avail, Bishop's knees pinning her arms down.

She tapped the mat three times, signalling defeat. The weight didn't move, so she tapped the mat again even as she started to struggle harder.

"How do you like that? Bitch!" Bishop spat at her, his full weight crushing.

"GET OFF!" she gasped. She threw herself to the side, unsettling him before he had her arms painfully pinned above her head.

"There's only two places for women," he said with an expression of pure fury. "In the kitchen and on your back, legs spread..."

She didn't allow him to finish.

"Ventilabis," she snarled, throwing her head into his nose as intense heat pricked across their skin.

"FUCK!" He automatically moved to protect his face, giving her the room she needed to kick out from underneath him.

Inhaling a lung full of air, she coughed, bending at the waist.

"What the fuck was that?"

"YOU FUCKING BURNT ME!" Red marks decorated his tanned skin, beside singed hair that was smoking. "That's cheating."

He went to grab her neck, his mouth howling in pain as her knee connected with his groin instead.

"Bishop, get up." Sensei scowled, tapping him with his foot. "You know the rules. Once a partner taps out, you stop."

"But she used magic!" he snapped back, eyes full of hate.

"And you would have let her pass out. This is your only warning, play by the rules or leave."

"It's my turn."

In all the commotion, Alice hadn't heard Riley move towards them, his face devoid of any emotion. He shot a look towards Alice before stepping onto the mat and removing his shirt. Alice stepped back, trying not to stare at the mesmerising tattoos.

"You can leave your shirt on, you know," she murmured.

Riley was a better match to Bishop, their sizes similar,

although Bishop wasn't as tall but meatier compared to Riley's toned strength.

"Is that who I think it is?" Sensei asked as they eagerly watched the two men circle each other. Alice noticed many of the other sparring couples had stopped to watch too.

"My stalker? Then yes, yes it is."

"Don't be a wise arse." He smirked down at her. "What's he doing here?"

"Probably wants to kick my arse, just like he's doing Bishop's."

Alice felt the kick as Riley's foot connected to Bishop's stomach, the move winding him completely. Alice tried not to smirk, enjoying the fight.

Payback's a bitch.

"Wow, that man can move," Sensei whistled, his complete attention on the match, "almost as well as myself."

Alice didn't comment, instead analysing everything both fighters were doing. It was akin to a sleek, elegant panther fighting an untrained puppy, Riley counterattacking and dodging every move with ease. His movements even seemed lazy compared to usual, his speed matching his partner when she knew he was faster. Much faster.

"I'm sorry, I didn't know he would be coming."

"Are you kidding? My students need to watch how he moves, and that includes you." He caught her eye, his attention going back to the fight a few seconds later. "Surprising isn't it? Considering who he is. I wonder who he trained with?"

A huge cheer as Bishop crashed into the mat, his breathing laboured as Riley stood above him, barely sweating. "Stay down."

"Fuck..." A sharp inhale as Bishop brushed the blood

from beneath his nose. "You." He staggered to his feet, fists lifted.

"Suit yourself." Riley leapt at him, turning into a roundhouse kick that flattened Bishop once again. This time, he stayed down. The room erupted into applause, every student having stopped what they were doing to watch.

"GET BACK INTO POSITIONS!" Sensei yelled, disbanding the crowd.

"I apologise if I was a distraction." Riley stepped forward, shaking Sensei's hand.

"No need to apologise, it was an honour to watch." With a bow he turned back towards his students, turning around only to give Alice a wink.

"What are you doing here?" Alice angrily whispered as she walked towards the changing room. "How much did you see?"

"Enough to know that you can move well," Riley said as he followed. "You had so many opportunities to beat him, yet didn't. Why?"

"I don't have to explain myself to you," Alice said as she pushed open the changing room door.

How dare he just turn up like that.

She punched in her locker code, opening the door when a hand slammed it shut.

"That was lazy fighting, and you know it," Riley glared.

"Bloody hell Riley, this is the ladies changing room."

She quickly regarded her surroundings, relieved that they were alone. From the sound of the adjoining showers and the women's underwear on the bench that separated the lockers they wouldn't be alone for long.

He continued as if she hadn't spoken.

"You move well, fast. But you continuously leave your left side open. You can't always resort to your magic..."

She tried to yank the metal door, before letting out a sound of frustration.

"If you were so bothered, why didn't you step in?"

"I knew you would be able to get out of it." His looked at her with a such pure focus that unnerved her. He pulled his hand away, allowing her to open the door. "Besides, it would defeat the purpose if I just saved you."

Alice had to grit her teeth from snapping back. She wasn't a damsel in distress, she was a trained Paladin.

"What are you doing here?"

"To see you. You're ignoring me."

"That's funny considering I haven't heard from you in months."

She slammed the locker shut once she had grabbed her bag, letting it drop to the floor by her feet.

"Now are you going to stand there and watch me shower or are you going to fuck off?"

His gaze intensified.

"Is that an invitation, sweetheart?" He gave her a slow teasing grin.

She knew he was joking, but she couldn't stop the heat that shot through her.

"Fuck. Off."

His lip twitched as he fought not to laugh.

"That's harsh considering you were inviting me into the shower only a moment ago."

"I swear Riley, I will..." Alice heard footsteps.

Pushing him back, she hid them behind the lockers, her palms on his bare chest. The woman sang as she dressed quickly, the changing room door swinging closed behind her after a few minutes.

She pulled her palms back as if she had been burned.

"You're going to get me kicked out." She caught his eye,

taken back by the unidentifiable emotion. His humour had gone, replaced with a stern expression.

Riley reached down to her bag and grabbed it before she could.

"We need to talk."

"Give me my bag." She went to snatch it, but he was faster. "RILEY," she snarled, not wanting to draw attention as another woman who had walked in, her eyes widening as she briskly made her way to her own locker. But not before she gave Riley a long look.

"We need to talk," he repeated. "Not here, it's too public."

"I'm busy."

"I didn't mean right now." He seemed annoyed. "I'll come by tomorrow."

"I'm busy," she replied again.

I don't need this crap.

"Doing what?"

"If you must know, I'm going to the Church of the Light."

"Why?" He handed her the bag before he folded his arms, making her eyes trace the tattoos along his pec. Her eyes shot up as her cheeks began to burn. Riley didn't seem to notice.

"None of your business." She enjoyed it when he clenched his jaw, eyes pinched in anger. He wasn't a man who was disobeyed often.

Riley cocked his head before he stepped forward, crowding her.

"Why?" he asked again.

"I'm thinking of converting," she shrugged, desperately trying not to touch him again. "Can you please put on a shirt?"

"Why, does it bother you?"

"No," she said too fast.

He growled, throwing on his T-shirt.

"I know you're part of that Spook Squad."

Alice just narrowed her eyes in response.

"Meet me at my place tomorrow... after your church," he added before she could protest, "and bring your sword."

CHAPTER 12

Alice stared at the ornate, but tired architecture that was the Church of the Light, the morning sun giving an almost ethereal quality to the off-white brick.

She must have walked past it hundreds of times and never looked up, never studied the gargoyles that crouched beside the tall but crumbling spires or the old bell through the broken stained-glass window.

The grounds, which must have once had fresh flowers and neatly trimmed shrubbery, had decayed into dilapidated courtyard with dead grass and aged headstones.

"The place has let itself go over the years," Peyton stated as he watched her expression. "Strange considering Brady's intel stated they charge an extortionate fee to join." His lip lifted.

"It's fitting they have gargoyles," she mused. "They're supposed to scare off evil."

Peyton's lip tugged again at the corners. "They consider Breed to be evil."

"What do you think?" she asked.

She turned to look at him, wanting to see his reaction. She still hadn't figured out what he was, knew he couldn't be human. At least, not entirely.

"Are Breed evil?"

"Breed is both evil and good, as are humans. That's the way of life," he said, left eyebrow arched. "Is that the response you wanted?"

"I have time to wear you down," she shrugged, smiling at his subtle head shake.

"We're going to be doing this my way."

He tugged at his tie as if he wasn't used to wearing one, the bright red a shock against the darkness of his tailored suit. Alice, in contrast, wore a pair of blue jeans and a slogan T-shirt that luckily her leather jacket covered, so she didn't look too casual.

Nobody mentioned dressing up, she thought self-consciously.

"Why are we here so early?"

His light eyes shot to her, his face impassive. He shook his head again before he crossed the street, confidently walking through the tall gates and towards the door as if insects weren't crawling across her skin. Trying not to squeak, Alice walked rigidly beside him, trying not to draw attention to herself among the other people. As she crossed the threshold, the sensation stopped as suddenly as it started.

"Did you feel that?" she whispered, looking around to see if anybody else had reacted.

What the fuck was that?

"Remember why we're here dear," he tensely replied, his eyes scanning the few people who were setting up extra seating beside the pews.

A woman wearing a yellow checkered jumper approached, a wide grin creasing her face.

"Are you the Noland's?" she said in a preppy voice. "Why you guys are early, service doesn't start for another few hours or so."

"That's us, ma'am." Peyton grinned, clasping her outstretched hand. "We know we're early, but we don't have time to stay for the service you see? My wife has a doctor's appointment for her fertility check-up."

Peyton grasped Alice's hand, patting it gently.

Alice's face broke into a fake, shy smile.

Bloody hell, he's good.

Peyton was playing to the recent propaganda that human numbers were falling compared to Breed. There was no evidence to suggest their fertility was failing. However, facts have never been strictly necessary to scare the general public.

"It was the only appointment we could manage," Alice politely added.

Peyton started to stroke Alice's hand gently, even giving her a little squeeze of reassurance.

"I appreciate you accepting my call the other evening, we didn't really know where to turn and have heard great things about your service."

The woman's eyes melted at the affectionate connection.

"Oh you poor dears, it's those damn Breeds, cursing us normal folk with poor fertility." She tutted and frowned, creating deep crevices in her forehead. "Feel free to have a look around, the only people who are here other than myself are a few volunteers who are helping to set up."

"Thank you kindly," he winked, before turning away.

"Come on dear, let's get accustomed to this magnificent church."

"Yes, honey." Alice smiled appropriately, letting her gaze take in the supposedly 'magnificent' church. The inside was only marginally better than the outside, the walls the same dull brick.

A gust of wind caught her coat from one of the broken windows, the cardboard that had once been taped up had fallen off, dropping the temperature in the already cold and open room.

"Excuse me, can I help you?" Another woman approached, her eyes unfriendly as she folded her arms. "We're not open right now, you'll have to come back later," she said, her tone short.

"Hi, my name's Gary Nolan, and this is my wife, Melissa." Peyton tugged at Alice. "We were invited by your friend to look around. We're looking to..."

"You're not wearing a ring." The woman interrupted, her eyes shooting to their joined hands where neither of them wore any jewellery.

"Oh, that's me," Alice chuckled, tugging her hand. "Miss ole clumsy."

"Ah, yes." Peyton started to laugh too, catching on to the situation fast. "My wife's an artist, gets paint everywhere. She recently knocked over a whole pot of paint, covering both of us completely."

"That reminds me honey, the rings need to be picked up from the jeweller's a week on Tuesday."

"Oh," the woman looked almost embarrassed by her hostility. "It's nice to meet you, my name's Mrs Lucinda Potts. I apologise if I came across as rude, we've had a lot of weird people wander in recently. I could have sworn they were Breed, but you know we can't always tell." She shook her head.

"I know exactly what you mean Mrs Potts, it's the reason we're here." Peyton moved closer, putting a reassuring hand on her shoulder. "Our neighbourhood is full of them, my wife and I are so worried about our souls being affecting by living in such close proximity."

He genuinely looked worried to the point Alice wasn't sure if he was acting or not.

"It can affect you if you're too friendly with them. But in the same breath, you don't want to upset any of them just in case."

Her eyes darted around as if she mustn't speak of such things. "I heard witches have the ability to suck your soul right out of you. So be wise."

"Oh no, really." Alice gasped, trying not to smile. "We don't live near any witches that I know of, it's those blood sucking vampires that worry me. How can they have a soul if they're already dead?"

"Tell me about it!" Mrs Potts said energetically before starting a lecture about vampires, blood and sacrifices.

"Lucy, can you please help out in the office? James is struggling." A deep set man asked as he approached. "I'll speak to our guests."

"Of course, my dear." She smiled shyly before walking off.

"I see you've met my wife, the names Gordon Potts. How can I help you today?" The gentleman smiled warmly, shaking both their hands before resting his own against his breast pocket.

Alice frowned, taking a second to recognise the man who stood before her.

"I know you, you were leading the rally in front of Parliament."

He had wanted public places to segregate Breed and humans. He was removed from the grounds, but not before giving an interview to the local news station.

Mr Potts grinned, the expression uncomfortable.

"That is just some of the work we do here."

Alice smiled but stepped back, feeling something off about him.

On the news footage he came across as confident, his gaze razor- sharp as he addressed the growing crowd. The man who stood before her didn't ooze the same confidence as he did on the TV, but something dark and ugly instead.

He looked genuine, his face clean- shaven and clothes pressed neatly, the only difference was he wore a leather eyepatch. She didn't know why she suddenly felt the need to recall her magic, her fire tickling her fingertips as she choked the urge down.

There's something wrong.

She wished Peyton had telepathy, it would make everything so much easier. But even if he did, she couldn't explain her gut feeling. That the pirate wannabe was a bad guy because the butterflies in her stomach told her so.

"Your Church is wonderful. My husband and I were fascinated by your wife's passion against vampires," Alice said.

"A personal favourite of hers." He smiled again, the emotion not reaching his one, pale brown eye. "I appreciate you visiting, as my assistant mentioned on the phone we're in need of some new members who reciprocate the same beliefs."

"That's why we're here." Peyton opened his jacket

pocket, pulling out a cheque. "Our admittance." He handed over the money.

"Mr Noland, this is triple our fee." Gordon popped it in his pocket before either Alice or Peyton could ask for it back. "Such generosity..."

"Such generosity deserves special treatment," Peyton finished for him. "Our mutual friend explained you have an inner circle, I believe both my wife and I would benefit from that service."

Gordon said nothing for a second, his eyebrows pinched in anger before he visibly relaxed. "Only those invited may join The Leader's circle. Why should I entertain your arrogance?"

"Because that cheque is just the beginning. I believe in this faith, therefore I am willing to invest in our immortal souls."

"Then Mr Nolan, we would be honoured if you joined us tomorrow night to meet with The Leader. The Leader's circle meets once a week, with only the privileged invited to attend."

"So you're not The Leader?" Alice asked, getting her an unimpressed look in return. "We were under the impression you head this church?"

"I'm merely his closest subordinate. He's the one who offers salvation, protection for our souls. You will meet him tomorrow night, and he will decide whether you meet his expectations." He grinned, showing off pearl white teeth.

"That sounds perfect, I look forward to meeting The Leader." Peyton shook his hand. "Melissa, let's go before we are late for your appointment."

He looked expectantly at Alice.

"Yes, we can't be late. It was lovely to meet you." She

nodded a goodbye before walking beside Peyton until they were outside the church grounds.

"So, what do you think?" Peyton asked as they walked side by side. His tone back to his usual closed off self while his smile disappeared along with his chipper personality.

"I think the place is toxic." Alice stopped walking once they were a few roads away. She wrapped her jacket more firmly around her, the temperature dropping as the sky above threatened more snow.

"Toxic? What makes you say that?" He stared at her intently, his eyebrows creased before he noticed their surroundings. Cars beeped around them as pedestrians made their way to work.

"We can't talk here, follow me." He guided them to a café, walking towards the back to an occupied booth. Brady turned to them as they approached, a half- eaten bagel clutched in his large hand.

"Brady," Peyton greeted as he waited for Alice to climb into the booth before him.

Alice narrowed her eyes, not wanting to be trapped against the wall. She stood there until Peyton sat down himself, shuffling to give her room.

"Don't you guys look cute," Brady observed as he sipped his coffee. "I'm just finishing up here. What did you find out?"

A large pot of tea was already on the table beside a jug of milk and two spare mugs.

Alice grabbed the mug closest to her, pouring the hot liquid before clutching it in her cold palms.

"What do you know of The Leader?"

Brady sat back, the plastic booth squeaking in protest at his excess weight.

"According to my intel, he *is* The Church of the Light.

Back in his youth he had a greater following, but as the years have gone by, he's only left with the single church."

"Who's your intel? Is it reliable?" Alice asked.

Brady shot her a look. "He's an old family friend. Both he and my father used to be part of the faith, believed in the greater good of humanity. They both left when I was a child, but he still pops in from time to time."

"Okay, do we know why the church is in such a state?"

"According to the paperwork, there was an accident around six months ago with the foundation."

Brady handed over plans, highlighting the original structure and grounds. It showed the church in its entirety, a spec drawing of every room.

"An accident? What sort of accident?" she asked, looking up from the images.

"The report doesn't say, but one that can shatter windows and crumble tombstones," he shrugged as he grabbed his jacket. "I have to meet O'Neil in five, can I leave this with you guys?"

Alice glanced at Peyton, who was studying the plans intently.

"Sure Brady," Alice said when Peyton continued to ignore him. "We'll sort it."

Brady grunted his goodbye.

"This might be why they're asking for admission fees." Peyton blinked when he looked up. "Where's Brady?"

Alice shook her head. "He had to leave. What were you saying about admission fees?"

"This might be why they're asking for admission fees, to help cover the recovery costs of the accident."

"Isn't that what insurance is for?"

"Interesting point. They either haven't got any insurance, or there's a reason behind why they didn't want to claim."

"Isn't it illegal to not have insurance for something like that?" Alice asked. Which left the other option.

"You're right, it makes them desperate."

"Exactly, and what do desperate people do?"

Peyton sat back in his chair, thinking, his tea completely untouched in front of him.

"They resort to desperate measures."

He looked down at his mug, frowning before gently moving the teaspoon away with the tip of his finger.

Alice frowned, watching the odd move. Why wouldn't he touch the teaspoon?

"Can you touch iron?" she asked casually as she swapped into Brady's old seat.

"Iron?" his eyes narrowed. "What makes you say that?"

Alice shrugged. "No reason."

Except he had tried to avoid touching the spoon.

Iron was an irritant to the Fae in the same way pure silver could cause painful burns to shifters. It had forced them to move out of cities until the industrial revolution, where steel was mass-produced instead for foundational building material.

Iron was still a small percentage in buildings, but not enough to get a reaction. The teaspoon wouldn't have much if any iron at all, but Peyton didn't necessarily know that.

He frowned at her as he grabbed the spoon, placing it next to his other untouched cutlery. His eyes danced with amusement when he caught hers, a slight smile tugging his lips. He knew exactly what she had asked.

Bastard.

"What do you think about Gordon Potts?" he asked, ignoring the spoon situation.

"He felt... off." Saying it out loud made her feel stupid.

"You saying he isn't human? You keep trying to convince yourself I'm not human, so I apologise if I don't take your word seriously."

"I never said you weren't entirely human."

Not to his face anyway.

"I also didn't say he wasn't human, just something feels off. I can't put my finger on it."

"I'll look into him, see if he has any criminal records." His eyes glazed for a second before focusing on her once again. "You have anything else?"

"No."

"Then I'll see you tomorrow, wife." He smiled, just a small curve of his lips.

He had an odd sense of humour, and she would simply have to add that thought to the very short list of other things she knew about Officer Peyton.

CHAPTER 13

Alice knocked gently on the wooden door that was supposed to be Riley's place, her temper flaring when she was made to wait several minutes with no response. Riley must have known she was there, the rigmarole of being I.D.'d at the front desk, glared at by security and then escorted into the private lift just to get to the front door.

She wasn't technically late to his demanded meeting, he never exactly specified a time. He had asked for her to meet him at his place after the Church of the Light, giving her no more information than the address. He didn't know she went early in the morning, then went for a jog, made fresh bread, and did pretty much anything else she could think of that delayed her.

She even spent a good twenty minutes appreciating the gorgeous, glass skyscraper that was in the centre of the Breed District. Each window mirrored, reflecting the city back beautifully.

She didn't want to be there.

She didn't want a Warden.

"About time you got here," a mechanical voice buzzed.

Alice looked around then frowned, not seeing where the voice could have come from considering the door was still closed. Riley's place was the only door on the entire top floor of what she thought was an office building.

When she had entered the atrium many floors below, she thought she had the wrong address. Men and women in suits seemed to be working, talking on their phones and generally looking busy. She even noticed a large board displaying names of a few businesses that operated inside the high rise, the name 'STORM' across the top.

It was peculiar, to say the least. Did he live at his office?

"Get in. We're towards the back."

We're? Alice pushed the door, realising it was unlocked. Closing it behind her she squinted at the darkly lit room, trying to make out the rough shapes of the sofa and large TV.

She tried to have a nosey before she heard a faint clanging followed by a deep growl. Figuring that was more interesting she followed the sound into a large room, just as poorly lit.

Dropping her bag onto the floor with an audible thump she waited to be noticed as Riley and Xander fought with swords, metal clashing violently as they attacked each other at full speed, their movements blurred.

Alice couldn't help but stare, watching both men move as if they were in a choreographed dance. They continued to snarl as they became faster, bouncing off their heels as they pushed and parried in equal shows of power. Both were shirtless with similar tattoos patterned across the majority of their chests, back and arms.

She still didn't entirely understand what the tattoos

meant, her father only having a simple design around his wrist. Riley hadn't exactly been forthcoming with an explanation, even though he knew she wanted to know more about her father's heritage.

"ENOUGH!" Riley growled as he threw down his sword, lifting his leg into a quick kick that connected with Xander's stomach. Xander huffed back, fist clenching around his sword as he stood there, chest heaving.

With a quick nod Xander placed his sword into a special frame on the wall before turning to the door. His eyes were the palest blue she had ever seen, almost white to the point she couldn't tell where his iris's began or even finished.

He shot her a glare, grumbling at her from the back of his throat before walking out.

"Light on," Riley said huskily, the light above reacting to his voice command.

Alice had to blink several times before she could see, her eyes taking their time to adjust to the sudden brightness. Riley stood in the centre of the room, arms folded, anger evident in the curve of his brow.

Fuck sake, what have I done now?

Refusing to be the first to speak, she studied the room, admiring the ornate swords and axes displayed on the walls. It was larger than she initially thought, twice the size of her house in square feet, at least. On the far right stood various weight apparatus, running machines and punching bags. The rest of the floor was empty, giving room for movement. For a home gym, it was impressive, although, she didn't understand why he would need so many machines if he lived there alone. There were even seven lockers, clearly well used and decorated with novelty stickers.

"Strip." A demand, not Riley's usual chirpy attitude.

"Excuse me?" she shot back, his attitude igniting her own anger. "What bug crawled up your arse?"

"I said strip, sweetheart," Riley said, dropping his tone as his eyes flashed silver. "Why can't you follow orders?"

"Because..." Alice started, hesitating as she thought of a reasonable response that wasn't childish or petty.

Fuck sake.

Huffing in frustration she ripped open her jacket, throwing it onto the wooden floor beside her bag. She was glad she had already changed into her gym clothes, satisfied she didn't have to give in to his demand. Although she felt overdressed.

Riley wore skin-tight shorts, ones that left nothing to the imagination as they stuck to every muscle possible. Alice fought not to look down, wondering if the tattoos that danced across his hips went lower...

NO! She scolded herself. She did not need that image stuck in her brain.

"What are you wearing?" he asked, his anger not as vivid as before.

Alice couldn't hold the small smirk back any longer. How could he possibly ask her that when he stood there virtually naked?

"It's a shirt," she said, playing ignorance. She watched as he tried not to smile, his anger starting to dissipate.

Her top read, *"I HAVE ABS-olutely no control.'*

She wasn't going to apologise for it. "Why is it so dark?"

"Xander doesn't like the light," he replied quickly, his bare feet making no noise as he walked towards her.

"His eyes?" she questioned, not really expecting an answer. She had only ever seen people with eyes that pale who were sight impaired. Yet, Xander walked confidently, showing no signs his eyes caused him any problem. "So, you live in an office building?"

"It's my building," he said. "I split my time between here and my other place."

"The building? You own the building?"

"Where else would I keep all my investments?" he said, eyebrows low as if the question confused him.

"Bloody hell, how much money do you have?" Alice was embarrassed as soon as the question left her lips. She knew it was rude, but couldn't seem to help herself even though the answer didn't really matter. Riley came from money, but she didn't really understand that he was a businessman.

"Did you come equipped?" Riley said instead, his grey eyes catching hers.

Nodding, she pulled out her sword that was strapped to a specially designed harness between her shoulder blades. As soon as she palmed the hilt the runes along the steel glowed eerily. She didn't acknowledge the flash of light, deciding to ignore it. She still didn't understand why the sword suddenly reacted when she touched it, couldn't find any difference in its performance. The runes themselves were just as confusing, the shapes unlike anything she had ever seen before.

It wasn't of witch or druid origin.

Riley observed the lights carefully, frowning at the patterns that continued to glow. Even he didn't seem to know why the blade shone, or if he did, he wasn't telling her.

"What's the matter?" she asked as he just continued to stand there. "You seem..." Riley leapt towards her, his leg curling around in a wide kick that made her jump back with a shout.

"You didn't react fast enough," he growled, his eyes flashing silver in an instant. She was still mesmerised, watching his unusual eyes turn from a storm grey to a mirrored silver then back again. It wasn't a druid trait, she knew that for certain.

No Breed had silver eyes, not even the Fae.

"Faster."

He threw his weight against her shoulder, disarming her with a quick flick of his wrist.

"Again." He handed back the sword, his features stern, almost disappointed.

"Fine," she said through clenched teeth. This time she lasted around two minutes before he rendered her unarmed, her blade clattering to the ground whilst Riley remained unharmed. The third time she lasted three minutes, then it was five, then seven.

Each time he left her unarmed without breaking a sweat. It was insulting.

"Again." She jumped at him this time, engaging the fight as sweat trickled down her back. Feigning a turn, she waited for him to react, as he spun to grab her she jumped back, turning the opposite direction and hitting out. The flat of the blade touched his hip, enough for her to grin, thinking she had the upper hand.

The sword was tugged from her grasp, thrown across the room as arms enveloped her, crushing. Alice remained calm, breathing in deep as she threw her head back, smashing into his nose.

"FUCK!" Riley roared as he tugged her back, flipping her onto the ground. "ENOUGH!" He put his whole weight onto her hips, pinning her as she breathed heavily beneath him.

"I got you," she smiled, even as blood started to trickle out his nose.

He gripped her wrists harder, holding them above her head as he ignored the slow descent of his blood.

"If this were a real fight, you would've been finished." She wanted to do a happy dance, elated at the small victory after all the times he had disarmed her with ease.

"You honestly believe that?" he said, his eyes intense as he studied her. "You should have made that move within the first ten minutes. You didn't even scratch me and you think you've won?"

He released her wrists, but remained above her, his weight on his arms.

"You seem to think this is a game. Like this isn't life or death." He hopped up, moving away to kick her sword further away. "Even now, you don't even realise how close you are to the edge."

Alice clambered up to her feet, wanting to argue.

"No, I'm not..." Then she felt it, the burning inside, the suffocating heat that was bubbling beneath her skin, threatening to explode.

"Alice?" A trace of concern on his face. "Look at me," he demanded.

Alice flicked her eyes to his, holding the grey spheres as they became molten silver. Those eyes weren't his, weren't Riley.

"Riley?" she questioned even as she started to taste smoke.

"Concentrate on me," he growled, his voice deeper than usual, hoarse.

Alice began to gasp for air, her power beyond her safe level. Flicking her wrist, she released as much of the fire as she could, concentrating on the burst of orange as it burned into a deeper blue. Letting out a breath she felt smoke tickle her nose as her fire started to burn the wooden floor. Sucking it back in she stared at the scorched mark, wondering what the hell happened.

"Hey, are you okay?" Riley was suddenly beside her, his hands holding her upper arms in a bruising grip.

"I haven't had a flare out in weeks." She never even felt her power breach the safety level, had been too busy with Riley. "How did you do it?" She tried to step back, but he gripped her arms harder.

"Do what?" He finally released her, but did not step away.

"It's you, being close to you..." she began even as she felt the fire begin to build once more.

"It might be the ley line. This place is built on one."

"You know I can't feel ley lines," she said angrily.

Ley lines were natural energies that seemed to connect ancient sacred sites around the world, undetectable to anybody who wasn't attuned to the earth. As a witch, she could see them through her third eye, but was unable to harness the natural energy, unlike druids.

"Look at me." Riley's hand shot out to grip her chin. The instant his skin made contact her inner fire calmed, retreating to a manageable level.

"How can you do that?" She stood there, welcoming the sudden feeling of peace. She could feel the pulse in Riley's palm, feel the warmth of his skin.

Riley smiled but didn't answer her question.

"This wasn't as bad as last time," he said, his thumb rubbing circles along her cheek. "However, we do need to figure out what made your power react in such a violent way."

Alice suddenly felt awkward, her cleansing calm being

replaced with distrust. Stepping back, she broke their connection, confused as to why she wanted to step back into his hand.

"Your chi is energy, an arcane you can manipulate and control." Riley's hand was suddenly covered in silver, a ball of arcane so controlled it was a perfect misty sphere.

Alice was captivated by it, enthralled. She blurred her vision, concentrating on opening her mind, opening her third eye.

The ability to see more than the mundane was something she took for granted, it showed her perceptions beyond ordinary sight. It showed her the Plethora ley line, one of the largest in the south of England that happened to be swirling around Riley's penthouse. Ley lines usually kept close to the earth, a rainbow of swirls and smoke that flowed from one site to another. Riley had had someone harness the ley line to encompass his whole building, or at least his penthouse, resulting in his own personal power socket.

"How?" she asked, watching the multitude of colours flowing across him.

"It's a secret," he said, eyes sparkling as he smiled. Her breath caught at that smile.

I need to go.

"I have to go," she echoed her thoughts. He was too distracting.

"We're not finished with training. You need to learn how to harness your power."

"Not today, I don't."

"Yes, today." Riley shot his arcane to within an inch of her face, the heat of the power touching her skin. "You have little control over yourself," he said as he began to get irritated. "Your affliction with your fire isn't normal, you need discipline..."

"Stop it, I'm doing fine on my own." She turned to pick up her blade, sheathing it in one practised move. "I'm a grown adult, I don't need to be babysat."

"You need fucking training." Riley raised his voice, the arcane extinguished when she turned back to him. "What about that flare up?"

"YOU were the reason for the flare up," she snarled, feeling her chi ignite.

Fuck sake. It was Riley that brought out these strange feelings, ones she tried desperately to suppress.

"Surely you know you're not simply a witch. You're more, your power reacts more like a..."

Alice cut him off with an empty laugh. "You don't know anything."

"Grow up, sweetheart," he snarled, stepping towards her aggressively. "This is my job, something I have been asked to do..."

"That's right!" she interrupted. "You're The Order's puppet. Or is it The Council's?"

Riley growled, his fists clenched as he began to speak.

Alice cut him off.

"Tell me Riley, have you been given the order to destroy me if this doesn't work?" She held her breath for the answer, his silence all she needed to know.

She began to laugh again, a full belly hysteria.

"Everything is out of my control. I have been told I have a Warden. I have been told The Council are concerned about me. I have been told my life is at risk."

"You think I don't understand?" he said through clenched teeth. "You know nothing of my life. Know nothing of what I've been through." He stormed towards her. "Why do you resist so much? Is it the training? Or is it me?" His nose almost touched hers as he bent forward, his eyes furious as he tried to intimidate. "You need my help. Not the other way around. Remember that."

"Fuck you."

His lips were on hers quick as a flash, their tongues battling for control as he pulled her head towards his. His chi was electric, sparkles across her skin as she absorbed his warmth like a woman desperate for touch, for connection. Her hands were everywhere, touching and shaping his body as his own clenched around her hips. She let out a moan, the feeling...

"Sire?" Xander's voice echoed in the room.

As if they were drenched in cold water they leapt apart, both panting uncontrollably.

"What is it Xee?" Riley didn't look towards his friend, his eyes too intense as he concentrated on Alice.

"Your father."

Alice tried to smile, her emotions raw. "Your duty calls."

Riley said nothing for a moment, just stared. "You have an appointment."

The statement threw her.

"What are you, my secretary now?"

He just glared at her before turning his attention to Xander. "Make sure she attends."

He lined up among the other boys, all shaking as cold water drenched their bodies. They had just finished a five -mile run in the rain. They weren't allowed to speak to each other. Barely even look.

But he glanced anyway, curious. He had been there six months before he saw anybody else other than the teachers. Not even his father, not since he came to tell him of his mother's death. They were all boys, almost men.

He had heard a teacher slip in conversation, saying they were the children of the strongest.

Bred specifically.

Who breeds for a child specifically?

Not his mother. She was peace. Would never have bred him into this world if she knew what they would do. Beat him. Control him.

They thought he was their puppet.

They were wrong.

There were seven of them in total.

Seven boys.

Seven beasts.

CHAPTER 14

"Get out of the car." Xander leant over her lap to force the door open.

Alice slammed it back closed as she turned to scowl at him.

"You didn't answer my question."

"I don't answer to you," he snapped, his jaw clenched as the steering wheel screeched beneath his palms. He had been silent throughout the drive, ignoring any attempt of conversation. She knew he hadn't been pleased with babysitting duty, something they agreed on.

Her gaze wandered to the hospital, nerves attacking her stomach. There was a reason Alice didn't attend her doctor's appointments. She didn't like doctors. Not necessarily the whole profession, just ones who looked over her like a lab rat. Ones who didn't see her as a person, but an equation they were struggling to figure out.

"Why am I here?" she asked him again as he refused to face her, his eyes hidden behind his wrap-around glasses. "Seriously? You won't even answer that?" She let out a noise of frustration. "It's not like I asked you about your special tattoos or why you called Riley 'Sire.'" She had been stunned at the title, wanted to know more.

His jaw moved, showing his irritation.

"Isn't your father a Druid?" he asked, surprising her.

She nodded.

"Then how come you don't even know your ancestry?" he bit out.

Alice didn't miss a beat.

"Because he's dead. Died when I was young."

Xander finally faced her, his expression softening as he murmured words in a language she didn't understand before switching to English.

"I'm sorry."

"What for? You didn't kill him," she said calmly, shrugging. "I don't know much about either of my parents."

Alice gripped the door handle, pulling it gently until it clicked open.

"They're not just tattoos, they're magic infused glyphs. Druids get them around their wrists when they come of age. It helps them to control ley lines, among other things."

Alice held the door, staggered he had answered. Xander had been vocal that he wasn't her number one fan, yet he had answered a question Riley wouldn't.

"Then why do you and Riley have so many?"

Xander remained silent, long enough that she didn't think he would answer at all.

"You're going to be late for your appointment."

Alice opened the door, her feet crunching on the small amount of snow that had settled on the footpath.

"Why am I here?" she asked once more, hoping he would finally explain why they wanted her to attend.

Xander leant across the seat, his face calm as he looked

up at her. It annoyed her that she couldn't read his eyes behind the glasses, couldn't decipher his expression clearly.

"You need to be careful. You need to attend as that is what The Council wants."

"Of course, they say jump, and you both ask how high."

He growled, the sound weird as if it started from deep within his chest. "Fuck The Council."

That didn't answer her question.

"What about you calling Riley 'Sire?'

Xander pulled the door from her grasp, speeding off a second later.

"Well, then."

She rocked back on her heels, the cold biting into her exposed cheeks.

What *did* The Council want?

It was the second time The Council had been mentioned when she discussed the tests. First with Dread, when she promised him she would attend and second with Xander. It made her cautious.

It also made her wonder why she was asked to undertake the tests at the General Hospital and not the hospital wing in the S.I. Tower. As usual, the corridors were painted white, matching the white tiled floor and ceiling. The artificial lights glowed eerily above her, guiding her further down the corridor until she came to Dr Richards' office. A man stood outside it, his face in a scowl as he spotted her.

"You're late," he grumbled, his dark eyes narrowing. "Get inside." He opened the door with one of his big meaty fists, pushing her through before locking the door behind her.

"Alice, how nice of you to come today." Dr David Richards smiled uneasily from his seat beside his desk, his eyes flicking to the small window in the door then back at her. "It's been, what, four weeks?"

Three and a half, actually.

"What's with..."

"So let's get started, shall we?" he interrupted, his eyes flicking to the door then back again.

"Okay," she said as she sat awkwardly in the uncomfortable armchair.

He nodded, his hands agitated as he shuffled through his papers.

"As you have missed other appointments, this is just a catch- up from the previous tests."

Dr Dave – as he liked to be called, frowned as he read through the notes, the eagle tattoo above his right eyebrow angrily judging her.

"As I'm sure you're used to now, the video camera will record every test and conversation in the room," he said as he pointed to the professional camera set up in the corner, the red light flashing ominously. "How has your general health been these past few weeks?"

Alice listed everything he wanted to hear, it was like a rehearsed speech she had memorised from the previous visits. All she ever got from these appointments were the facts she was generally healthy, and that they had no clue what caused her power flares.

Pointless.

"What about flares?" he asked, "when was your last one?"

"Over four weeks ago," she replied instantly even as his eyes narrowed at her answer.

He knew she was lying.

"Fine," she huffed, her eyes glaring into the camera then

back to him. "It wasn't exactly a flare," she lied again. "I just became overwhelmed."

"Overwhelmed? In what situation were you in?"

Alice felt her face begin to burn, it took all her control to keep her face relaxed.

Fuck you, Riley.

"I was training."

"Training?" Dr Dave repeated, his attention on something behind her.

"Oh, let me get that..." He stood up quickly from his seat just as his arm swung and hit the camera off its mount.

The camera crashed to the ground in an audible thump. He promptly ran to the equipment and placed it back onto its stand, only for the red record light to be turned off.

Alice wanted to ask if it was safe, decided against it as Dr Dave gazed towards the locked door.

"We only have a few minutes or so before they notice the camera feed has stopped." He sat back in his chair, face concerned as he kept flicking nervous glances towards the camera and the door. "I need you to know that I do not work for S.I. nor The Council. I give my findings directly to Commissioner Grayson, do you understand?"

"Yes." Dread trusted him.

"I have only just recently been informed about your ancestry. Unfortunately, that also means The Council know, which is probably why there is so much attention on figuring out your power limitations. I'm hoping they will be satisfied with the video footage, but I can't promise I can keep them from trying to continue their experiments."

"Excuse me?" A man wearing a dark suit burst through the door, someone Alice didn't recognise. The man who pushed her through the door stormed in behind him.

"Can you not see I'm with a patient?!" Dr Dave barked. "You're interrupting."

"Apologies Dr," the man said without any sincerity, "the camera isn't working, so this session cannot continue."

"Oh, is it not?" Dr Dave turned towards the camera, reached over and flicked a switch. "I knocked it over a minute ago and didn't realise it had switched off. Are we working now?"

The man stood there for a moment, his face unfriendly before he nodded. Without a goodbye he left with his friend, closing the door behind them.

"What's with the suits?" Alice asked before she remembered they were being watched.

Dr Dave thought about the question before answering, his head nodding towards the camera.

"I believe they work for the new team that reports directly to The Council. I've been informed you will be seeing them around The Tower too."

Great, just what I need.

"Seems friendly."

"Let us get back to your results. All your tests have come back as expected for a woman your age. At the moment we're running on the theory that your ancestry has given you a greater ability to harness energy than the average person."

"Should I be worried?"

"That remains to be seen. We have been asked to keep a close eye on you until we recognise a pattern with your power flares. Until then I'll be researching other descendants and see if there is any record of anything similar."

"So, this was a waste of time."

Again.

"Forever the optimist," he chuckled. "We need to test

your stamina and heart rate again," he said as he turned on the running machine beside his desk. "You know the routine."

"Yes," she sighed, removing her jacket.

Whatever Dread had planned, it better be worth it.

CHAPTER 15

Alice stroked her fingers through Sam's glossy hair, the smooth movements comforting as he stretched across her lap in a distinctively feline way.

He chuckled at the movie they were watching, his hand reaching out to grab the popcorn in the bowl by the floor. Alice darted her eyes up to the screen, watching the clearly fake vampire bite into his busty victim's neck. She couldn't see clearly, the mid-day sun streaming through the gaps in the curtain, so she went back to stroking Sam's hair, enjoying the heavy silk through her fingers.

"Watch this bit," Sam laughed. "You can clearly see how fake the blood is."

They both had the majority of the day off, and had decided to catch up with their weekly movie. It was Sam's choice, which was why they were watching a poorly rated B-movie with the worst acting she had ever seen. She loved him, but he truly had the worst taste in movies.

"Hey, did you see it?" Sam moved onto his elbow, his

hair pulling from her hands as he turned to check. "Are you even watching?" His eyebrows came down in concern.

"How can I not watch the man with those abs?" she smirked, knowing it would get a reaction. "Remind me again why you chose this specific film?"

He grinned, the leopard showing unrepentant mischief in his eyes.

"You can't say I don't treat ya." He popped another popcorn into his mouth before relaxing back onto her lap, his head resting on her thigh.

As soon as he started to laugh at the film once more she allowed her smile to drop, her hands busying themselves in his hair once more.

She couldn't concentrate on the screen, her brain overthinking every little detail of the past few days. It was actually comforting to sit with Sam, to hear his untainted joy at such a simple thing. He was her rock, kept her down to earth. He knew all her secrets, her nightmares, her worries. And he loved her anyway, flaws and all.

"That was one of the worst films you have ever made me watch," Alice said an hour later. "Not even the abs could make up for it."

"Nah, it wasn't that bad." Sam stretched his arms above his head, turning to look at her. "Your choice next week, you can torture me with one of those sci-fi's," he groaned, pouting.

"I've decided on a superhero one, actually," she grinned, knowing he secretly loved all things fantasy and sci-fi just as much as she did. Last year she had gotten him to dress up as a green monster for a convention, he groaned the whole day but she knew he loved the attention. It wasn't like she wasn't dressed up too, in the matching monster outfit.

"So you've been quiet," Sam commented as he sat up.

"Did you want me to talk through the whole film?"

He poked her nose. "You know what I mean," he smirked. "How was training?"

Alice looked away, not sure what to say. "It was okay."

"You're not telling me something."

"I don't think I want to continue training with Riley," she said as she stood up, stretching her legs.

"Riley? Why?" Sam pulled her back down beside him.

"I... I." She didn't know how to explain how she felt. "I don't trust him." Which was true, she didn't trust him, not entirely at least.

"You need to train," Sam stated, shaking his head. "Don't be an idiot baby girl."

"I can do it on my..."

"No," he said, cutting her off. "You need the help. You know it even if you don't admit it yourself." He sighed as he reached for her hair, tangling it around his finger. "Riley isn't Rex."

Alice couldn't help her flinch. "Why would you say that?"

"Because I know you, more than anyone else. They're both men of authority, you're afraid the pull you feel towards him is being manipulated, like the bracelet."

Alice sat there dumbfounded, staring into his amber eyes. *Shit.*

"You're allowing what *he* did to influence your emotions on the one man that can train you. And you do need the training."

"Okay, who are you and where have you put my best friend?" Alice pulled away.

Sam let out a mock growl before he bounced to his feet.

"Sometimes it's my turn with the helpful advice," he

grinned. "Anyway that's enough of my superior guidance, I need to get ready."

Alice couldn't help but smile even though she felt confused. She had to think about what he said. Sighing, she swung her legs onto the sofa, lounging back. "I didn't think you're working today?"

"I'm not." He caught her eye, his leopard flashing across his amber irises. "I have a date."

"A date?" she spluttered. "But you don't date!"

No, Sam was a once, maybe twice casual sex guy. He didn't do commitment.

"Who is she?"

"*His* name's Zachary, and I met him the other day." Sam gave her a slow grin. "You okay on your own?"

Alice felt her smile tighten. "I'm a big girl, I'm sure I can look after myself." She could distract herself.

Sam read her expression, his own smile wavering.

"I can stay," he said, sounding unsure.

"And miss your hot date with Zac? I don't think so." She jumped up from the sofa. "Go, have fun. At least one of us should get laid."

Sam smirked. "Maybe it should be you," he winked before he moved upstairs, the shower starting a few minutes later.

Alice stood there for a moment, staring at the rolling credits on the screen. She couldn't stay there, moping around. She needed to do something, anything.

Decision made she grabbed her jacket, locking the front door behind her.

W*ell, I guess this was a good enough distraction,* Alice thought as she stared at the portrait of a dragon.

She had already memorised every scale, every flame and curl of smoke. Large eyes, like emeralds glistened as razor-sharp teeth snarled. One claw curled around a pearlescent orb, protecting it while the other clutched at a rock, one that teased the edge of a mountain.

Even as she looked at the painting, her own face mirrored slightly by the reflective glass, she couldn't comprehend how she could be called a dragon, a beast so beautiful it took her breath away.

A beast of mythology, one that didn't exist. But it also made sense, a dragon the symbol for the Draco's, a family name so old it was said they existed around the time of The Goddess, the alleged creator of the witch race.

At the beginning of time she gifted four humans with an element, she gave the ability to manipulate water to a Diluvi, earth was given to a Terra, air was gifted to an Avem and fire was for a Draco. Over the years the original elemental powers became diluted through generations combining, creating modern witches' ability to control magic. At least, that was how the legend went.

Dread had told her to visit the exhibit, she had used as many excuses as she could not to go. She hated to admit that she was afraid, afraid of what she was, afraid of what she could be. She didn't have her parents there to ask, to seek comfort. But she wasn't a child, she was a fully grown- arse woman who needed to understand her heritage if she was to grow further.

No more hiding.

She had felt drawn to the portrait almost immediately,

but what really caught her attention was the poem engraved beside it, the same poem that was messily written on a coffee stained napkin in her pocket.

With steady breaths, they ride towards the dawn.
Mortals cower in the dark, defenceless, prepare to mourn.
Shadows move across their souls, as darkness, corruption and power grows.
The four elements, magnets against mortal breath.
Generations of lies, of wrath.
Power in its truest form, made physical with greed.
Are they saviours who wish to lead?
Famine destroys along the path, against Pestilence in his wrath.
Death stares and waits his turn, as War's flames turn to burn.
The apocalypse they bring to earth, destroying it for all it's worth.

It was the same poem recited to her by a dying Daemon, one who called her not only Dragon, but War.

"Excuse me, ma'am," a voice from behind her gently asked. "You've been staring at the painting for a while now, could I be of some assistance?"

Alice gripped the red velvet rope, not wanting to look away from either the dragon or the poem. Peeling her fingers back, she turned to the voice, noticing the balding gentleman wearing a smart suit and lanyard. Behind him only a few people remained, the museums closing time coming up fast. She really had been staring at the painting for hours.

"Do you know much about that poem?" she asked.

"Ah, it's a beautiful one," he smiled as he looked at it.

"An old poem with no author." He shuffled closer. "It's the prediction of the apocalypse as believed by The Knights."

"The Knights?" she asked, frowning at him even though his attention was on the poem. She had never heard of them before. "What have they got to do with the Original Elementals?"

"It's because this particular poem dictates that true-blood Elementals were manifestations of the four horsemen of the apocalypse."

He grinned, obviously enjoying her shocked reaction.

"It's also why the original families have been hunted, leaving no known descendants but a room full of artefacts." He gestured to the large room, Alice only just noticing the other portraits and relics on display.

When she had entered a few hours ago, she instantly felt herself drawn to the dragon, completely ignoring the three other portraits placed equally spaced along the wall, each representing an element. The first was earth, a large crystal gargoyle perched on top of a mountain, the sunlight splintering through in a beautiful rainbow. Water was depicted by a three- headed hydra, the scales shimmered as if water physically flowed across the painting. Last was air, a pure white gryphon in mid-flight. Each feather was meticulously painted, the talons and beak dangerously sharp.

Large glass cabinets stood beneath each portrait, holding various memorabilia from crystals, drawings to a few black and white photographs. Alice studied the photographs, scanning them to see if she recognised any of the men and women who posed stone-faced for the photographer. Of course she didn't, the date stamped on them almost two hundred years old.

"Where do you get the items from?" she asked as she pointed to the photos. "Can't these just be anybody's?"

"Donated mostly. Some are lent to the museum by people who collect such things, and some are from historians who can approve their authenticity. The photograph in the middle is the last known picture evidence of any of the Elementals."

Last known picture?

"Why do you say there are no descendants?"

"Well, I'm sure many people originate from them, but there are no known true descendants, ones who have the same ability as their ancestors. The legend is that King Arthur himself was scared of their combined power, so worried for his people he sought out the Celts who predicted that it only took one true descendent in any generation to cause true devastation. If all four true Elementals got together then... well... it would cause the apocalypse."

"That sounds ridiculous."

"Well it does now I suppose, but back then they truly believed it. Believed it to the point the Terra family became known as Death, Draco's became War, Diluvi's became Pestilence and Avem's Famine. The original four elementals became The Four Horsemen of the apocalypse."

He pulled at his lanyard, frowning.

"It caused the families to go into hiding, protecting themselves from the king's obsession. He would get his Knights to destroy towns and villages all from a whisper or even a rumour that an Elemental could be found there, even though only a true-blood could actually control their ancestor's magic."

"I didn't think The Four Horsemen legend was a Breed story?"

"Ah, many renditions of the same tale can be found among most religions and Breeds. In the same way, many religions believe in different variations of a comparable god. It was the same with King Arthur, he thought it was his job to make sure the prophecy could never come to be, so he organised his Knights to hunt down the families and slaughter them."

"So they were made pariahs," Alice said, clenching her fist. "What do you believe?"

"Excuse me?"

"Do you believe there are family members still out there? From any of the elements?"

"It's impossible to tell. It's believed that The Knights are still hunting today, believing that even now, the descendants could bring hell on earth."

Alice kicked an aluminium can away with her boot as she walked to the bus stop.

She felt drained, as if her whole life was a lie which, technically, it was. She didn't know who she was, who her parents were. She kicked the can again, enjoying the clatter it made across the pavement, the snow having already disappeared.

At least I have control over this, Alice thought as she kicked the can once more, *the existence of an inanimate object.*

Alice lifted her boot to kick the can again, hesitating when she heard something crunch behind her. Spinning, she swept her eyes across the empty street, unable to tell where the noise came from. It was late, but not late enough in the city to be so quiet. She flared her chi, trying to sense if she was truly alone or not. Nothing, either she was going crazy or whoever was there had concealed their aura.

Senses on high alert she slowly bent to grab the can, throwing it in the bin before she began walking once more.

Another crunch, closer this time.

It could just be a cat, Alice thought as she forced herself to remain calm, to not hurry her pace.

Crunch.

She flared her chi again, hoping it was just Kyle.

Crunch.

Alice casually turned down a dark alley, luckily London was full of them. As soon as she was out of sight of the street, she ran to a dustbin, crouching behind it. She held her breath, waiting. A few seconds passed before she heard it, someone walking into the opening. She slowly stood up, making sure she was hidden in shadow. A man she didn't recognise stood at the mouth of the alley, his face stern.

Now, who are you?

The man grunted, walking forward. When he passed, Alice stepped out from behind the dustbin, intending to follow him. He stopped in his tracks, his head swinging from side to side as mumbled something beneath his breath. A ball of light shot out of his right hand, suspended in the air for a few seconds before floating towards Alice.

Alice leapt back, the ball of light following. The stranger turned, his eyes wide when he realised she was behind him.

"Who are you?" she asked, watching his light carefully. "Why are you following me?"

"Shit!" He threw his hand forward, the ball of light expanding, lighting the dark alley in an unnatural light. Alice had to squint, the light blinding.

"Hey!" she shouted as her eyes began to water. "Who are you?"

"BUTIO!"

Alice rolled away just as the ball burst into sparks, barely missing the spell as it shattered around her.

A hand was around her throat, pinning her to the cobblestones as he rummaged in his pocket, finding a small glass bottle while his knee pinned her shoulder. Eyes narrowed he went back into his pocket, pulling out an identical glass bottle. He pulled out the cork with his teeth, muttering beneath his breath.

"Somnum ante lucem. Somnum ante lucem. Somnum ante lucem."

Alice scratched up his hand, forcing him to release his grip just enough so she could smash her fist forward, cracking his nose. His hands loosened completely, enough for her to fling herself to the side, dislodging his knee.

"Fuck, my nose!" he cried as gripped his face, the glass bottles smashing at his feet. A vapour cloud curled around his legs, slowly crawling up his body before disappearing.

"Who are you?" She gripped his collar, pushing him against the brick wall with as much strength as she could. Luckily he was small for a man, a size similar to herself. "What was in the bottles?"

"You... ca... blllerrrrrrt..." the stranger slurred, his eyes becoming unfocused.

Alice shook him.

"Pay attention!" When he didn't, she slapped him. "Why were you following me?"

"Bloooo... me... foo."

"Oh, for fuck sake." She released him, allowing him to crash to the street, head slumped back with his legs at an uncomfortable angle. A second later he was snoring softly.

Alice stared at him for a moment, then the shards of glass a few feet away. The hand at her throat hadn't been strong, he never intended to hurt her, just keep her still long enough before he could grab the potion.

The man snored gently, his breath hitching at intervals before he groaned.

A sleep potion.

The glass crunched beneath her boot as she crouched down, staring at the remnants of the two bottles. One was obviously a sleep potion, and the other...

"Fuck," she cursed, recognising the flower on part of a shard. A forget-me-not.

Angry she kicked at his leg, getting her a soft grunt before he continued to snore.

"A fucking amnesia potion," she moaned at the unconscious man. "Really?" She kicked him again, savouring his grunt.

She hoped he had bruises in the morning, or evening, or whenever the spell wore off. Opening his coat, she rummaged through his pockets, finding three more bottles and a wallet. Popping the bottles in her jacket, she opened the wallet.

Burt .P. Lince
The Magicka
Department of Magic & Mystery
Officer ID – 74692-6

"Great, just great, He's a fucking Officer for The Magicka. Shit. Shit. Shit."

She grit her teeth, tucking the wallet back into his coat. She couldn't just leave him there, not if he belonged to The Magicka, the witches' official congregation. While a witch held a seat within The Council, The Magicka specifically governed their own Breed on a day- to- day basis. Every witch was supposed to present themselves to the congregation to be ranked into a tier system, something Alice never went to.

What was The Magicka doing following her?

Alice eyed the glass shards once more, biting her bottom lip.

Well, at least he isn't going to remember what happened.

CHAPTER 16

Munching on a noodle, Alice grinned crazily at the jogger who was giving her an odd look. She didn't think it was weird for someone to sit on a bench eating from a box with chopsticks. Everybody else who walked past seemed to disagree.

She ate another mouthful, ignoring the black wolf that sat and stared from the shadows. It was small, closer to the size of an average domestic dog than a shifter. But she recognised those arctic eyes.

"Go away Roman," she murmured into her box.

He just tilted his head in response. She would have thought it was cute if she hadn't known why he was there. At least she didn't mind this particular stalker.

"I'm not interested." She didn't want to help find his older brother, didn't care what happened to him. Probably. "Tell Theo I say no."

The wolf whined, scratching at the pavement with his claws.

"You been here long?"

Alice jumped up from her seat, having to scramble to catch the takeout box she threw into the air in panic.

"Bloody hell Peyton!" She shot him a scathing look. "You trying to give me a heart attack?"

She had purposely sat on the bench across the street directly in front of the church, allowing her a decent visual of the entrance as well as all road access. He seemed to have appeared from thin air.

"You need to wear a bell," she mumbled into her food, finishing off the remaining noodles.

"You should be more cautious," he said, looking unimpressed. "How long have you been here?"

"Not long." She hadn't realised how late it was when she left the museum, but luckily had enough time to grab dinner – after leaving Mr Lince slouched against a lamp-post. He was going to wake up struggling to remember the night before, with all his potions missing. Plus a few extra bruises.

She didn't feel guilty at all.

"Why do you think they have these meetings so late?"

She tossed the takeaway box into the bin beside the bench, glancing up at the gargoyles on the roof. She swore they moved, but knew the thought was crazy. Yet she couldn't tear her gaze away, their snarling faces fascinating. Alice blinked several times before she turned to Peyton.

"Bit suspicious, don't you think?"

"Maybe," he mumbled. "What's with the wolf?"

"Wolf?" she said as her gaze slid to where Roman sat, blended into the shadows. "What wolf?"

Peyton just gave her a pointed look.

"Fine. As long as it doesn't compromise tonight, I don't care."

Alice stared at him, eyes narrowed.

How did he know Roman was a wolf? A human couldn't have been able to tell, in fact, most people wouldn't have been able to tell. He didn't look like a traditional shifter.

"We ready to go?" she said instead of asking the question.

She moved so she stood beside him, hiding her arm that was warning Roman to stay. At least, she hoped it was.

"Hmm," he nodded, his eyes intense. "Your instinct was right by the way, about Gordon Potts. Convicted and served time for ABH to his previous wife, including coercive behaviour and battery."

"Previous wife? What happened to her?" she asked as they slowly made their way across the road.

"Meera Potts disappeared several years ago. He was brought in for questioning, but there was no evidence to suggest foul play. Mr Potts went to court to get her classed as legally dead a year or so after her disappearance."

"She not have any family?"

"If she did, they didn't speak up. In fact, not one person would make a statement against him."

"Sounds like a great guy."

"So what we thinking, is he a changed man under the eyes of their god..."

"Or is he their muscle that deals with the issues?" Alice finished for him.

"Bingo." Peyton smiled gently, the expression softening his otherwise hard face.

He looked relaxed in his jeans and chequered shirt with his white blonde hair neatly brushed. His blue eyes weren't as meanly pinched as they usually were. It didn't suit him, at least, didn't suit the image she had in her head of the hard arse police officer.

"Are you ready?" he asked as they came to the gate.

No.

The last time she had felt like she was being eaten alive. Something to add to her growing list of 'no fucking idea.'

"Of course, dear." Alice accepted the hand he held out, concentrating on the connection as a million insects started to crawl across her skin. Luckily it only lasted a few minutes, stopping entirely just as they entered the church.

Alice didn't exactly know what to expect, her mind pushing out ideas of an AA meeting or even a book club. Disappointingly it was nothing like she imagined, the main hall eerily quiet as they were guided through.

The pews had all been neatly arranged from the earlier session, large copper bowls placed at each end, begging for donations. They followed the green carpet that had been rolled down the centre, towards the stage that had hundreds of melted candles, still lit.

"Through here," a man encouraged them, pushing them into what looked like an office hidden behind the stage. "Please get on your knees before The Leader."

Peyton dropped down, pulling Alice with him. The room itself was too small for the number of bodies, the floor space barely enough room for the twelve or so to fit. A man sat quietly at an old desk, his head framed with inspirational quotes that hung limply behind him on the wood panelling.

'When we put our care in his hand, he puts peace in our hearts.'

'The pain that you're experiencing is nothing compared to what they will get in their damnation.'

'Faith is seeing the light in your heart when all you see is darkness in others.'

Alice would have been amused at the quotes if her knees didn't itch from the threadbare carpet. She wanted to tug at her jacket and scarf, the temperature inside the small room increasing dramatically as everybody settled before the man, Mr Potts standing towards his right.

Each religion had their own ideologies regarding a divine, whether they were one person or more. Witches generally believed in The Goddess, more of an entity than a god while many Vamps kept to their human beliefs.

Alice didn't believe in anything, not since she witnessed her mother's death. She was jealous though, that someone could believe in someone or something that could help guide them. Or someone they could blame.

The man who sat at the desk remained silent as he appraised everyone on their knees, his eyes hard as he studied everyone individually.

This must be The Leader, she thought as she tried not to fidget, her blade feeling exposed under the scrutiny even though it was hidden beneath her jacket.

Alice let out a gasp, the crescent scar on her hand throbbing intensely, the same as it did when she was with Kyle. She fought not to look down at her hand, not wanting to draw attention.

She felt Peyton flick her a look of concern. Shaking her head gently she clenched her fist, fighting a groan of pain as she concentrated on The Leader, noting his similarities to the one and only Saint Nic. His hair was pure white, matching his long beard and bushy eyebrows. He was on the larger scale, with a pot belly that strained the buttons on his pale shirt.

'He looked like Santa. Old, chubby with a white beard. Said he could give her a special drink. Make her better again. Santa can do that, you know? He's magic.'

The memory of Mia describing the fate of her friend was still vivid in her memory. The so-called Leader looked the part, an influential man who could use his words to convince a vulnerable and desperate woman into something she didn't want to do.

"Ah, who do we have here?" The Leader stood up, coming around the front of his desk. The wood squeaked as he relaxed his weight onto it, leaning back. "New blood in my herd."

"They were the ones we spoke of earlier, my Leader," Mr Potts said from beside him. "I thought they would be trustworthy to join us."

"While I trust your judgment, my good friend. I always choose who's worthy of an audience with myself." The Leader sneered, his eyes suspicious when he looked at Alice and Peyton. "Why are you here?"

"We seek guidance," Alice said before Peyton could begin. "We worry for our mortal souls."

"My wife is right." Peyton lifted his hand to grip hers, squeezing it in reassurance. "Breed have overtaken our neighbourhood. We need like-minded individuals who support our views on them."

"And what exactly are your views?"

"That they shouldn't exist. They are inhuman abominations that need to be cleansed so the earth can thrive once more."

"Perfect answer." The Leader smiled, his face softening. "Gordon, my friend. Remind me, why do you believe these two were respectable of the leader's circle?"

Gordon leant across, whispering in his ear.

"Ah."

The Leader turned his attention back to Alice and Peyton.

"Your generosity has brought you amongst us, but you must prove yourselves worthy."

"Of course."

"Friends, please join me in welcoming our new members." The Leader clapped, encouraging the others to join in before he opened his arms wide. "Now, what are the updates?"

Members spoke up in turn, excited as they discussed upcoming rallies and protests. She even recognised a few from earlier, including Mrs Potts who sat towards the front, close to her husband. Her eyes were closed, a silent smile on his lips as she listened to her friends casually discussing disrupting hospitals where Breed were known to work, as well as charity events to raise money for the church itself.

"I would like to thank you for all your noble work, and I would like to discuss some great news," The Leader said, smiling, showing off a full set of veneers. "As we know, the press doesn't understand that we are trying to cleanse the world, but today they have confirmed that those fanged beasts have been cursed, struck down where they stand."

Alice risked a quick glance at Peyton, who just subtly shrugged. She didn't think the information had been released to the public yet. The Gala had been dealt with quietly, the press stopped from reporting.

"I thank you all for your sacrifices in the name of our divine, but our work is far from over. The world is still full of those Breed, and until they have been extinguished, we will continue in his name."

People quietly murmured in agreement.

"Bless you."

"Hail divine."

Alice clenched her fist harder, the pain resonating through her palm as Gordon's expression changed, his mouth set in a grim line. He quietly excused himself, leaving through the door beside the desk.

Where does that go to?

She noticed Peyton checking out to the door too, his jaw set as he watched for it to re-open. That door wasn't on the blueprint.

Alice finally glanced down at her hand, the burning and throbbing becoming unbearable. Almost thinking it was on fire, she gently traced the crescent scar with her fingertip, not understanding why it was reacting in such a way again.

"My Leader..." Gordon Potts stepped back through the door, a strained look on his face. "I would not interrupt if it wasn't important."

The Leader glared for a moment. "My children, unfortunately this meeting will have to come to an abrupt end, I have business to attend." He nodded towards everyone, a friendly smile painted across his face. "Let the light guide you."

Everyone replied in unison, almost perfectly synchronised.

"Let the light guide you."

CHAPTER 17

Alice eyed her car in the driveway, the blue rust bucket taunting her as she shivered in the cold.

"Bloody thing," she cursed as she unlocked her front door, stamping her feet of the excess snow before stepping inside. It just had to start snowing as she walked home, the sky covering her in the delicate white fluff that bit into her skin.

She hated the winter.

"Sam?" she called into the darkness. "You home?"

Alice frowned, her senses on high alert.

The air was still, the house silent, but she couldn't shake the sense of urgency, like she was being watched. Her eyes settled on the corner of the room, the light from the street lamps failing to penetrate the dark space. She slowly reached for the switch, her back pressed against the door.

"I hope you don't mind my visit," a girly high-pitched voice said from the darkness.

Alice flipped the switch as she pulled out her sword, the

tip pointed towards the intruder's throat before she even recognised the vampire.

"Valentina."

Alice held the blade steadily, her ears straining to make sure they were alone. Pointless, considering vampires were silent predators.

"I didn't see you."

Why were you hiding in the dark?

"Then I will forget your manners this one time." Valentina stared at the runes on the blade, ones that were alight and glowing. Her eyes flickered in annoyance.

Alice had to make a conscious effort to sheath it, fighting against her better judgment.

"Does Dread know you're here?"

"Nobody knows I'm here," she smiled, causing shivers to rattle down Alice's back. "It's why I'm alone and haven't got my guards with me."

She looked around the room, the darkness of her hair and dress a stark contrast to the pretty white wallpaper Sam had just put up.

"Interesting home, I see you haven't finished unpacking?" She nodded towards the pile of boxes.

"Is there anything I can help you with?" Alice asked, irritated but remaining polite. She wasn't interested in small talk, not even from a member of The Council.

Valentina ignored the question, instead went to touch one of Sam's half-naked men's magazines on the table, flicking through the pages as if she had never seen such a thing.

"How is your training going with Councilman Storm's son?"

"Fine."

Alice dropped her bag, nudging it under the side table

so it wouldn't be in the way. She kept her back to the door, keeping the sofa between them.

"Only fine?" She looked up then, the light catching the red ruby necklace that hugged her throat. "It surely cannot be merely 'fine' now, can it? Is this Riley not good enough?"

"No, no, that's not what I'm saying."

"Then it must be more than fine. You need to learn control if you are ever going to be of any use to us," she said sternly, her eyes narrowed as she looked Alice up and down. "You look strange."

"Strange?" Alice looked down, wondering what she was on about. She looked as she usually did.

Maybe she had some smeared makeup?

"Yes."

Valentina finally put the magazine down, her gaze arctic as she slowly moved around the sofa, her fingertips reaching across to trail down Alice's cheek.

"Like a pretty girl next door." Her voice was distant, almost a whisper before she snapped her arm back. "It doesn't suit you."

Alice fought not to flinch at the sudden movement.

Fuck. Fuck. Fuck.

Her hand twitched, itching to grab her sword. Up close she knew Valentina hadn't fed, could tell by the absence of humanity in her gaze. Vampires came from humans, many keeping the same characteristics and personality traits after the turn. Valentina's eyes, when they connected, were old, ancient with a ring of red around the irises. If Alice didn't know any better, she would have said she had never been human, just... other.

"I see your soul, child. You're just like me, dark, full of horrors many people couldn't survive."

She opened her mouth, her fangs elongating to twice their length.

"It makes us powerful, strong."

Alice stepped back, moving away from the door and Valentina's reach while her pulse thumped against her throat, adrenaline rushing through her veins. A normal reaction when faced with a predator, and that was precisely what Valentina was, a predator. Just one that was shaped like a young girl, with dark tresses and large eyes in a pale, porcelain doll face.

Valentina moved forward as if she were a magnet, her face granite as the twin fangs peeked through her lips, too long for her petite mouth. Alice slowly reached for her hilt, wondering how long she could survive against someone as powerful as her.

"Why are you here?" Alice asked, trying to distract her from the hunger.

"I want to know what is happening with my vampires in this city." Valentina's voice was eerily soft when she replied, her eyes no longer as hard.

"That's what I've been trying to figure out."

"Tu es trop lent," she snapped angrily. "Too slow. I want to return to my home, to Paris. I need this absurdity to end."

"We're working on it."

"We're?" The oily black pools of her eyes receded into narrowed points. "Ah, yes. The police force you seem to be working with. Smart move by Monsieur Grayson, getting all the Norms on his side." She smiled, the emotion not making Alice feel any better. "Now tell me why you have been interested in the Church of the Light?"

"How did you..." Alice wanted to kick herself.

"We are watching until you are no longer a liability."

"I thought that was the point of Riley, or should I say, Danton?" *And Mr Lince,* Alice wanted to add but doubted Valentina had anything to do with The Magicka.

"You think I would trust those druids?" She let out a high pitched laugh. "A bit of advice, don't trust anybody. You'll survive longer."

"So I shouldn't trust you?" she replied without thought.

"Very clever, Alice." A predator smile, a warning. "Danton was one of my guards before I lent him to Grayson. You're pouting like it was a dirty secret, but Dread knew all along who he belonged to."

"How long have you been watching me?"

How long has Dread allowed it to happen?

"I'm growing bored with this conversation." She gave a dismissive wave. "Now tell me about the church."

"It's a church who hate all Breed, what else do you need to know?" Alice spat, allowing her anger to shape her words.

Valentina spun and hissed, her hands turning to claws as a black wolf growled, his electric blue eyes glowing.

What the... Alice quickly accessed the situation.

"Bad dog," she scolded the wolf, placing herself between them cautiously. "I'm so sorry - he should have been in the garden."

How the fuck did he get in?

"That is not a dog," Valentina said, her voice hoarse, her eyes never leaving the wolf.

"Of course he is, picked him up from the pound only a week or so ago." Alice wondered if Valentina could hear the lie from the change of her heartbeat. She hoped not.

Valentina looked unamused when she finally met Alice's eyes, her face wary.

"Be very careful Alice, remember who your superiors are. My patience is wearing thin."

"We're still investigating. Once I figure out what has been happening to the Vamps, I will be able to make a report."

Valentina stared for a moment, completely immobile as if she were a statue, not one twitch of a muscle.

"I will find out your dishonesties Alice, then you will answer to me."

"I'm invested in this too. I have friends who are at risk."

"Then get results." Valentina reached up slowly, ignoring the wolf's warning as she brushed hair off Alice's face. "Tick tock."

CHAPTER 18

Blood Bar was busy for a weeknight, almost every table taken as music flowed from the band on the stage.

Fighting through the crowd, Alice found a seat beside the bar, allowing the music to calm her nerves. She couldn't relax once Valentina had left, not even with a wolf who seemed to be stuck in his animal form. He wasn't exactly one for conversations, and he just sat, staring. What was she supposed to do with that?

"Can I get you anything?" The bartender asked as he flicked a rag over his shoulder.

"Vodka martini, please."

"Coming right up."

Alice waited for her drink, cuddling it to her palms once it was presented in a flourish. She wasn't sure what she was doing there, didn't know who else to talk to. She couldn't speak to Dread, not yet. Not until she knew more. So it only really left her with one option.

The deep husky voice of the man in question broke

through the music, his low rumble pleasing the crowd as he introduced the next band onto the stage. Alice sipped her cocktail, sighing at the delicious burn of the alcohol. The crowd continued to murmur excitingly behind her, forcing her to spin in her stool to face the stage out of curiosity.

Riley Storm was one of London's most eligible bachelors, at least, that's what the magazines had said anyway. He oozed sex appeal as he teased the crowd, his blue-black hair pulled back from his masculine face, his stubble longer than the other day. He wore the same uniform as his staff, the casual form- fitting T-shirt suiting him as much as a thousand- pound suit would.

Alice took another sip of her drink. She hated the fact she couldn't look away, the same as the many females gyrating for his attention on the dance floor. He had something about him, a magnetism that instantly got her back up.

But Sam was right, her wariness of him was because of the past. Riley wasn't trying to manipulate her emotions. He seemed just as confused by their magical connection as she did.

He saw her then, his smile faltering before he quickly recovered. He didn't seem pleased to see her sitting at his bar. She wasn't exactly delighted she had no one else to talk to, so it was mutual. Sad really.

"Hey, do you want a drink?" the man beside her asked, grabbing her attention. "I'm buying." He winked, smiling to show his fangs.

He was dressed pleasantly in a white shirt and smart jeans, his blonde hair combed off his face, highlighting the impossible beauty of his skin.

"No, thank you," she smiled back. "I already have a drink." She nodded towards her cocktail.

"I'll get the next then," he continued, undeterred.

She shook her head. "I'm waiting for a friend."

"You only said friend, not boyfriend." He grinned, sipping his own red drink. "You at least open for donations?" He meant blood, his eyes tracing down the line of her throat.

"Sorry," she shrugged.

She would have enjoyed the disappointment in his eyes if he hadn't been staring at her like a popsicle. She never understood the lure of vampire sex, didn't want to be a midnight snack.

"Do you know I work with a vampire?"

"Oh?" he said, his drink at the edge of his lips.

"Yeah, he's a real pain in my neck."

The man burst out laughing, choking on his drink. "You sure you're not open to donations? Or even a dance?" His eyes glistened.

"Sorry, I'm not your blood type."

"Hey, Will," another man walked up, placing his hand eagerly on his friend's shoulder. "A girl is giving up free sips in the corner. She's wearing this cute little fluffy cardigan."

"Not now Glenn, I'm talking to a pretty girl."

"She's not interested." A tattooed arm appeared between them.

"Riley!" she squealed at his abruptness. "I'm so sorry..." she began to apologise to the man, but both he and his friend were already gone. "Riley, what the hell was that about?"

"Why are you here?" he asked, eyes hard as he studied her. "We haven't got training planned."

"I wanted a drink."

"At this specific bar?" He began to relax, leaning back against the free stool. "You sure it wasn't to see me?" he asked, smug, crossing his arms across his chest. It brought her attention to his tattoos, glyphs as Xander had explained.

A flare of irritation. She had asked Riley on numerous occasions about her father's heritage, but druids were secretive bastards. He had told her barely anything. Yet, a short car ride with Xander gained her that information.

Her eyes shot up, Riley's expression curious as he caught her staring.

"I'm not here to just see you." She was, but she wasn't going to admit it. "Besides, aren't we friends?" The word surprised her, because they were friends, she just hadn't realised it.

Riley just smirked. "Come on, follow me to my office."

He guided her past the dancers towards a set of private stairs, his office on the floor above. Alice had to ignore the death glares from the other females, instead concentrating on not spilling her drink when the dancers bumped her.

They passed through a door at the top of the stairs, the hallway pitch black as she stumbled in the darkness.

"Riley..." She reached out blindly, feeling his hand grab hers.

A spell was on the tip of her tongue as he pushed open another door, allowing a small amount of light to penetrate.

"Now tell me why..."

"Riley darling, about time you came up. I've been waiting."

A redheaded woman sat cross-legged on the small wooden desk, her short skirt riding up to show baby pink lace underwear, a teasing smile on her magically enhanced lips.

"Mandy? What the fuck are you doing here?" Riley demanded, growling as he flicked on a switch, lighting up the hallway behind them.

"You never returned my calls," Mandy petulantly replied, swinging her long legs to stand. "Your other office said you were at your new bar."

Her eyes slowly judged the room, taking in the small, gloomy space in one sweep.

"I don't know why. It seems... cheap."

Alice finally recognised her from the Gala, the one with the pillow breasts that had been Riley's date.

"Do you want me to come back later?" Alice said dryly. "I seem to be interrupting something important."

"You. Stay!" Riley snapped before returning his burning gaze to the redhead. Alice couldn't confirm if she were a natural redhead or not, the quick flash they received too fast.

"Oh, and who are you?" Mandy glared, flicking her hair over one shoulder. Her short skirt showed off her impressive legs while her top was cut low on the front, highlighting her breasts. A gold chain glittered between them, drawing the attention.

"Mandy, you need to leave." Riley reached past her towards the old handset phone, dialling for security.

"What? I thought you would have wanted to see me?" she whined. "You would rather spend time with... that?" she huffed as she pushed past Alice, standing beside the door.

Alice stepped away, sipping her drink while watching the drama unfold.

"Leave or be removed."

"But darling..." she purred.

"Leave."

"Fine, I'm going." She dropped her voice to a whisper, shooting Alice an evil look. "He isn't in proportion anyway."

Alice tried to hide her smirk behind her glass, waiting until Mandy was out of earshot before turning to Riley.

"Did you want me to leave? You're obviously interested in humping her."

Humping? Did I just say humping? I've been around Sam too long.

"Humping?" Riley burst into a grin, his question echoing her own thoughts. "I think you mean fucking sweetheart, besides, it's you who's thinking about me humping her."

"No, I wasn't." Alice felt her cheeks burn as she started to imagine his sweaty body moving... *oh, for fuck sake.* "Anyway, I assumed she was your girlfriend."

"Why, jealous?" he teased.

"No," she replied a little too fast. "Besides, from what she said, I don't think I'm missing anything special."

Riley erupted into laughter, his hands unbuckling his belt on his jeans. The fabric sagged, dropping to show naked flesh, no underwear.

"Haven't we been through this before? Except last time you were tied to a chair."

"I try to forget." She looked away, having no desire to see whether the redhead was right about his proportion or not.

She considered the room instead, his office small, the overhead fixture missing its bulb, so the only light was from the bar below, the back wall made of glass. Photographs were tapped to the exposed brick, covering the whole available space in small square Polaroids. Posed pictures of employees smiling to the camera as well as some action shots, including Sam, who was shot serving a drink with a smile on his face. On his weathered desk was a single landline phone and a computer. It was basic but had character.

"I have never dated nor have I fucked Mandy," Riley

said as he buckled his belt back up. "She was just conveniently available for an event."

"Why are you telling me? You're a big boy, I'm not your keeper."

"Say that big boy comment again," he said, eyes gleaming mischievously.

Alice rolled her own eyes instead.

"What happened with Sam?" She nodded towards his picture.

"He had a better offer." Riley shrugged, coming to stand beside her. "He also dislikes me, makes it hard to work together."

"He doesn't dislike you," she frowned, turning to face him.

He was close enough that she had to tilt her head to see his face.

"He didn't understand why I had to leave. Sometimes the best thing for someone isn't what you want." Riley frowned, his eyes catching hers before he looked away, hiding his expression.

He snatched her cocktail from her hand, downing the last remaining liquid before placing it onto his desk.

"So you going to tell me why you're really here? Or was it simply to scare away my customers?"

"I wasn't trying to scare them away," she glared.

"Then tell me the real reason you're here."

"Valentina."

"Valentina?" He gestured for her to come further into the room before he clicked something that made the low hum of the background music mute. "The room's now secure. Tell me what happened."

Alice began to explain how Valentina had turned up at

her house, wanting information on the poisonings amongst her vampires.

"My father never mentioned her still being in the city." Riley sat at his desk, the cheap seat squeaking at his weight. He looked like he belonged, not someone with a multi-million -pound estate. To be fair, he never really acted like he came from money, he seemed to always enjoy doing everything himself, his hands reflecting his hard work. Unlike Mandy, who branded the place 'cheap.'

"Valentina said that she didn't trust the druids."

Riley thought about it for a moment.

"And what about you? Do you trust the druids?"

She knew there was a right and a wrong answer.

"'You are a time bomb waiting to go off. We shall see if your fate matches the rest of your family,'" she quoted instead of answering.

"I don't understand."

"Your father said that to me."

"Did he?" Riley reached to a drawer, bringing out two fresh glasses and a decanter. Popping off the lid, he filled two glasses up with the amber liquid, pushing one glass towards her. "My father says many things."

"What do you know about my family?"

"Other than what you have told me? Nothing."

"Surely your father must have said something."

"Why do I feel like you're implying something against my father?" He sipped his drink while Alice ignored hers.

"My family is the reason for the warden, he must have mentioned something."

"No, I don't need that information, and I never asked. Alice, what are you trying to say?"

Alice moved away, pressing her hand to the glass wall. "Is this mirrored?" The dancers below never looked up.

"Alice..." Riley growled.

"Fine. I've recently found out that I'm a descendant of Draco, one of the original elemental families. I believe that knowledge was one of the reasons my parents were murdered."

Alice hesitated, watching the dancers.

"Your father said I was a time bomb, and that my fate could match that of my family."

She pushed away from the glass, turning so she could see Riley's face, read his expression. He seemed calm, his eyes soft as he listened to her. She couldn't see any recognition; no tell-tale signs he already knew her past.

"So to answer your previous question, no, I don't trust the druids."

A loud bang broke through the tension.

"Excuse me sir," a man shouted through the door. "We have an emergency."

"I'm busy." Riley never took his eyes off her.

"But, sir..."

Riley looked annoyed but opened the door to show a worried bouncer, blood on his hands as he raised a fist to knock against the door again.

"What happened?" Riley snapped.

Moving through the dancers was easier the second time around, most of them outside crowding around the scene.

Alice quickly surveyed the situation, noting how the vampire on the left was already dead, his skin starting to peel and dehydrate in front of her eyes.

"Don't touch him!" Alice barked out the order, making some of the crowd jump back.

She recognised the dead as one of the vamps at the bar, the friend to the one she was talking to. A woman knelt beside him on the hard floor, blood turning her fluffy white cardigan into a pink mess. Blood poured down her throat from the several holes, her blood refusing to clot.

"Stay down," she grabbed the woman when she tried to scramble away.

"Get off me," she snarled, trying to scratch up Alice's arm.

"If you don't stop moving, you'll bleed to death."

"What?" The woman's eyes took on panic, her hands trembling as she grabbed her throat. "I'm bleeding? Why won't it stop?"

Alice almost felt sorry for her, almost.

"Alice, how can I help?" Riley asked calmly, his bouncers working on keeping the crowd back.

"Keep pressure on her wounds."

Riley replaced the woman's hand with his own, trying to stem the flow before the ambulance arrived. Alice stood back, trying to see if anybody else could have been affected. The crowd seemed in equal measures curious and shocked, but no one appeared to have drunk from the woman.

She took a deep breath, noting how many of the customers still clutched at their cocktails, cocktails made with blood.

If the drinks were contaminated...

"Riley, where do you get your blood from?"

"Blood?" He looked at her like she had lost it.

She turned to him, the front of his shirt soaked in red.

"For your drinks, where do you get it from?"

"A local supplier," he frowned. "Why?"

"I have a..." *Shit.* "You need to close the bar."

Sirens drowned out his reply. The paramedics began shouting out demands almost instantly. They ignored the vampire, his death evident as they moved Riley to start working on the woman who still continued to bleed.

"She's going to die," he said gently as he stood beside Alice.

She said nothing as she watched the woman start to cry, deep painful sobs that racked her whole body.

"No. No. It isn't supposed to be like this, they said it wouldn't be like this," the woman bawled.

"Who said it?" Alice tried to reach the woman, her efforts falling short when she's forced back by a paramedic. "Who said it?"

The woman looked at Alice, her eyes glazing over as her lifeblood soaked into the street. "May the light burn you forever more."

CHAPTER 19

Alice stood outside the supply store, staring at the red neon sign that glowed against the dark brick.

She should have gone home, blood still dried beneath her nails even as she had tried to scrub her hands clean. But she couldn't get the idea of contaminated blood being sold out of her mind; that an innocent person could be infected, dying a painful and unnecessary death. Because it was an infection, a toxic point of view just as much as the physical contagion. If her deduction was right and whoever was behind the genocide had been able to taint bottled blood, the death rate could be catastrophic.

'Blood on the Go' was the only local supply store in the city, part of a larger chain that dominated across England and Wales. Apart from the red sign, the storefront was achingly white, giving it a cold medicinal feel. Alice had been standing there for a while, patiently watching a few people enter the brightly lit store, to be escorted around the side alley towards the back.

"Hello, welcome to Blood on the Go. Are you looking to

donate today or purchase?" a clerk asked when Alice finally entered, her perky attitude not reflected in the clock which stated how late it was. Or more likely early.

"I'm not sure yet," Alice replied as she looked around. It was a simple layout, a desk that separated the room in half with several industrial -sized refrigerators full of blood covering the back. Pricing was pinned to the wall, showing that you could buy a single glass bottle of blood type A for £4.99, while blood type B rhesus negative was £7.99. There were also several options for the 'specials' which started at £9.99 per bottle.

Bloody hell, Alice shook her head. *I'm in the wrong trade.*

"Don't worry, it's completely safe. We supply all across the country." The clerk looked sceptical, her friendliness disappearing.

Shit. Maybe she didn't look like a typical donator?

Alice started to scratch along the inside of her arms, trying to appear as shady as she could.

"Do you require medical records to donate?" Alice asked, hoping the answer would be yes. Or, at least they tested the blood for abnormalities. "I need the cash real bad."

"Nope, we don't ask questions. We give twenty pounds for one pint of blood, which you can donate a maximum once per week."

She smiled, showing shiny white fangs. They looked weird, almost fake.

"Is this something you're interested in doing?" She looked smug as she grabbed a piece of paper and a pen, confident.

"Maybe." Alice scanned across the simple contract,

noting how they asked for your full name and address. "It says here about photo ID?"

"It's fine if you don't have any, we lose paperwork all the time."

Alice signed the piece of paper, giving fake details. "Do we do it now?"

"A few people are waiting, but I can take you around to have a look."

Alice followed the woman around the back towards the alley beside the building.

A side door was wide open, a beaded curtain concealing inside. Several people hung around the door, glaring as Alice passed through the beads.

"It's just in here." The woman guided her in, pointing out the booth covered by a dirty curtain. Inside was a man wearing a sweat- stained white vest. He didn't look up as he inserted a winged infusion needle into the arm of a painfully thin man, his eyes glassy enough to give the impression that he was high.

The floor was a crusty brown, blood staining the once white tiles to the point it looked like rust. Small refrigerators hummed beside them, blood smeared across the front while used needles were thrown in the corner, beside a full contaminated materials bin.

Alice couldn't believe the health and safety issues.

"How can you be sure the health of your donors if you don't ask for their medical records?"

The clerk looked shocked at the question but answered anyway. Her regular clients must not care.

"We advertise to vampires who can't get infected with anything. It's not our problem if others choose to drink," she shrugged. "Like, we ask you some general health questions, and if we think the blood will be below our standard, we will not pay you the full fee."

She tried to move Alice back, away from the men.

"Why, are you worried about something?"

"So you don't check the blood for impurities?"

"No, why would we?" she frowned, her eyes dashing to the man who had turned to look at them.

"What about storage? How long do you hold the blood before being sold?"

"We aim to sell it in within a few days, but it lasts weeks." A slight frown pinched her eyebrows. "What is this?"

"Do you keep a record of who donates on site?"

"We do as it's the law. We can't accept more than one donation per week, which is why we keep names." She folded her arms. "I'm sorry, you a health visitor or something?"

"Or something." Alice eyed the man with the needle, his gloveless hands clenched as he stood up. "I need to see your records over the past month or so."

"What?" the woman asked, her eyes wide as they flicked towards the man again. Clearly the boss.

"Excuse me, are we going to have a problem?" The man in the vest growled, trying to intimidate. "You can't look at our records without a warrant."

"You need to stop accepting donations immediately," Alice stated. The number of bottles of blood she could see just in the small space worried her, especially blood that hadn't been vetted. She wasn't sure of their client base, buying bottled blood a new concept but if just one contaminated donor got their blood sold...

"On whose authority?"

"That would be the city of London." Detective O'Neil

walked in, followed by Officer Peyton in full official gear. "I would like to examine every vial of blood donated in this establishment. While our investigation is going on, you will be unable to accept any donations."

"This is bullshit!" The vested man steamed as he grabbed the bit of paper O'Neil handed him. "We're an honest business..."

"If you're an honest business, you have no need to worry," Alice added. "Although I would re-examine your health and safety."

The place really was disgusting, she wouldn't be surprised if the donators left with infections or even sepsis.

"If you do not co-operate we will come back with a warrant that could result in permanent closure. What would you prefer?" O'Neil stood his ground.

"Fuck sake," the vested man cursed, his face glowing red in anger. "Fine, I will co-operate."

"Oh, hey Alice." Someone wearing a white bodysuit walked in, taping up the room.

It took her a few minutes to recognise the voice.

"Hi Jones, you checking out all the bottles?"

"Don't you know it." He started to whistle to himself, unpacking a bag onto the floor full of different sprays and cotton buds. "Just checked out the front, who'da thought bottled blood would be so pricey?"

"Agent Skye," Detective O'Neil nodded in greeting.

"Thank you for coming so quickly."

"It was a good shout, lucky the owner has agreed for us to take a look. You think we will find anything?" he asked her genuinely.

Alice looked around the room, the different bottles marked with different batches and blood types. There must be at least one- hundred different donors in the back room, not including the ones in the front.

"I don't know. But if we catch just one contaminated bottle, we could stop it from spreading."

O'Neil grunted, his eyes tired. "Either way, we will be comparing samples. Jones has an appointment with someone in The Tower." He sighed, pinching his nose. "Peyton has updated me on the church, but until we get solid evidence we have no chance. You guys have done a great job of getting in, but without a solid ID on The Leader we have nothing. Even then, a dead woman's word doesn't stand in court. You need to find something."

"We're working on it."

She stepped outside, the people waiting to donate long gone once the police turned up. She was beyond tired, the whole day taking its toll. Yet her brain wouldn't quit, she couldn't stop thinking about who was behind the genocide. It was small because they were only targeting vampires, what would happen once they turned their attention to other Breed?

"Agent Skye," Peyton greeted, his face calm. His blonde hair was wet, making it darker than usual. "Did you really have to call us this early?"

"Probably not," she smiled, wondering if there was a coffee shop nearby.

"I get it. I got a few hours asleep at least before O'Neil called. I couldn't let myself relax until I figured out The Leader."

"You find anything?"

"No. Other than the fact he looks like Santa, which is one person's description. Also hard to compare this time of year when many people dress themselves to represent the season."

"Oh, bollocks." He was right. She never celebrated the human holiday, Dread not exactly one for the festivities when she was a child. "That means Winter Solstice is coming." She closed her eyes, pinching her nose. The months had really gotten away from her.

"Without his full name we have nothing. He was only ever called 'The Leader' or 'My Leader.' I even spoke to a few people as we were leaving trying to get his background, but that was useless."

"There's something wrong... something..." Alice couldn't explain it. A feeling? Gut instinct? Then there was her scar, the pale crescent piece of skin that was colder than the rest of her body. It had ached while she was there, then stopped as soon as she had left. "Do you think this is the guy we're after?"

"If it's not, it's a real coincidence." Peyton folded his arms, watching the other officers corner the whole area off as Jones continued working in the small back room. "We need to search that church."

"O'Neil has already said we can't do anything without physical evidence." Stupid if she said so herself.

"No, we can't go in under force," he said, eyebrows creased. "But we need to find evidence before they strike again."

Alice remained quiet. She wasn't hired directly by the Metropolitan Police, wasn't under the same strict rules and regulations. Either way, she had an idea.

"We'll figure something out."

He pinned the teacher to the ground, a strong grip on the older, more powerful man's neck.

"Let go," the teacher wheezed as he struggled beneath his palm.

He tightened his fist, wanting to end it for them all. This sadistic teacher that smiled at the bruises. Smiled at the broken bones. He had gotten bigger, stronger than they intended. They didn't understand that he wasn't their sheep-dog, wouldn't follow their exact order. It confused them which pleased his beast.

"Let go." A voice of reason this time, the voice of a friend. Meeting Xander's eyes gave him clarity. Eyes as silver as his own, almost mirrored so he could see his own reflection.

He glared down at the teacher, watching his face turn purple even though the other instructors quietly murmured from the sidelines. They would let him finish what he started, they wouldn't interfere.

How tempting.

"You're not worth it," he growled as he released his teacher, watching as the pathetic man gasped for breath. He wasn't worth it, wasn't worth the beatings. Wasn't worth the anger from his father who would say it would put their family to shame in front of the Archdruid.

Not that he cared. It was the old man who decided to put him through this training, a great honour for his father who was to become the next Archdruid. So he stepped back, crossed his arms and allowed his friends to stand beside him.

United. An alliance. A force to be reckoned with.

They didn't expect that either, didn't understand.

The total loyalty of all seven.
Brothers.

CHAPTER 20

What the fuck am I doing?

Alice stood at the back gate behind the church, the chilly air dampening her mood as she worked on the lock.

"Stupid bloody thing," she snarled as if scolding it would help. The metal clanged as it fought her picks, the sound echoing across the headstones just beyond.

With an exasperated sigh, Alice scowled. She was running out of time, the sense of urgency fuelled by the man who stood across the street, watching her. He wore complete black, his face slightly obscured by the brim of his hat. He didn't seem to care that she knew he was watching her, wasn't trying to hide when she kept checking to see if he was still there. At least he was open with his stalking, which made a change.

She turned in a burst of frustration, glaring as the man casually leant against a lamppost. She was a fully trained Paladin who was efficiently trained with a blade, yet, she was struggling with an old as fuck lock.

"Typical, bloody typical," she muttered as she waved at the man. She didn't expect a reaction, so was surprised when he waved back as if they were good friends. When she responded with her middle finger he wasn't as pleased. He flashed her a fang, his hiss carrying in the silence. At least it confirmed he was one of Valentina's goons.

Chuckling to herself, she turned back to the gate. She had spent the day studying the blueprints of the church, memorising every nook and cranny until she had fallen asleep at the table. It was Sam who had woken her up after his shift, an amused smile on his face. So she had left later than intended, already behind schedule even before the lock gave her problems.

Luckily it was winter, the sun not rising for a few hours yet.

With a click the clunky lock fell to the floor, allowing her to push the gate open with a squeak. The graveyard was in poor condition, the names of the deceased either scratched off or unreadable as the marble and limestone slowly dissolved from the rain. Overgrown grass and weeds covered the remnants of the graves, making them indistinguishable from one another. It was a shame. The dead didn't deserve the disrespect.

Breed didn't bury their dead, preferring to burn them to ash, that's if the deceased didn't naturally disintegrate on their own. Why bury something that was going to be worm food? You could still grieve a memory.

Please don't let there be any ghouls.

Alice slowly made her way through the grounds, carefully stepping over the graves.

Vampires had a very small success rate. Before protocols came into place, many of the freshly turned became ghouls, a feral fledgeling that only had basic instincts and close to zero intelligence. As part of the transition, humans who had their blood drained and then replaced with their creators' would be buried under the following moon. As cemeteries were already full of the dead, they became prime places to bury the fledgelings.

It was one of the main reasons Paladins were created, to hunt down the feral Vamps and then their irresponsible creators. While it was now illegal to transition without passing a strict test, it still happened. Hopefully, the graves were all empty, no fledgelings waiting to rip out her throat and the bodies moved to a place where they could be mourned properly.

Alice was prepared for the painful sensation, had psyched herself up as the prickling invisible insects bit all along her skin. Gritting her teeth, she concentrated on the lock for the back door. As a deterrent, it was effective. She did not want to be there, would have happily turned right back around, especially when the newer lock was also giving her hassle. Then she felt it, the final pin clicking into place as the door swung open.

Breathing a sigh of relief, she stepped past the threshold into the small, country style kitchen.

Fuck me, that's painful.

She took a minute to collect herself, her skin sensitive even though it looked unmarked. It wasn't real, she wasn't really being eaten alive. That fact didn't make her feel any better.

The kitchen was clean but cluttered. More baking equipment than anyone really needed was stacked up on almost every available surface. An unfinished, hand-painted poster was draped over the table. It was weird to see that the church did regular fundraising when they weren't all protesting about Breeds going to hell.

Alice huffed as she carefully opened the swing door that led into the main hall, the waning crescent moon giving very little light through the windows. The pews were pushed against the walls, leaving a vast emptiness that was creepy in the moonlight, dust in the air giving the echo of ghosts floating across the room. The broken windows were crudely repaired, and floorboards taped back together. For somewhere that charged as much as they did for entry, the money wasn't going back into the church.

She tried to walk slowly, the floorboards squeaking beneath her feet every time she moved. The office was the same as she remembered, the quotes catching her eye even in the dark. The only furniture was the desk, a chair and a bookshelf full of several different well- known novels. The desk was clean of everything, not a single piece of paper, or a pen could be found.

The drawers came up empty, a fine layer of dust inside indicating they had been empty for a while. Alice frowned, checking all the drawers several times just in case.

It's an office, where is everything?

Alice tried the bookshelf, searching through the books finding nothing. Each novel looked brand new as if they had never been used. Some still had their sale stickers. There weren't any folders, no information regarding money or details about the upcoming events that were discussed at the meeting. Nothing.

"Bugger." She slammed her hand down on the bookshelf. "There has to be something." Surely there would be administrative paperwork?

Her attention slid to the only other door in the room, the one Gordon Potts had disappeared into. It wasn't on the blueprints, so was added after the church was built.

It opened without resistance, a strange draft teasing her

ankles as soon as she stepped onto the first metal step. She stood at the top, listening intently for any signs of a presence. It was early, but not early enough for her to be confident she was alone.

She slowly took another step, listening intently.

Nothing.

Silence.

Self-assured she continued her descent, noting a harsh light beneath the heavy metal door at the bottom. As well as an electronic keypad a chain was wrapped around the metal, the lock loose with runes engraved inside. She wouldn't have been able to simply pick it open even if it was locked, the design magic infused to stop any intrusion by force.

Either someone was down there, or they had forgotten to lock it, the keypad stating 'OPEN' in big green letters.

"Why would you need a magic lock?" she asked herself. "What are they trying to keep in?" *Or out,* she mentally added.

The door opened, revealing a laboratory around double the size as the office above with several closed doors. It looked newly built, the tiles and surfaces too white, especially compared to the age of the church. There were no records of anything beneath the church, the basement built illegally, without permission. It was probably why the church was crumbling.

What the hell is this?

Shiny cupboards lined the walls with silver pipes crisscrossing the concrete ceiling. A metal table was in the middle, empty glass beakers sitting on the top alongside a computer, the screen dark.

Alice stepped further inside, eyeing the see-through plastic box, a tube with black liquid locked inside. A low hum buzzed, the sound consistent as she searched through the folders and notes left on the side.

Something moved behind her.

Spinning, she let out a gasp, her heart beating a hundred miles an hour as she noticed Roman sitting by the stairs.

"You need to stop doing this," she said quietly, trying to calm herself.

How could he have moved down those stairs silently?

"Why are you here?" She kept her voice low, quiet.

Roman just tilted his head, his arctic eyes looking at her puzzled.

"This would be easier if you could talk."

He just continued to stare, not even barking.

"Go home."

No response.

Fuck sake.

Deciding to let him be she turned her attention back to the room, finding paperwork in messily written handwriting beside a microscope. Unfortunately, she had no idea what any of it meant, the words and equations gibberish.

A soft snort behind her before Roman pawed at the metal table. Frowning, Alice examined underneath, finding a hidden drawer. Opening it slowly, she noticed the small notebook.

October 26th
The trial will begin in the next few weeks, my followers have all agreed to be part of the next phase. Gordon has already prepared the poison, we now just have to decide our course of action.

November 30th

Another success, the night dweller didn't know what hit him. It seems that consumption is the easiest way to get it into the system, although I was not told the effects it would have on my people. I pray that our sacrifice is enough.

December 10th
It wanted more. Mason promised salvation, but the consequences seem too steep. Have I made an error in blindly accepting a Breed's advice? The very same Breed I wish to cleanse from this earth? Only the holy can judge me now.

Alice read through the notebook several times, a diary of every detail behind the genocide. She couldn't believe it. The hate The Leader had for Breed was beyond comprehension. It wasn't merely hate, it was fear. He feared them.

Fear made people reckless.

'*Mason promised salvation.*' Alice touched her finger to the name, able to feel the impression of the pen. *Surely it couldn't be?*

A quiet growl brought her head up, Roman staring at the door opposite, his ears flat against his head.

"We're running out of blood," a muffled voice murmured.

Alice froze, panic building as she concentrated on the direction of the voice. She set the book down, making sure it was placed precisely as she first saw it before closing the drawer.

"Now, now. That is your job, I was only supposed to introduce you to it. I have no idea why you have asked me here."

Shit.

She looked towards Roman who was edging towards the stairs. In a split second decision, she made her way through another door, hiding behind it as Roman quickly followed her heel in a huff of annoyance. She shot him a glare before closing the door to a sliver, able to make out some of the lab.

The stench of bleach assaulted her nose immediately, the smell burning as she tried to keep from sneezing. Roman moaned beside her, his nose turned to her thigh.

"Mr Storm, you are a part of this just as much as me. When I have problems, you have problems." The Leader's voice was clear as he stepped inside the room.

"Nonsense," Mason said, his eyes pinched as a metal squeal closed the door behind him. "I introduce you to it, and you organise the removal of as many vampires as you could. That was the deal."

You have got to be shitting me.

Alice watched as one of the most powerful men in London looked around the room in interest.

Shit. Shit. Shit. Does Riley know?

"Well, I want to change the deal!" The Leader barked, shuffling further into the room. "You didn't make it clear how many of my flock I would lose. That alone deserves compensation."

"You want more money?" Mason sniggered. "I thought this was about your belief in cleansing the world?"

"I am but one man. One man that needs money, otherwise I have nothing to help my campaign." The Leader sat at the metal table, his fingers racing across the keyboard. "I'm still recouping the loss of this facility alone." The computer dinged.

"I funded this facility," Mason said, his attention on the beakers on a high shelf. He picked one up, studying the liquid contents then putting it back. "How much?"

"You funded this place but at what cost to me? The damage to the church..."

"How much?" Mason asked again, his voice sharp in irritation.

"One million."

Mason's head shot round, face stern.

"What do I get back for my money? You have only killed a handful of vampires. You didn't even get the Commissioner or my fellow Councilman, and I put them both in a room together for you."

"It wasn't my fault they didn't drink. I can't force it," The Leader growled.

"What about your Summoner? What's he doing?"

"He's been working with it, what do you expect?" The Leader pushed away from the table.

"If he's working with it, then he can get more blood." Mason slammed his hand against a cabinet.

Alice flinched, stepping back as something cracked beneath her boot. Freezing, she waited to see if anyone had heard. Roman tensed beside her, his ear twitching as he concentrated on the conversation. He shot her a warning look, annoyed that she dared to make noise.

"It's asking for more payment."

"Then pay it." Mason patted down invisible creases in his jacket, his face smug.

"I can't just give it..." He seemed to hesitate, his forehead creased in a frown. "They're innocent."

"Then find people that aren't so innocent." Mason smiled, the look making him look evil. "Whatever helps you sleep at night."

The Leader looked defeated as he moved back to the computer. "You at least made any progress with the boy? We need him."

"Are you really in a position to demand anything from me?"

"You know he would be easier to handle. We would be doing exactly the same without the risks."

"Your Summoner thinks he can control him?"

"If the slave bands are not compromised, then yes."

Slave bands?

"My intel says he's still in the city, probably watching his sister." Mason's face sneered. "She isn't going to be a problem, her lack of control will be her downfall."

"Can we not use her?"

Mason thought about it for a moment before shaking his head.

"She belongs to The Council. Besides, it's her brother that we need."

"I apologise if I don't trust your fellow Breed."

"Such disgust in your voice, John."

"It's Leader." A snarl.

"Remember who is paying for all this." Mason turned to leave, stopping at the electronic keypad. "I will give you the extra million, but do not call me again. I want results, not excuses."

"Of course." The Leader put in the code, his body hiding the number sequence before following Mason out. The door clicked closed behind them.

Moving away from the door Alice waited for a few minutes, listening out for anymore voices. Quickly peeking down she tried to dislodge the glass shard without making anymore noise while Roman sat on his hind legs, panting. The room was dark, the bleach stench still burning.

"Lux Pila," she quietly murmured, her eyes taking a while to adjust once the ball of light popped into existence.

Holy shit!

She had found the culprit for the bleach. The floor was stained red, bleach soaked rags left beside buckets full of murky water. The room was twice the size of the lab, half concrete and half tiled. The tiled side held a grey plastic chair that reminded Alice of the dentist, but one with leather straps. The concrete side held two closed metal cells, the red stains fresher inside.

Alice could just make out a faint circle marked across the concrete, the bleach smearing the lines. Stepping closer, she felt her scar start to throb, aching in time with her heartbeat. She ignored the pain, trying to make out the shapes that were once painted.

What are they?

She touched one of the runes that remained, unable to understand its meaning. She could feel power still pulsating from the circle, the magic charged as if it was still activated.

But the circle wasn't anchored, the marks that would have been the five elements destroyed, except one.

Opening her third eye, she tried to suppress the cold heaviness that wrapped around her chest, constricting her lungs. The concrete secreted dark magic, tendrils of orange power shooting out of the ground like lightning.

She didn't understand. A circle had to be anchored to the five elements to work, fire and earth were the two fixed points, with air and water allowing the natural flow of magic through the circle then spirit to close. The fact magic still flowed was supposed to be impossible.

She reached for the bleach, tossing the abrasive liquid over the remnants of the circle, hoping to remove the last symbol, closing the loop. She choked out a breath, the bleach stench unpleasant but better than it was.

"Salt, I need salt." Salt was a catalyst, could break the remaining enchantment.

Roman yipped, nudging a large burlap sack in the corner. He bit into the side, ripping the fabric until salt poured onto the floor. She felt the magic start to dissipate, but too slowly. Smoke sizzled beneath her feet, the vapours black before disappearing altogether.

"I need to get out of here," she cried as the electric sensation became overwhelming, even as the salt fought to break the spell. She opened the door back into the lab, slipping through with Roman quickly behind.

She paused to grab the notebook before she pushed her weight against the metal door, her attention swinging to the keypad.

"You've got to be shitting me!" She pushed it again, knowing it was useless without the code.

They were locked in.

Fuck.

"What do we do now?" she asked Roman, looking at him expectantly.

He shook his head, his eyes wide as he started to shake anxiously.

"Hey, are you alright?"

She reached for him, petting him awkwardly. He calmed instantly, pushing his weight against her palm as his heavy panting quietened. She had forgotten he had been kept in a cage, forced into a transition he didn't want. He was the reason Rex had done what he did, sacrificed her for his brother.

"It's going to be okay."

We're only locked in a secret underground lab behind a thick, key code locked metal door. Casual workday.

Alice snorted at her own sarcasm, gaining her a worried glance from Roman. She scratched behind his ear, analysing the doorframe.

A bang against the metal made her jump up, pushing Roman behind her. Unsheathing her sword, she gripped the hilt, flinching at another loud bang. The metal screeched, a high-pitched shrill that set her teeth on edge.

She stepped back, pulling a snarling Roman with her just as the corner curled in. She knew for sure it wasn't The Leader, a human couldn't physically make a dent, never mind pulling the door from its hinges. Neither could a druid... usually.

Alice gripped her sword tighter.

Danton released the door from his grip, the metal clattering to the floor. He stood there, his dark eyes looking around the room before they settled on her.

"Ma petite sorcière, how nice to see you."

Roman leapt forward, snarling as D showed off his own, impressive fangs.

"What are you doing here?" Alice relaxed her arm but didn't put away her blade.

D looked at her pointedly, his dark eyes holding a controlled anger.

"Why did it take you so long to remove the barrier spell?" His fangs grew longer in his mouth, forcing his lips open. "Merde. It hurts, bâtards sanglants."

"Barrier spell?" *What's he on about...* "Oh, you mean the deterrent?" The horrible sensation of insects biting across her flesh.

"You shouldn't be here, It's dangerous."

"Danton..." A stranger hissed from behind the broken door. "La maîtresse?"

"Non." D shot back in French. "Ne l'essaie pas."

The man tensed, the brim of his hat clutched in his hands. He moved past D to face Alice, his expression tight.

"The Mistress sends her regards," he said in a deep, gravelly voice. Guess he didn't really appreciate her hand gesture.

D's hand shot out, sending the stranger smashing through the wall, head cracking against the concrete.

"It's time to go," he snarled at Alice.

Alice chased after him, ignoring the stranger as he peeled himself off the wall.

"I need to ask about Valentina..."

"I cannot speak to you of it." He climbed the stairs, assuming she would follow. "Do not make a habit of this, ma petite sorcière. I cannot keep rescuing you."

"But you were watching me because she said so." Alice came to a halt inside the church, begging for D to turn and face her. They had been friends for years, was one of her first partners as a Paladin. Had it all been fake?

D stood in the centre of the atrium, the moonlight giving him an eerie pale aura. He turned his head, his dark hair catching the breeze from one of the broken windows.

"Oui, I'm her soldier. Have been for centuries."

"Tell me D, did you mean any of it? Was it all a job?" She wanted to hurl something at him, the urge to hurt him strong but instead she clenched her fists.

He spun to fully face her, a frown creasing his brow. He appeared in front of her, the speed knocking the wind from her lungs as he gripped her jaw.

"A long time ago, she saved me. She gave me back my life, for that I serve." He gently released her, his skin ice cold. "I help you because you need it, you're reckless like a bad-tempered child. If I hadn't been there over the years..." he hesitated, eyes flashing. "You're my friend. I help my friends."

"Friend?" Alice stepped away, not wanting him to touch her again. Roman stood beside her, his ears pinned back as he watched the vampire. "You didn't help me, you served your Mistress."

"You're too young to understand loyalty, ma petit Alice."

"I know you don't fuck over your friends."

He started to laugh, holding his pale palm over his chest.

"Être juste, I wanted more than simply friends. But you never fell for my la passion." He grinned, the usual flirtatiousness that she was used to back before his eyes hardened. "I was assigned to watch over you, over the years, it no longer felt like a job. You might not understand right now, but you will." He bowed his head, moving away. "Be careful of The Mistress, she is of old and likes to collect unusual and beautiful things."

"WHO'S THERE?" a voice called through the church.

Alice spun to the voice, a flashlight blinding her as it swept across her face.

"PUT YOUR HANDS UP!" the voice shouted.

"Okay, okay." Alice squinted past the light to the officer. "I'm Agent Alice Skye, I heard a commotion, so I came to investigate."

"I SAID PUT YOUR HANDS UP!"

Alice made a sound of frustration, her eyes darting around the poorly lit room in search for Danton, but he had disappeared.

Fuck sake.

"Call Detective O'Neil." Warm fur settled against her leg, the weight comforting as she slowly reached for her ID. "I'm part of the Spook Squad."

CHAPTER 21

Alice blew into her Styrofoam cup, the aroma of tea soothing as she cupped it for warmth. Morning light streamed through the windows as several officers milled around, flicking her looks of uncertainty when they thought she wasn't looking. It took her an hour to convince them who she was, then another hour of her sitting on one of the pews, forced to wait for her team.

At least they gave me tea, she supposed.

"Agent Skye," a voice barked, strong enough to carry through the church. "What happened?" O'Neil angrily stopped in front of her, his eyebrows pinched and eyes tired. She wasn't sure if he was angry at her, or the situation.

"I decided to stake outside, heard a commotion and thought I should investigate," she lied.

She carefully watched his expression, trying to make out any tell-tale signs he knew of her deception.

"I hadn't even taken a few steps until Officer Gunner intervened." She shot a friendly wave towards Gunner, with whom she had spent the last few hours chatting. He seemed like a nice guy, relatively new to the force but she wished she didn't know all his ex-girlfriend's names, nor the fact he had one leg longer than the other.

"Why are you just sitting there?"

"I was asked not to move." She tried to hide her annoyance, apparently not well enough by the nudge from Roman. She tried to push him away, which resulted in him settling heavier on her feet instead.

O'Neil frowned at the wolf but didn't comment. Which was good considering there was only so many times she could explain that he was a stray and that no, she couldn't get rid of him. She had tried.

"You have full authority here, you shouldn't have been treated like that." O'Neil reached for a cigarette before fisting his hand. He gave an irritated glance at an Officer who handed over an evidence bag before returning his attention to Alice. "I was told you found this notebook?" He held up the bag, the word *'EVIDENCE'* printed in red across the plastic.

"I found it here, someone must have dropped it." Another lie, but one that benefited them. "It contains journal entries admitting to the genocide."

"Detective, we have a visitor." Peyton cut her a sharp glare as he approached, a knowing glint in his eye.

"WHAT'S HAPPENING?" A commotion as an old man shuffled through the main church doors, his arm shook as he used a walking stick. "THIS IS A PLACE OF WORSHIP, GET OUT, ALL OF YOU!" The Leader waved his free arm angrily as an Officer approached, trying to calm him down.

"Well, isn't that interesting." O'Neil nodded towards Peyton, who unhooked his handcuffs.

"Hello, my name is Detective Sullivan O'Neil, and this

is Officer Peyton. Can you please come take a seat?" O'Neil held out his arm towards a pew.

The Leader glared at Peyton for a moment, frowning before he made his way over. He heavily sat down, his shoulder slumped. He looked frail, old. Nothing like he came across before, in the meeting.

"What is this? On whose authority...?"

"Sir, could you please start with your legal name." O'Neil interrupted, bringing out his little black book.

"My name's The Leader." His eyes moved to Peyton again, narrowing. "Do I know you?"

"I don't need to explain the severity of the situation," Alice said as she joined the men, Roman hot on her heels.

"What severity? No one has explained why you are here," he snapped before he recognised her. His eyes went wide, flicking between Alice and Peyton. "Traitors," he snarled, the weak- old- man- act disappearing. "You... you." The Leader leapt up from the pew before being forced back down. "I knew we shouldn't have trusted you," he spat towards them.

"If you don't calm down I will charge you with aggravated assault towards a police officer," O'Neil warned. "Now, what is your name?"

The Leader hesitated, a note of uncertainty in his eyes. "John Smith."

"John Smith, can you please explain why you have an unregistered laboratory built in your basement?"

"I think I need to speak to my lawyer."

"That indicates you have done something illegal," Peyton muttered. "Have you done something illegal?"

"Answer the question," O'Neil asked.

"I don't know what you're talking about."

"So you have no idea about the lab built underneath

your church? I checked, you have no planning permission, which means it was done illegally."

The Leader remained silent, a slight smug look on his face.

"What about the cages? Or the circle you so crudely tried to hide?" Alice added, watching his reaction.

Still no response.

O'Neil eyed him with measured interest.

"Mr Smith, we can do this the easy way or the hard way. We have enough evidence against you with the notebook..."

"You have nothing. Anybody could have written those letters, they don't prove anything."

"No, but the DNA found on the letters will surely match the DNA you have so freely given us." Peyton pointedly looked at the blob of spit by his boot. "Not even mentioning the clear fingerprints from the smudged ink."

"Sloppy if you ask me," O'Neil added, a slow smile creeping across his face.

"It wasn't me. It wasn't. I'm a man of god, only the divine can judge me. I was persuaded for the greater good..."

"The 'greater good'?" Peyton snorted. "I'm sure your god or deity encourages mass murder."

"It wasn't me, it was Gordon. Gordon Potts. He's the Summoner."

"He's a witch?" O'Neil asked The Leader while looking at Alice.

She just shrugged. She didn't know, it was hard to tell someone's Breed by just looking at them. Flaring her chi to see if she could feel someone's aura was the simplest way to know if they were a magic user or not, but that didn't determine the exact Breed. Although, that was only if they weren't concealing their magic.

"He told me he wasn't, that he was normal. But he had ancient knowledge so he could practice magic without compromising his soul."

"You believed what you wanted because it helped you," Alice stated.

The Leader caught her eye. "I believe in what is for the greater good of humanity. You wouldn't understand that," he sneered.

"Who else?" O'Neil asked. "From the state of your church you don't have the funds to orchestrate it alone."

"Mason Storm," Alice said before The Leader could answer. "Was it only Mason from the Storm empire?" Alice asked, panic underlying her tone.

If Riley was involved...

The thought sucked the air right out of her lungs.

"Mason approached me, remember that." The Leader confirmed. "I think I've said enough. I would like to speak to my lawyer."

Alice felt her anger snap. "You pretend to be righteous, but you're just an extremist hypocrite disguised as a religion. You don't deserve the..."

"Agent Skye, step back," O'Neil warned.

Alice moved away before she said anything else. She didn't know what would happen if one of the most influential men in London, if not Britain was found guilty of such a heinous crime. Someone who, in the public eye, had been very vocal in equal rights as well as open about generously donating to various charities.

Shit.

Peyton came with her, his face stern as he moved her away from anyone else.

"What the fuck did you think you were doing?" His

eyes flashed in anger, his lips a hard line. "You could have compromised the whole case."

Alice opened her mouth to lie, deciding against it. Peyton saw through her excuses.

"We needed evidence, I found it. Do not tell me you wouldn't have done the same thing if you could."

Peyton's cheekbones sharpened through his skin, his eyes searching hers.

"What are your thoughts?" he asked, voice softer than before, but his eyes no less intense.

"That I want Mason locked up with the key thrown somewhere far away."

Actually, she wanted something darker to happen to him, something that reflected what he did to those innocent people.

"We will never be able to get him."

"What makes you say that? We have all this evidence..."

"We have his name on a piece of paper and a confession that will be thrown out of court."

"I saw him..."

"You saw nothing as you were never there. Otherwise all the evidence will be compromised." Peyton's jaw clenched. "He's going to have the best solicitors money can buy, we won't be able to get this to stick."

"Your rules are ridiculous." Breed authority might have been more barbaric, but in the circumstance it would be justice. Unfortunately, the structure was to inform the head of the specific Breed of the crime – which would be Mason.

"You Paladins have no structure. Just point your sword and stab."

Alice couldn't help but laugh. "You can't say it doesn't get the job done."

Peyton smirked in reply.

As a Paladin, she knew the justice system well. Knew the corruptions and scandals influenced by The Council. They ruled by fear, allowing the human justice system to do its job until they were forced to step in. They wouldn't have agreed to give over their power. They would have said anything to make the Norms happy, even giving them a false sense of entitlement. It was only the extreme cases when the crime was deemed too serious that the Breed's governing body took over. It was the reason why she was allowed to use lethal force. Someone with razor- sharp claws, preference for blood or could turn your skin inside out was a lot more dangerous than the usual human.

"Do you know who he is?" Alice asked.

"If you mean his Council status then yes. Nobody is above the law, not even them."

That's what he thinks.

"What about a confession?" Alice said, knowing he would never see the inside of a cell, at least, not a normal one. She's sure The Council had their own special ones, especially for people like him. Or worse.

"How likely are we going to get that?"

CHAPTER 22

Alice paid no attention to the beautiful woman who sat behind the glass desk in front of Mason Storm's office, his door closed beside her. The woman looked up, her expression like a fish as she watched Alice push open the door, bursting inside unannounced much to the fluster of the receptionist.

"Excuse me, excuse me!" her red lips gasped. "You can't go in there..."

She came to a halt, her eyes huge, round.

"I'm so sorry Councilman Storm, she just..."

"Louise, it's fine," Mason said calmly, his grey eyes narrowed as he glared coldly at Alice. "Could you please move my next appointment."

"Sir." Louise nodded before closing the door behind her.

"Are you going to explain why you're here?" Mason asked.

Alice said nothing as she looked around the office, analysing his masculine, expensive taste. She knew it would irritate him, her blatant disregard to his question. She needed him angry. To fracture his calm demeanour.

So she remained silent.

His desk was oversized, covered in paperwork with his family name embossed on the front. An oil painting decorated the panelled wood wall directly behind him, what looked like a warped beast snarling. Everything was in masculine shades of navy, pewter and grey other than the burst of green through the floor to ceiling windows. His office was on the sixty-eighth floor that faced directly opposite the nature reserve that was a burst of life in a city of steel and glass.

It would have been breath-taking if she had time to appreciate it.

'We're live. Try and get him to admit his involvement without leading the conversation,' Detective Brady said from her hidden earpiece. *'Be careful, we don't know how dangerous he is.'*

"I'm waiting," Mason asked, his tone like ice as he sat down behind his desk. "Why have you made such a rude entrance?"

He relaxed back into his seat, the painted beast surrounding him until it gave the impression they were one. It made him look powerful, a force to be reckoned with. Which was probably the point. She could imagine him there, negotiating his business deals with ease. For the bastard he was, she couldn't dispute him as a businessman.

She gave him a slow smile, enjoying the slight narrowing of his eyes.

"I'm working."

"Oh, yes. Aren't you part of that new inter-breed partnership? Ridiculous, teaming up with the Norms," he sniggered, clasping his hands together.

"I'm surprised you seem so opposed, wasn't it The Council's idea?" she drawled, baiting him.

"Nonsense, why would I care about such a ludicrous concept?" He remained calm, his attention following her as she walked around his office. "Tell me Alice, how is Rexley Wild?"

Alice froze at the name, knew he had said it to gain a reaction, to take back control of the conversation.

"I wouldn't know, haven't seen him." She had done well not to think about him, that man didn't deserve any of her attention, even if it was only her mind. At least, until recently.

"You haven't spoken to him?"

Mason stood up, slowly walking around his desk to stand in front of her. His height dwarfed hers by almost a foot, made her neck ache to look at his face, but she refused to step back.

"Weren't you lovers?"

"Are you asking if we fucked?" Alice asked, using the profanity on purpose. "I don't think that's any of your business." Mason knew exactly what to say to unnerve her, something he could use against her. She wouldn't allow him to get the upper hand.

"How crudely put. I think being betrayed like that is fascinating." He slowly smiled, leaning forward into her personal space. "Someone who knows you intimately and still chose to betray you, how... embarrassing. Or is it more pathetic?"

Alice didn't respond.

"I don't understand what he saw in you. All I see is a girl who's in way over her head. A pathetic excuse of a witch who can't even control her most basic energy. It's... disappointing."

"Isn't it a shame I don't respect your opinion."

She didn't even see him blur before her head cracked against the glass window, a strong arm pressed forcibly into her throat. She kept the eye contact even as she struggled to breathe, not daring to give him the satisfaction.

'What was that?'

She had forgotten people were listening in, could only hear and not see what was happening.

'Agent Skye, this is your ten- minute warning before we're coming in. Get the confession.'

"I can still feel you leaking energy. Has my son not taught you anything?" Mason asked with a dissatisfied tut.

He released a slight pressure from her neck, giving her the chance to suck in a much needed breath.

"We're not here to talk about me." She enjoyed his frustration as she remained calm, even as fire tingled in her fingertips.

"You're a bomb waiting to go off," he spoke against her cheek, his breath intimate across her face. "You may look relaxed, but I can feel it beneath your skin, your chi's electric. All I would have to do is..."

Alice gave a startled gasp, could feel her chi blazing as Mason touched it with his own. It felt similar to Riley, how he could make it charged just by being close. But it wasn't the same, it was darker, toxic, like a thick tar across her senses.

"Cute trick," she spat at him, not hiding her disgust. He felt... wrong. "Do you do kids parties too?"

"You're like a personal ley line, a power socket that I could syphon," he whispered in her ear. "Maybe that's why everybody is so fascinated with you. It's what made me so fascinated with your mother."

Alice heard the blood rush from her head, her eyes blurring as Mason sniggered. She pushed against him, allowing her energy to coat her palm in a burst of crackling blue. Mason stepped back just in time, an unreadable glint in his eye.

"Don't speak of her," she snarled. She could see her personal Tinkerbell floating from the corner of her eye, the ball of flame sparking at intervals to match her temper. It was times like this when she hated the thing, a physical manifestation of her weakness.

"That's what they want to do, you know. To use The Dragon child. Use you," he said, casually looking her up and down. "Although, you're no longer a child, can't be as easily manipulated. At least, that's what my fellow councilmembers believe."

"You know nothing about my family."

Alice jumped at his burst of laughter.

"Your ignorance is amusing."

'Five-minute warning.'

She wanted to ask him more but knew it wasn't the time.

"Where were you around five-thirty this morning?"

"Why should I answer you?" he smirked.

"Because you've been accused of being a conspirator in a recent genocide."

She watched his reaction, saw a flash of panic before he quickly recovered. Alice tried to hide her satisfied grin.

Got yu.

"This is utter nonsense." Mason walked to his desk to pick up the phone, dialling his receptionist. "I grow tired of this conversation. Leave before you're thrown out."

"Forensics are currently collecting evidence against you for your part in the poisoning," she calmly explained. "I wonder what everybody is going to think..."

"Your uncontrollable surges have clearly affected your mind. I will make sure I report it to The Council Immediately. Your accusations are treason against a councilmember."

"Do you mean the same councilmember that organised the murder of another?"

Masons face turned cold, his eyes guarded. He settled the handset back into its cradle. "What do you want?"

"I want to know why."

Mason stared at her for a few seconds, his grey eyes unreadable.

"Everything I do, I do because it needs to be done."

He moved slowly towards her again.

"Your brother, for instance..."

Alice saw her Tinkerbell sparkle, annoyed that it was giving away her emotions.

"Yes, your brother is very much alive. I've been looking for him actually. He's a danger to the general public."

"You don't know that," she shot at him.

He kept speaking as if she hadn't spoken.

"You know nothing of what I have to do. The decisions I have to make. Valentina has become a threat, she has taken too much power, has become sick with it, her and her night dwellers."

Mason moved closer once again, his movements uncharacteristically rigid. Alice concentrated on extinguishing the Tinkerbell, but left the flame in her palm, not allowing him to get too close.

"It is what I do, it's part of why The Order was created. We neutralise threats to keep the world safe. Are you a threat Alice?"

He stepped closer again, a bare inch away from the magic she coated across her palm.

"Are you following in your parent's footsteps?"

"Don't speak of my parents." Her fire crackled. "You don't deserve to even mention them."

"Druids can become addicted to power, crave it. My ancestors chose power, became corrupted by the darkness of it..."

"Daemons," Alice finished for him as the realisation clicked. "Your ancestors were the first Daemons."

The passage she read months ago flashed across her memory.

'For one to 'Become' age-old one must sacrifice a vessel of clean magic. Doing so will give the bearer the ability to transcend into the next stage, giving unbelievable power over the darker arts, their body reflecting the high power bestowed on them by the mother of everything.'

"The Originals. We're now taught from birth the consequences of choosing dark, choosing power. It's a burden we live with, the curse of our blood."

'One-minute. Keep him talking.'

"Your mother was a power your father craved," Mason continued. "He chose her over The Order, even over The Council. They became dangerous, first when he didn't disclose who your mother was, and then when he refused to hand her over. So they both had to be neutralised."

"Neutralised?" Alice choked out the word.

"It was a shame something as beautiful as your mother got in the way. She would have made a great pet."

"It was you? You led the Daemons to them."

Alice felt her hand start to pulsate, the flames crawling up to her elbow.

"You killed them." The fire began to build in her other palm, an uncontrollable element.

He smiled. "I'm a businessman Alice."

"GET DOWN!" Voice's boomed as the door was kicked open. Three uniformed police including officer Peyton stormed through the door, pointing their weapons at Mason.

"ON THE GROUND!"

Mason was quickly pinned and handcuffed, his smile turning to a snarl as he was manhandled.

"GET OFF ME! DO YOU KNOW WHO I AM?"

Detective Brady approached Alice cautiously, his eyes worried as the fire crackled loudly. She could smell burning, knew if she didn't calm herself, she could suffer a flame out.

"Agent Skye?"

Alice closed her eyes, concentrated on breathing in and out. Smoke tickled her throat, the intense heat decreasing with every passing second before she finally extinguished it. She opened her eyes, instantly searching for Mason, unable to hide her emotion as she watched the sneer carved into his face disappear. Replaced with her death.

Alice wanted to smile, wanted to laugh hysterically as she watched the man who admitted to murdering her parents be taken away in handcuffs, she wanted...

Riley stood in the threshold, his eyes completely silver, unreadable.

An apology instantly bubbled up her throat, one she swallowed. She had nothing to apologise for, the devastating knowledge of what Mason admitted plastered across her face. Instead, she stood there, frozen, unable to break the eye contact.

She felt cold, hollow.

Riley blinked, the captivating silver replaced with steel-grey that darkened with impatience.

"Agent Skye?" Brady nudged her, forcing her attention.

She looked up at him expectantly, having to blink to clear her vision.

"We've got exactly what we need. We're done here."

"Yeah, okay," she replied, voice husky. Lifting up her top she ripped the microphone off, ignoring the acute pain from the sticky tape. Handing it to one of the officers she turned back to Riley, an explanation on the edge of her tongue.

But he didn't give her the chance.

She quickly searched for him, following back through into the reception where she was met with concerned stares. They had all heard his father's confession, knew one of her darkest secrets, at least partially.

And she didn't care.

Couldn't care while she felt this strange sense of urgency to find Riley, an irrational feeling that something was wrong. Something...

A sharp bark snapped her out of it. Roman whined low in his throat, his tongue lapping at her fingers. She instinctively reached out to his fur, anchoring herself in the warmth. She had no idea how he had arrived up there, but thankful that he had.

"Come on, let's get you home."

CHAPTER 23

Alice tried not to smile as Roman played with the air currents, his mouth open in a wolfish grin as he caught the wind from the open car window. He was lucky that Sam knew how to replace a tyre otherwise it would have been public transport. Except, even that would have been difficult since shifters were banned from being in public in their animal form. Alice chanced another look at him, his pure black pelt shinier than she remembered.

He was small for a shifter, could possibly have pulled off the deception if no one looked into his eyes. Too intelligent, you could never mistake a shifter for any animal, never mind a domesticated one. Yet, as far as she knew, Roman had not shifted back to his human form, his wolf having taken over back when he had been captured. He should have been showing signs of deterioration, the beast becoming more permanent. However, he didn't. It was peculiar, but she didn't want to jinx it. If Roman needed more time to come to terms with his captivity, so be it.

As Alice drove up the driveway to White Dawn's compound, she felt herself panic, an irrational reaction considering she knew she wasn't in any danger. Anxiety wrapped around her chest, restricting her lungs into panicked gasps.

Roman looked over to her, feeling her angst.

She closed her eyes, shutting everything out. She was still so angry, angrier even more so that she couldn't ask questions of the man who had, willingly, handed her over to a cult. A man for whom she'd had feelings for, with whom she had slept with.

She knew why Roman's quiet whine was reminding her, but she still couldn't control the sudden energy spike. Heat prickled her fingers as she clenched her fists, hard enough she felt her nails cut into her palms.

She hadn't achieved closure, not really.

A warm tongue licked across her cheek. Opening her eyes, she turned to Roman, his own eyes dark with concern. It wasn't his fault.

"It's okay," she murmured, giving him a reassuring smile as she got out the car. She didn't really want to be there. Had no interest in the pack who couldn't, or wouldn't answer her questions.

The old manor house was just as she remembered. Even so, her heart skipped a beat once she saw Theo open the door, her brain seeing his twin instead. Blinking away the illusion she assured herself it was indeed Theo and not the man she never wanted to see again.

"Hello, oh Roman, there you are." Theo smiled at his brother, making the large scar that started from his forehead, across his nose and distorting his upper lip stand out. "Wondered where you had gone off to."

"He keeps popping up," Alice said dryly.

Roman barked before wandering to sit beside Theo, his ears twitching.

"Have you thought about the offer?"

"I'm sorry," she said, her voice humiliatingly hoarse. "I can't." She couldn't face him, not yet. She needed to understand her feelings first, needed to know if they were real. If anything was real.

"We will pay you anything," Theo said as he stepped out of the doorway, a desperate edge to his voice.

"This isn't about money."

Roman snorted, forcing Theo to whip his head towards his brother. He looked at him like he could understand – which maybe he could. Theo growled, the noise disconcerting coming from a human throat. Roman barked in response before moving to slump beside Alice instead.

Theo looked frustrated but didn't say anything.

Great, now she was in the middle of a brotherly spat.

"Look, I need to go."

"Please, you don't understand. We need to find him before Xavier. I can't make you forgive him for what he did to you, but surely you can recognise the reasons behind it."

Alice saw red.

"How dare you say that to me," she snapped, irritation igniting her already high energy level. She took a controlling breath, concentrated on calming her chi. "You go find him."

"Do you not think we have tried?" His eyes flashed blue, his wolf reacting to his own spike in anger. "You're our last option."

Alice opened her mouth to give a retort, but nothing came out. They were desperate. She knew what it felt like to be searching for a brother. Alice wanted to run away, screaming. Wanted to leave Rex to it; a fitting punishment.

But was it though?

She searched Theo's eyes, not sure what she was even looking for. Rex had betrayed her in every way possible. Tricked her. Used her. Yet, she knew she couldn't allow him that fate if she could help it.

"What does Xavier want?" she asked as Theo closed his eyes, his breath coming out in a slow exhale.

"Thank you."

"I haven't agreed yet." She had heard Xavier was one of the most ruthless council members, gaining his position by killing his predecessor. Shifters didn't have The Magicka like witches or The Order like druids, where there was a majority panel to decide your fate. They only had Xavier. His decision was final.

"Yes, you have."

Alice looked away, the wind catching her hair as she gazed out towards the trees surrounding the compound.

Fuck. Fuck. Fuck.

She was going to regret this.

"What leads do you have?"

Alice sat in her car, blinking up at the clearly lived in shed.

"This can't be right?" she frowned, checking the crumpled paper map for the hundredth time. "Stupid, bloody..."

Alice smelt smoke, the edges of the paper alight and quickly burning though.

"SHIT. SHIT. SHIT!"

Alice flung herself into the open air, stamping on the map with her boot.

She hated maps. It was her own fault, her satellite navigation unit needed to be repaired, the crystal inside broken, so she had been stuck with the old- fashioned way.

She eyed the remains of the directions, wondering if she was simply born with bad luck. Or it could be that she let her magic go unchecked, which was also her fault.

Great, just great.

She puffed out a breath as she gazed at the crudely made wooden house, hoping it was the right place. She was in the middle of nowhere, the building made from felt, wooden slats and nails which was surrounded on all sides in a thick brush. The only way onto the property was the thin dirt driveway that was clearly handmade. The ground beneath the structure was darker than the rest, the earth charred as if something else had stood there before.

"Well, this is a good place to kill someone," she laughed, the sound hollow.

Why had Theo sent her there? He had given her a vague direction, explained she was to meet with someone who could help. She had no idea what he could do when she couldn't track him. And she had definitely tried to track him. It was like Rex had vanished into thin air.

Or that could be just wishful thinking.

"Hello?" she called, trying to peer through a dark window.

"Who are you?" A man emerged from the forest, his pitch-black eyes guarded as he stayed in the shadow of a tree.

"Oh, hi." Alice tried to approach but stopped when he stepped back. "I'm supposed to be meeting someone here."

"You here for the wolf?"

"Ah, yes. That's me." She gave an awkward wave.

"I told him I don't work with wolves."

"Well, I'm not a wolf."

He tilted his head, staring at her from a distance.

"Your aura is weird," he finally said.

"I'm sorry, what?" She sensed it then, something brushing against her chi. It felt strange, dark.

Where did Theo find this guy?

The man stepped into the light.

"How did you do that?" she asked, blinking stupidly at the vampire. He had just tested her chi. But vampires didn't have magic.

She studied him, wondering if she was simply seeing things. It wouldn't be the first time. His hair matched the darkness of his eyes, spiked in every direction possible with his fangs at full length. He was dressed like a hiker, with heavy boots, jeans and a chequered shirt. Goth meets country. It was a creepy combination.

"I will do this for you because I'm interested in what you are," he stated. "It is not for the wolf."

"I'm just a simple witch." If she kept telling herself that it might be true.

"Just a witch, as I'm just a Vamp," he grinned, emphasising his unnaturally long canines. "But not a wolf," he quickly added, the smile disappearing.

Alice warily watched him, his gaze uncomfortable before he finally invited her inside. She followed cautiously, not really wanting to be too close to him.

The inside was modest, a single camping bed sat next to a chimney and a basic kitchen. Copper pots and crushed herbs covered almost every available surface while dead birds, rabbits and other little critters hung bleeding from the ceiling.

"So what's your name?"

"Unimportant. Unimportant. We do not exchange names. I have no interest in yours. Yet. Maybe? No, no names. Now..." He clapped his hands together. "Your wolf mentioned a bracelet?"

He stood by the chimney, his fingers absently brushing the corpse of a rabbit, his attention never leaving her.

Alice grabbed the leather cord from her pocket, handing it over.

"Do you know what it is?" She hadn't seen the bracelet since it was removed from her wrist, thought it was lost. She was most surprised when Theo presented her with it.

"It's fascinating," the vampire said as he studied it eagerly. "Bought on the black market, incredibly illegal."

His eyes were excited when he looked up, his movements unnaturally jerky as if he had forgotten how to act normal, human.

"The leather would be entwined around the hair of the person they would want to track, then soaked in the owner's blood."

"Hair?" Alice instantly touched her own.

"Yes, yes, hair. It's easy enough to obtain without the victim knowing."

He licked his lips as he held the moon pendant up to the light.

"Now, this is interesting."

Unnerved by the intensity of his gaze, Alice looked at the pendant.

"It would have emphasised emotions towards the person who gifted it, made them heightened. Anger, jealousy..." He made a sound of choked amusement. "Lust."

Alice felt a chill at the back of her neck. Her emotions had been fake, forced. The thought made her skin crawl.

"How heightened?" She held her breath, waiting for the answer.

"The emotions would already be there, but once in the

presence of the owner of the bracelet, they would be amplified. General annoyance could become rage while simple attraction could change to intense passion." He licked his lips again, eyes excited.

"So, it can't force emotions?"

"No, no, no. Emotions already there, just amplified. Maybe a little manipulated."

He made a sound of annoyance.

"If emotion isn't already there, the bracelet cannot fake them. That is called Pathokinesis, which this bracelet is not." He snorted, throwing the bracelet onto his bed. "This will be sufficient payment for my services."

"Wait, I never agreed to that."

"Do you not want my help?" he asked, his fingers clawed in a threat. "I'm sure there are many people around that can do what I do."

Fuck.

What exactly could he do?

"What of the effects of the bracelet? What will you do with them?"

"Magic is no longer... it's..." He seemed to struggle for the right word, as if English wasn't his native tongue. "Broken."

Alice thought about it.

"Fine."

She didn't really have any other options. She wanted to curse Rex for doing what he had done, curse Theo for asking her for help.

"This way, this way," he clapped as he pushed his bed over. Beneath was a neatly drawn pentagram in blood, his symbols stylised in a way she didn't recognise.

Alice felt goosebumps break over her skin even as she

stepped away, the circle secreting dark magic. It was thick, like oil that clung to her lungs with every breath.

"Stay there," he demanded as he cupped his hands, murmuring incoherently before stepping into his circle. A dome appeared around him instantly, his aura bland, completely colourless.

How can he do magic? It was impossible. It was...

"You're a familiar," she said as the realisation hit her.

Familiars were magical partners to witches, sharing their chi. They were usually a cat or another small domestic animal, the reason being that the witch would borrow their familiar's aura in spells, substantially expanding their own chi. As it caused intense pain and left the creature without an aura to protect themselves, it was ruled as black magic, therefore illegal. The practice of making a person into a familiar was forbidden.

The vampire looked up, his eyes entirely encased by black, his head tilted inquisitively. He would have been tortured every time his master practised magic, something like that would have left many people with a few marbles missing.

Although he had obviously learned a few things along the way.

"You share your master's aura." It was the only logical reason the vampire could practise magic.

He gave her a wicked grin.

"Where is...?" She couldn't bring herself to call the person a 'master' again. It implied he was a servant, a slave. The idea he was seen as an object someone could own made her feel ill.

The Vamp burst out laughing, his shoulders shaking violently as his hands continued to be clasped tightly together. A small light broke through the cracks between his fingers.

"Ladybird ladybird, fly away home," he sang in an eerily detached voice. "Your house is on fire, your children have all gone, all but one that lies under a stone..." He cackled away, the light flickering in his fist before flashing brightly. "All done," he said chirpily as he bounded over to her. "Give this to your wolf, he will be able to track his own blood."

Alice opened her hand as he dropped a small pebble, the surface intensely cold as it hit her skin.

"Blood as in brother?"

"Either or," he shrugged before wrapping his arms around himself, his fingers clawed into his chequered shirt.

Was this all Theo had wanted?

She closed her fist, trying to ignore the fact she thought the pebble had a pulse.

"Thanks."

"That was fun. I haven't done that in a while." His gaze drifted off to stare at the bracelet.

That was her cue to leave.

Even as she transferred the pebble to the glove compartment in her car she felt uneasy, wondering what sort of dark magic had made it. One thing for sure was that she couldn't wait to be rid of it already. She caught herself looking at the charred earth beneath the shed, only just noticing how some of the trees surrounding were also singed.

"Ladybird ladybird, fly away home," she sang to herself, remembering the nursery rhyme. "Your house is on fire, your children have all gone, all but one that lies under a stone, fly thee home, ladybird, ere it be gone."

She really hoped it was simply a rhyme, and not something more sinister. From her gut feeling, she doubted it.

CHAPTER 24

Alice smiled politely at the man who swiped her into the basement morgue in the London Hope Hospital. It wasn't a place she often visited, which she was glad about because the place reeked of bleach and formaldehyde. She was trained to track and detain Breed, not deal in dead bodies. Not usually, anyway.

"You're late," Detective Brady complained once she entered into the room. "You were supposed to be here over thirty minutes ago."

"Traffic," Alice said as if that was an excuse. She didn't get stuck in traffic, but they didn't need to know that. She would have been there sooner if she hadn't stopped back at Theo's, wanting to get rid of the pebble as quickly as possible. She literally threw it at him, driving away to his confused 'thank you.'

She had done what he had asked, it was up to him to find his brother. She just hoped it kept Roman away. She had enough problems, she didn't need to babysit an unstable shifter too.

"If you planned these meetings better, I wouldn't necessarily be late," she whispered beneath her breath as she stood beside Jones and Brady, three sheet- covered gurneys in front of them. Jones lit up when she smiled at him, unlike Brady, who looked unimpressed with her explanation.

"Where's O'Neil and Peyton?" she asked, louder this time.

"O'Neil's busy, and Peyton's an Officer," he said as if that was explanation enough.

"Right, is everybody here?" a man asked as he stepped through the door. "Ah, if it isn't my favourite girl." Dr Miko Le'Sanza grinned when he noticed Alice, his arms wide as he went in for a hug.

"I didn't think you would be on this case?" Last she heard Miko had been hired directly under Dread for The Tower.

"You'll understand why in a moment," he said, eyes gleaming mischievously.

"You know each other?" Jones asked, his attention more on the gurneys than the conversation. It was weird to see him in regular clothes compared to his usual white full - body suit. He wore a pair of worn jeans and a basic logo T-shirt with his brown hair messy, like he just got out of bed.

"Can we get down to business?" Brady crossed his arms, straining his jacket across his thick arms. "We're all here, so why don't you explain why you've had us come down here Dr Le'Sanza?"

"I'm sorry, is there somewhere more interesting for you to be Detective?" Miko asked in a clipped tone.

Alice tried to hide her smirk.

She had known Miko for years, met him on one of her many contracts. He had a fun, flamboyant personality befitting a Brazilian carnival dancer, as was his father's heritage.

Until he became aggravated, then he became an icy bastard Alice loved to tease.

Brady clenched his jaw, his skin darkening around his cheekbones, but he remained silent.

Miko glared for a few uncomfortable seconds before he nodded towards Jones, signalling for him to pull off the first sheet on the left. The body was reasonably well preserved, the man looking more like he was asleep than dead. Other than the large Y stitched across his sternum. That was a big giveaway.

"I would like you to bring your attention to patient 'A'."

Jones whistled, admiring the cadaver. "Is this the one we spoke on the phone about?"

"Nope. There's more to come," Miko smiled, his infectious cheerfulness back as he wiggled his eyebrows.

"You mind filling us in?" Brady asked, annoyed.

Alice didn't bother to hide her smile this time, understanding how Miko and Jones would become quick friends. They both worked in a similar field, Miko was a Pathologist while Jones was a Forensic Technician. Both their jobs entailed finding out the cause of death.

Miko pointed to an open wound, highlighting the dying cells.

"Patient 'A' is one hundred per cent human and has been confirmed as being a carrier. We have discovered a lack of platelets and blood glycoprotein, which resulted in severe haemorrhaging, causing death."

"We know this already," Alice said, pointing to the puncture marks on the neck. "The humans fed their victims and then would bleed out when their blood didn't clot."

"Yes," Miko confirmed. "It seemed to start from the access point, in the humans it's ingested. It gets into the bloodstream through cuts in their mouth or once it starts to be digested. The main reason humans don't see symptoms sooner is that the human body can take six to eight hours to fully digest and absorb."

"Why do the Vamps get symptoms faster? If they used to be humans?" Jones asked, frowning.

"Vampires don't have a digestive system as they don't eat. When they are put into the ground to start the turn, their internal organs shut down."

Brady looked over to Alice, who shrugged. She had no idea vampires had weird insides. She had never personally looked.

Vampires were private, rarely sharing their secrets with anyone. The knowledge of the turn was only made public when one fame hungry vampire invited a news crew to witness the whole transition. The newly formed vampire slaughtered the entire crew live on air before anybody could gain control, resulting in a dramatic legislation brought in by The Council. Nobody could be turned without the consent of another master. It made human screening even harder. The newly turned vampires were also connected to their creator until they showed enough control to become their own master.

"Whatever a vampire ingests gets directly absorbed into their cells, which results in a quicker reaction time."

"What about the substance they're ingesting, do we know what that is yet?" Alice asked.

"Ah, that is why it has been flagged by The Tower," Miko's eyes twinkled as he grabbed a clipboard, handing it to Jones who frowned.

"It's blood," Jones murmured, squinting at the paper.

"At least, part blood," Miko confirmed, his eye contact penetrating as he concentrated on Alice. "It's similar to another case where we identified the deceased as being in a Daemon transition."

Of course it is.

Alice instinctively gripped her crescent scar. Brady noticed but didn't comment.

"We knew that already," Jones stated as he studied the paperwork. "But it wasn't one-hundred per cent confirmed until now." He handed back the paper. "So it's Daemon juice?"

"We're confident the other case was a failed Daemon transition, this blood, however, is more distinctive. Defined. It's also mixed with other, unknown materials. Either way it's deadly," Miko nodded. "Okay, let's look under sheet two." He pulled at the fabric, revealing another body, this time female.

Alice recognised the woman from the Gala, a newer vampire who was on her table. She wanted to look away, not wanting the image stuck beneath her eyelids. The woman looked like a ghost, her skin so pale it was transparent. The Y incision hadn't been closed completely, the thread still visible through the ripped skin. Her arms looked wrong, bent at an impossible angle.

"This is one of the first victims, we call her patient 'B'. We have estimated from consumption to time of death being around thirty minutes. The protein started to degrade the cells instantly, resulting in softening of bone and shrunken, dehydrated skin."

He touched the paper-thin skin of the woman, showing how little pressure he had to add to make it disintegrate beneath his fingertips.

"She was found slumped against the table, her spine crumbled."

"This isn't why we're here." Jones eagerly eyed the last gurney.

"No, you all already know most of this, but Patient 'C'..."

Miko pulled off the final sheet, revealing another male body.

"This isn't a vampire..." Alice said at the unveiling. The body was a mixture of the two others, his skin pale and dehydrated but not paper-thin. His jaw was slack, showing regular teeth, no fangs.

"You're right, it's a shifter," Jones said, excited.

"They can be affected?" Brady asked, concerned.

"Apparently so."

"I did some research once you called me," Jones stated. "I don't work directly with bodies, so I had to look into some medical journals, but shifters have the closest physiology to humans. So I'm interested to understand what happened to him."

"Patient 'C' died of haemorrhaging but at a lot slower rate. It is possible he didn't even notice until he was too weak to do anything. Shifters have an incredible ability to heal due to the fact that when they shift from one form to another, their skin rips and bones break. His body was trying to restore even as the substance started to eat away at his cells. It resulted in mild bone deterioration but not enough to cause death. In my opinion, if he had simply ingested it like the humans he probably wouldn't have seen any effect at all, his body would have worked its way through it."

"He didn't ingest it?"

"The substance was found directly in his bloodstream." Miko pulled at one of his arms, showing the small puncture marks.

"He injected it?"

Miko nodded. "Patient 'C', also known as Richard Pail. Arrested for possession of a controlled substance, possession with intent to supply and GBH. We can find no evidence of any other puncture marks other than the ones along his arms and between his toes. We believe he didn't have a chance to spread it."

"They could be branching out, targeting junkies," Brady said, stepping back. "It isn't unheard of that they will swap a feeding for a fix."

"Vampires sometimes seek junkies out specifically for a feed, it's the only way they can gain a high," Alice confirmed.

Brady started to slowly smile, it was uncomfortable besides the bodies. He turned to Miko, who was in a quiet discussion with Jones.

"Where's the case report? We need to know everything about where this body was found."

CHAPTER 25

"What the fuck is that?" asked Detective Brady as they walked beneath a motorway crossing bridge just outside the city.

Alice followed his line of sight, silently cringing at the grotesque goblin that was trying to peacefully eat his bowl of unknown meat. It smelt of a mixture of fish guts and stale chicken, the odour strong even through the general aroma of waste and unclean bodies. The goblin snarled when he noticed them, baring the screws he used as teeth in warning.

They were unfriendly creatures generally, keeping to themselves. While they usually were around four foot, the goblin that was watching them with its beady black eyes was taller, around five foot. Alice quickly checked around, seeing if he had friends. They liked to work in groups, using distractions to pickpocket.

Alice politely nodded as they passed, his long green ears twitching in irritation.

"He's nothing you should be concerned about," Alice replied.

At least, as long as we don't piss him off.

Goblins were classed as Fae, and while they had little magic they made up for it in strength. A strength Alice didn't want to go up against, especially as their skin was thick enough to absorb most damage.

"Corvus oculum corvi non eruit," the goblin muttered.

"What did it say?" Brady asked, his eyes narrowed as he evaluated the situation.

Alice shrugged. "Something about ravens, or maybe it's crows."

"Crows?" he frowned. "What the fuck has anything got to do with crows?"

Alice sighed. "He said 'a crow will not pull out the eye of another crow,' or something around those lines."

"That doesn't sound right," Brady muttered.

"Do you want to try and translate then?"

She spoke Latin. Sort of, anyway.

"Well, what the fuck does it mean?"

"It means something like honour among thieves."

"Well that's fucking great," he growled as they walked beneath the large underpass.

The overhead line crossing sheltered the homeless from the worst of the winter weather. In the shadows beneath, the ground was dry of snow, but the wind threatened the flames that crackled in the metal barrels strategically placed around.

It was the home to a mixture of people, some homeless, some junkies. A man shuffled towards them, pushing a shopping trolley full of discarded home appliances and sleeping bags. When he noticed Brady, his face drained of colour, his eyes darting around before he quickly made his way past.

"Did you really have to dress like a cop?" Alice said as a few more people recoiled away from them.

Brady frowned, looking down at himself. "What do you mean?"

"I mean you look like a police officer who also wrestles on the weekend." She pointed to his smart suit and black overcoat. She could even make out the small bulge on his hip where he hid his gun.

"This is how I normally dress." He shot her an aggravated look.

"I think it's best if we split up," she said. "We can cover more ground."

"Fine," he grumbled as he approached a man who was trying to warm his hands by a fire.

Alice stayed back for a moment, scanning the fifteen or so men and women who called the underpass home. Cars sped high above, the disorderly noise irritating even as road debris rained down after every other car.

"Hello?" she asked the man who sat alone in a foldable camping chair, his sleeping bag rolled out ready beside him.

"What do you want?" he asked as he drank from a wine bottle.

Alice guessed his age to be around the late twenties, the dirty beard and sores making it hard to tell. A needle and spoon were carelessly thrown nearby, confirming why his eyes were glassed over.

"I'm not open for business. Come back in eighty-two and a third days," he mumbled.

"I'm here to ask about Richard Pail? Do you know him?"

An incoherent murmur before he licked his lips.

"What about Stacey Simpson? She was a working girl that..."

"Hey, over here." Alice turned to the voice of another man a few feet away. He didn't have the same dazed out look like his friend.

"You talkin' about our Stacey?" He eyed her suspiciously. "You not a reporter, are ya?"

"You know Stacey?" she asked the even younger man, possibly in his late teens. "No, I'm not a reporter."

"A fucking cop?" he snarled, showing cracked teeth.

"Do I look like a cop?"

He squinted at her, taking his time to decide. "S'pose not."

"What's your name?"

He took his time to answer again, a massive grin erupting across his face. "You can call me anythin' ya want beautiful."

"Can you tell me about her? Who she spoke to? Why she was down here?"

"Well, well. It's been a while ya know. The memories all..." He hit his finger against his forehead three times. It brought his arm into clear view, highlighting all the needle pricks against his pale flesh.

"Will this help?" Alice went into her pocket to grab a few notes, handing him the cash. Between her and Sam they could barely make ends meet, yet she couldn't help but want to give the man more money. Just because he made bad decisions did not make him a bad person.

The man appraised the money, licking along the edge before folding it up into a tiny square and tucking it underneath his black cap. "What exactly are ya if you're not a reporter or a cop?"

"I'm a friend."

"Friend? We need more friends down 'ere." He nodded, almost to himself. "It wasn't an accident, ya know. She was tricked."

"Tricked?"

"Yeah, yeah. I liked Stacey, you know? She came down here sometimes, brung us food, sometimes herb," he said, grinning. "Nice gal. She used to sleep down here with us, ya see, before she met that man of hers. Real Prince Charming him."

"You said she was tricked? What do you mean?"

"She doesn't touch the gear anymore, you know? She's clean. Her Prince Charming helped her, got her a flat and everything. The papers said they found needle tracks along her arm." He shook his head.

"Who's her usual supplier?"

"Nah man, I ain't giving that shit up."

His eyes darted around before they settled back onto her.

"But I remember the guy she spoke to last time, before the papers. He's a new dealer, tryin' to push his stuff on us, ya know?"

"New dealer? What does he look like?"

"Fucking weirdo man. I won't touch his stuff, gives me the creeps. He doesn't even accept payment. Just favours."

"Favours? What sort of favours?"

"Don't know man, refused to talk to him. You should ask Ricky, he was chatting with him only the other day."

"Ricky as in Richard Pail?" When he nodded, she continued. "What does this dealer look like?"

"I don't know," he mumbled, scratching along the inside of his arm. "Medium build, dark hair. I think his eye is fucked up or something?"

"His eye? Does he wear an eyepatch?"

"Nah man, but he should though. It's like a prune, all shrivelled and shit. I overheard him saying he can help us all make money."

"Alice, you find anything?" Detective Brady asked as he came up behind them. "They're not talking to me."

"Aw shit man, you said you weren't a cop."

"I'm not." She handed him some more money. "Thank you for talking to me." Alice gently smiled. "There's a shelter not far from here, that money will get you the bus fare as well as some food along the way."

He started to chuckle. "Yeah, yeah, man. I'm sure I will."

"You know that's going to go on drugs, right?" Brady said as they stepped away. "You should never give them money."

Alice just shook her head. "He confirmed Gordon Potts has been lurking down here, and that he talked to our vic several days before his death as well as Stacey Simpson."

"I'll reinstate the APW," he said as they headed to the cars. "It was good that you were here. They wouldn't have said anything to me." He gave her a sideways glance, a hint of a smile. "I appreciate it."

"Aw, don't get all soppy on me now detective," she sniggered.

His small smile tightened. She seemed to be growing on him, probably.

"You coming back to the station?"

Alice thought about it. "No, I have some bits I need to do. You'll ring if you need me?"

Brady nodded, lifting his hand in a half wave as he drove off, leaving her standing by her rust bucket beetle.

"I thought he would never leave."

Alice reacted, her sword in her hand before she even

processed the thought, the tip facing Mason Storm as he swaggered from behind a concrete pillar.

"Back off," she snarled.

"Oh Alice, that isn't how to greet a Councilman, is it?" he said, his mouth twisted into an evil smirk. "I thought we were friends." His eyes danced with laughter as he slowly walked towards her, his arrogance overwhelming.

He wore entirely black, the outfit so tight it was like another skin. It was disconcerting, she had never seen him in anything but a power suit.

"I see you made bail."

"Of course," he said as if it was obvious. "As if simple human laws can keep me contained."

"What about Breed laws?"

Mason stopped when he was only a few inches from the edge of her blade, the runes highlighting his face in little bursts of light. He didn't give them a cursory glance, his attention entirely on her as he sized her up.

"I am the law."

Mason smiled as he leapt forward, knocking her sword from her outstretched hand as if it was a fly swatter. It clattered to the ground, the runes disappearing as the blade settled into a puddle. Alice kicked out, her foot connecting with his stomach with enough force for him to growl.

Her fist shot out, catching him in the chin before he gripped her wrist to the point of breaking. Twisting out of it she blocked his punch, his speed and strength nowhere close to Riley, yet faster than a shifter.

"*Ventilabis,*" she shouted as she forced him away, the heat of her chi searing her fingers a second later. Mason dodged the flame, his face screwed up in annoyance. "*Scintillam.*" She shot a spark towards his face, using the distraction to run to her sword.

Alice gasped, crashing to her knees even as she reached for the hilt, her fingers trying to grasp it as she was torn away. Her chi was on fire, electric as it felt like it was being painfully pulled from her.

"This is getting tiresome." Mason dug his fingers into her skin, dragging her across the concrete before throwing himself on top of her. His fist hit her in the eye, cracking her head against the floor. "Is this all you got?"

She tasted blood as she screamed, her aura throbbing as Mason manipulated it.

"ADOLEBITQUE!" she spat, satisfied as an instant burn started to bubble against his cheek, the skin darkening before splitting open in a burst of red.

"ENOUGH!" He hit her again even as he pulled her magic. It was like when Riley had done it to help her with control, but this time it was forced from her, the pain excruciating even as she gasped for breath.

Hands restricted her neck, his thumbs digging into the hollow of her throat.

"Why didn't you just die in the first place," he growled. "Then you wouldn't have been in the way."

Alice scrambled against him, her body pulsating in a great wave as she fought for control. She could see from the corner of her eye a burst of flame, her power leaking as Mason syphoned.

"You could have been magnificent, little dragon," he whispered against her.

Alice felt it then, like a dam had broken, an overwhelming energy that had to escape. Screaming through the pain, she shot her head forward to connect with his nose, the crack loud as his hands loosened from her throat. Her fists shot into his chest, sending him several feet in the air before he fell to the concrete in a crash. She shakily stood up, her hands up to her elbows completely encompassed in bright blue flames licked with green. She had never felt it so alive, so powerful.

Mason struggled to stand, the wind knocked out of him.

Bending down she grabbed her sword, the blue flames covering the steel within seconds, the runes flashing beneath. She felt like she was attached to a power socket, the energy burning through her too much. Throwing out her hand she let some of it loose, concentrating on extinguishing as much as she could as Mason finally came to his feet.

"Arma," she whispered as her breath came out in smoke. Her shield surrounded her, the beautiful film of her aura protection until she could get herself together. The fire still crackled loudly, but no longer growing uncontrollably.

Mason just stared, his face expressionless as he watched. The burn across his cheek looked sore, even more than the break in his nose, the injuries marking his otherwise beautiful face. She didn't feel guilty, her wrist bruised from where he had almost broken it and her eye was already starting to swell.

Neither of them said anything as the wind picked up.

With a nod Mason stepped back into shadows, leaving Alice alone to figure out what the hell had just happened.

CHAPTER 26

The key turned in her front door when she felt something move behind her, swinging her arm out she threateningly held her keys in her hand, pretending it was something scarier.

Xander stood there, his face furious as a single drop of blood dripped down his cheek where the edge of her key caught him. She didn't apologise, straining to keep her arm from waning as she watched him. His muscles were bunched, eyes hidden behind his glasses so she couldn't confidently tell when he was about to move.

You've got to be shitting me.

He wasn't alone, five other men stood quietly behind him, all dressed identically in black leather. She didn't recognise any of them.

"Where is he?" Xander snarled.

It took Alice a second to understand his question. "How do you know where I live?"

Xander moved like lightning, his hand snapping out to grab her neck, her back smashing into her front door in a matter of seconds. Without thinking she punched his jugular, kicking him in the shin at the same time he dropped her to clutch his own throat.

Dropping the keys, she unsheathed her sword, holding it between them.

The other men moved then, fanning out in a perfect semi-circle. They all were large, at least six foot plus with similar black and red tattoos patterned on any exposed flesh. If any of them moved like Riley, like Xander, she was fucked.

"You fight dirty." Xander choked out the comment, coughing. He lifted up his fist, asking the men to move a step back. They didn't. Instead, they unsheathed their own weapons. Two had swords, thick metal almost the size of Alice's thigh, two went for their handguns while one went for his scythe, as if he was the Grim fucking Reaper.

Alice didn't think before she released some fire in an arch an inch in front of their boots, making them step back or risk being burned. She hid her grimace, her chi still recovering from Mason as her eye ached in time with her heartbeat. She stared at each in turn, she was too tired and sore for this shit and wanted them to know. The fire gradually got larger until one by one they sheathed their weapons.

Accepting that, she extinguished the flame.

"Where is he?" One of the men asked, the one with black hair spiked as if he was an anime character.

"Who?!" she bit out.

"Riley," Xander growled, baring teeth.

"I haven't seen him since I helped arrest his father," she spat back.

"Holy shit, really?" the anime haired man laughed.

"She's telling the truth," another one of the men said, his expression less happy.

"Wait, you arrested Mason?"

All her sudden confidence seemed to disintegrate, she had to relax her arm before the men noticed it shake. She spotted a few curtains twitching across the street, nosy neighbours getting their gossip. They probably thought she was about to have an orgy or some other nefarious thing. Mr Jenkins glared from behind his own curtain, eyes judging.

"He isn't replying to our call," Xander stated.

"I don't know what you want from me."

"You need to tell us exactly what happened," he aggressively took a step forward.

Alice ignored him, kept her ground. "Well, I arrested Mason..."

"No, from the beginning."

She described how she had broken into the church.

"Why did you break into there? It's just full of extremist nutters."

"Shut up Sythe," Xander roared before he turned back his attention to Alice.

"I was trying to figure out who's behind the vampire deaths," she explained.

"Who says it isn't natural?" Sythe asked, ignoring Xander. Sythe looked at her like he was examining a rat, his eyes a pale caramel brown that contrasted against his dark hair. One arm was bare, showing off his tattoos while the rest of him was covered in black leather. A gun was on his hip while two short swords crisscrossed his back.

"Let them all die, vermin anyway," another of the men said, his hair a beautiful honey brown that was styled to try and hide the red scar that sliced down his left eye.

"It's not natural," she clarified. "Humans have been purposely poisoning themselves."

"What has this got to do with the boss?" The men started to bicker.

"Is this about his bar?"

"That fucking place? A stupid idea that was," Scar face laughed.

"He had the idea while he was drunk."

"All his ideas come from when he's drunk."

"SHUT UP!" Xander snarled at the men, stopping them from squabbling between themselves. They just sneered back.

"Alice, tell us what happened."

"I found evidence that Mason was involved in the genocide."

The men said nothing, their expressions closed off.

"That doesn't explain why Riley's gone."

Alice began to speak when she caught her neighbours glaring again.

"Look," she said harder than she intended. "I don't know what you want from me, but I need to go." She opened her door, planning to close it quickly behind her before a thick boot pushed past the threshold.

"We're not finished here," Xander growled as he used his weight to keep it open. "We need to figure out where he is."

"I'm not inviting you in," she said as she stared into his sunglasses, wanting badly to read his eyes.

"Please."

Alice clenched her jaw, her face tired.

"Fine." She stepped back, allowing the six men to crowd her living room. Three of them awkwardly folded themselves onto her sofa, their massive frames barely fitting.

Xander and scar face stood by her door while Sythe casually walked through into her kitchen. She heard banging and crashing before he returned holding a bag of frozen peas, throwing them at her with a smirk.

"Your eye looks like shit."

"Thanks," she muttered as she held them to her face. Luckily the swelling had already gone down, her eye open and clear although she felt a bruise.

"Who are you guys?"

They all turned towards Xander, who remained silent.

"You're not even going to introduce yourselves?"

That's just rude.

She sighed. "Why are you here? I have already said I don't know where he is."

"He's your Warden..."

"And?" she interrupted. "It's clear neither of us wanted it."

"I like her," the man on the furthest left of the sofa grinned. His face was movie star beautiful, his lips a little too full. His hair was dark, cut military short.

"You don't need to know who we are," Sythe said as he looked curiously around the room. "All you need to know is we're here for Riley." He started to prod through her things, moving some of the boxes she had stashed under her stairs. She ignored him.

"You think he's in trouble?" She eyed Sythe, watched him tense as he shot a quick glance towards Xander.

They all remained silent again.

"If you're not going to talk, you might as well leave."

"We don't trust you." Xander broke their silence.

"You came to me," she said, frustrated. "Now, what has happened to Riley?"

"Why do you care?" One of the men from the sofa stood up, his movements agitated as he stared her down. He had the most beautiful shade of red hair, like the heart of a ruby. His eyes were dark, hard and angry.

"Are we really going to have a pissing contest now?" Alice couldn't believe it. "I care because he saved my life."

"So you owe him?" he spat it out like it was offensive.

"Kace," Xander growled. "Calm down."

"Well, Kace..." Alice stepped up to him, shaking her bag of peas in his face. It would have been more threatening if she wasn't almost a foot smaller and the peas didn't make little tingling noises every time the bag moved. "I do owe him. But not only that, we're friends." She thought so anyway. Were they? It was complicated. "I help my friends."

A loud chuckle. "I really like her," the man with the beautiful movie star face said as he winked at her. "Come on big guy, come be moody over here." He unfolded his long legs from the sofa before reaching over to Kace's shoulder, pulling him gently away.

"Alice, when was the last time you spoke to Riley?"

"I didn't speak to him, but I believe he overheard Mason's confession..."

"Confession?"

"It was more of a gloat."

"Can you get to the point?"

Alice thought about what to say, decided on the truth.

"He overheard how Mason was behind the death of my parents."

She let that sink in.

"How he led the Daemons to their house. This house, in fact. Where the Daemons murdered them in front of me."

"Fuck."

"What?"

"No way?"

Xander stood rigid, veins in his arms visible as he clenched his fists.

"Everybody out!" he shouted to the men. They all looked at him until he growled, a deep vibration that made them move. Once they had gone he approached her, pulling off his glasses so she could see his eyes. "I need you to stay away."

"Why?" She held those eyes of pale blue, almost colourless.

"Because you're a liability." He breathed into her face. "And I don't like you."

Alice felt herself grin. "I wasn't a liability when you came to me for help."

"Which you didn't provide." He took a deep breath, placing his glasses back on his face. "Stay away from Mason. He's dangerous."

"Is he? My eye wouldn't know."

"Well, he didn't kill you. That's something."

"You seem to think I'm easy to kill."

He smirked, tilting his head like a dog. She noticed because Riley had done it too, something a shifter would do, not a druid. "You have a ghost."

Alice felt ice cold, her spine rigid as goosebumps broke out across her skin. She didn't need to know that. "What?"

"Your gnome is haunted," he nodded towards Jordon who had suddenly appeared on the sofa, his grinning face turned to them. "Be careful Alice, you shouldn't trust the dead." With that he followed his men out, slamming the door behind himself.

"Jordan?" she asked the gnome, knowing he wouldn't answer.

Great, what do I do now?

He looked out into the field they were being made to run in, him and his brothers.

They had all grown, bigger than even the teachers. The last of The Elders had been proud of their progress, had not been upset at the teacher's lack of control.

They did as they were asked out of respect for their people, not the teachers.

His father looked pleased, even if his face was as closed as it always was, even more so since he became the new Archdruid. The opposite to his mother, who was a ray of open sunshine. He allowed her memory to shape him, not let the training shape him into a drone.

His mother had taught him the old ways. Respect for the hierarchy, it's how his people had been for centuries, an old Breed proud of their heritage, yet hiding dark secrets.

He guessed that was why they were created, trained, beaten. A force to take on the ancestors who made mistakes.

Not that they thought it was a mistake.

The wind howled, calling his spirit beast, wanting release. His brothers were the same, yet different, their spirits. All forced on them as children, disguised as a gift. Chosen for a purpose. He wasn't sure what purpose, surely it wasn't just for hunting his prey? He saw the humour in that.

They trained them to be as bad as their prey, stronger, faster. Prey that were ancestors, blood. Someone had to do the job, and it was just bad luck they were chosen.

The sons of the important.

The sons of the strong.

The sons of The Elders.

CHAPTER 27

Alice heard a high-pitched whistle once she had finally convinced the officer to let her beneath the police tape. O'Neil appraised her bruise, his eyes darkening as he flicked a cigarette between his fingers.

"What happened?" he asked on an exhale, smoke coming out his nose like a dragon.

"I thought you were quitting," she said instead.

He just glared at her, the cigarette burning between his lips as he waited. The orange flare highlighted the grey hairs in his goatee perfectly.

"You should really see the other guy," she laughed. She knew he was overreacting, the bruise barely visible anymore. "Seriously, it's fine."

"You been getting yourself into trouble again?"

Alice turned to Brady and Peyton, smiling politely as they joined them on the porch. She had been called to an old mansion in the outer suburbs where there weren't any neighbours for miles around. The place itself didn't look as expensive as it should, the wood around the windows poorly painted black, matching the dirty grey wood cladding on the second floor. Dark red rose bushes guarded the pavement to the front of the house, their thorns abnormally large and sharp. The majority of the windows had been boarded up while some were a spider's web of cracks.

"The whole team here?" she asked, looking around for Jones.

"Jones is inside."

"What's this about?" She tried to hide her chills as they stood on the creaky decking just outside the front door.

"Four dead..."

"Vampires?" She thought The Leader was behind bars.

"No, we believe them to be witches. Although, we think it's connected."

"What makes you say that?" she asked even as she frowned. Something was off, her aura reacting to something she couldn't see. Looking around, she found the culprit hanging from a wooden beam.

The sticks were manipulated around small pieces of bone, tied together with twine. Alice stepped towards it, raising her hand but not daring to touch the talisman. They were held in the position of a full moon between two crescent moons. Skin was pulled across the shapes, making them glow a faint red when the sun hit it at just the right angle.

"What is that?" O'Neil asked.

"It's the symbol of The Crone," Alice answered, fighting the shiver that rattled down her spine.

"What does it mean?"

"It means this is probably a dark coven, they use this symbol to ask The Crone for protection."

"Who is this Crone person? He doesn't sound..."

"She, it's a she." She pulled her hand away as a fly

buzzed greedily around the rotting skin. "In witches' lore, it is believed the first humans were given their ability to manipulate the elements by The Goddess, thereby creating witches. She would empower them with her gift if they were to be good, kind. Her sister, The Crone, despised The Goddess. Out of spite she tricked the humans into accepting her gift, the ability to manipulate death and blood, but only if they would sacrifice something to her."

"Sacrifice?"

"Yeah, that's where the origins of black magic come from, although, most modern witches doubt the existence of either The Goddess or The Crone."

"Sounds thrilling," Brady said dryly.

Alice held back a chuckle. "You have no idea."

The men stared at the talisman quizzically for a moment and it worried Alice how little they knew about Breed. Especially considering the general knowledge was taught at school, math, science and 'why is your neighbour eating their dog?' classic classes. Breed had been recognised citizens for almost three hundred years. They had lived and worked alongside Norms for enough generations that there shouldn't be any prejudice. Yet they needed to hire a Breed consultant because none of her team had enough knowledge alone. She didn't know if it was plain ignorance or naivety.

Pursing her lips, she followed them through the door, the smell of meat, blood and rotten eggs instantly striking her nose. The mansion must have been abandoned before it was taken over by the coven, the stairs to the floors above broken beyond repair. Floorboards were missing, leaving gaping hazardous holes and graffiti had been sprayed across a few walls. Two arches on either side of the stairs led off further into the house, the left – Alice could just see, looked like a kitchen with windows facing towards an empty swimming pool. The right led towards a room that was splashed with red, body parts torn apart and thrown across the large space.

"Fuck me," Alice gasped, her brain trying to piece together what could have happened. The room was empty of any furniture, the walls painted over with graffiti, the same as the foyer.

A large pentagram had been scratched into the floorboards, each of the elements drawn in their own circles at each point. Dry blood was splattered across every surface of the room, yet was most consistent inside the pentagram.

"It's a summoning circle," Alice confidently said.

"A what?"

"A summoning circle. It looks... yes," she murmured to herself. "A normal circle is anchored into place using the elements fire and earth with water and air filling the space between. This circle is anchored with all five elements."

"What do you mean, 'five elements'?"

"I mean, there would have been five people, each standing in one of the elemental circles." She pointed out the five separate circles, each touching a different point of the pentagram. "Each person would have represented their element, someone for fire, someone for air... you get the idea. They would light it in sequence before finishing with spirit, which would complete the circle."

"Have you seen anything like this before?"

"Kids are taught this in school, it's how you get students to learn to work together. This is a more brutalised version, made to keep something inside the circle while protecting the people outside."

"What exactly were they protecting themselves from?"

Alice took a second to reply, the scar on her hand aching before she clenched her fist.

"Daemons." The smell was what tipped her off. It's a smell that will be eternally embedded in her brain.

"That's what I thought. Fuck." O'Neil scanned across the room, his eyes narrowing on the body parts that had settled. A large window was towards the back with thick blackout curtains partially pulled. A head sat eyeless, its mouth forever open in a silent scream.

"I thought you said the circle was supposed to protect them?"

"Well... erm." Alice bit her lip, trying to think. There was no literature on Daemon summoning, nothing on black magic in general. Since The Change, everything regarding dark magic was either destroyed or quarantined for the safety of the public.

So who the hell has this type of ancient knowledge?

"The spell either failed or one of the members let the circle drop."

"You need to explain what the hell you mean," Brady remarked as he looked down at part of an arm, his expression open but disgusted.

It was sad that she had gotten over the smell. That actually being this close to a number of dismantled bodies no longer bothered her as much as it clearly did to both Detective Brady and O'Neil. She was more professionally interested than disgusted. Peyton didn't seem repulsed either, neither did Jones when he waltzed in like it was a family wedding rather than a massacre.

"Hey guys, you like the party?" he chuckled.

"You're disgusting," Alice said with a grimace. So she wasn't as affected as others, but she wasn't as bad as Jones.

"We're discussing how one of the five bodies could have broken the circle..."

"Four. There are four bodies," Jones chirped, smiling. "We have counted enough times to be confident."

"No, this spell requires five people. They wouldn't have been able to summon anything without all five."

"Well, there's only four people here. Do you think the fifth person made a run for it?"

"There are tyre tracks just up the road," Peyton said.

"Did you know, it was only a month or so ago that I thought Daemons were like unicorns. They didn't exist." Brady mumbled, his dark skin taking on a slight ashen colour.

"Hey Brady, you ever heard of Hansel and Gretel?" Alice said, trying to hide her smirk.

"The kids and bread crumbs?" His wide eyes shot to hers. "You saying it's true?"

"Well, the original Grimm story didn't say that the children were simply human, but changelings."

"Changeling?"

"Yes, Fae children that have been swapped at birth with a human. Probably why they ate the witch in the end..." she let the story train off.

"Alice, stop winding Brady up," Peyton interrupted, but she could tell he was amused.

"What? I haven't even explained Cinderella yet..."

"That's enough," O'Neil stated, a slight smile on his face. "Alice, what do you see?"

"I see four bodies that have been ripped apart. There should be a fifth, but according to Jones there isn't one."

"No, the house is abandoned other than this room and part of the kitchen where there are a few rucksacks full of candles and books. Upstairs is completely unreachable," Jones confirmed.

"So, the only purpose the coven came here was to create the summoning circle?"

"Seems to be. We have four female bodies who have been here long enough for larvae to be implanted in some of the flesh. We have found no toiletries, mobile phones or change of clothes. Nothing to indicate that they planned to stay overnight or for any longer than a couple hours. The plumbing doesn't even work."

"I'm not surprised by the no mobiles. It's known that an electric pulse can break a weak circle, so it makes sense to leave them behind." Alice shrugged.

"So are we believing that the Daemon killed them?"

Alice thought about it. "I can't be positive." She had no idea. She only had the sulphuric smell to go on. "An enraged shifter could deal the same damage."

"Isn't this your job?" Brady frowned.

"I do apologise that I'm not familiar with all forms of dark magic," she said, sarcasm dripping from every word. "It makes the most sense that the Daemon broke free and slaughtered the witches. But then why would it have left one alive?"

"So, the question is," O'Neil mumbled. "Where is the last witch?"

CHAPTER 28

Alice stared at her phone for the hundredth time. It remained the same as it did an hour ago, the same as the last few days, no messages. She wanted to launch it across the grand atrium of Riley's building, allow it to smash into smithereens in a burst of rage.

How dare he ignore her!

Alice gripped the phone, heard the screen screech in protest before she shoved it into the pocket of her jeans. Riley hadn't answered any of her calls.

Petty, so fucking petty, she growled loud enough to make the man in front give her a wary look. She shouldn't have to explain herself, and she shouldn't have had to drag herself to his penthouse because he wasn't answering his damn phone.

Alice took a deep breath, calming her face before she plastered on a fake smile. When it was her turn, she approached the desk clerk.

"He's expecting me," she battered her eyelashes.

"Surely you recognise me from before?" She had only been there a few days ago.

"You're not on the list, ma'am." The clerk looked down at his notes.

"He invited me here, do you want me to ring and disturb him?" she huffed, pretending to scan through her phone. "He isn't going to be happy."

"You're more than welcome to wait here in the atrium, ma'am. If you do have an appointment, Mr Storm will make us aware." The clerk said, emphasising that he didn't believe her.

Crap.

"Fine," she grumbled, taking a seat across from the desk beside a bunch of potted plants, giving her a clear view of the whole room. "Riley will hear about this poor service." The clerk just smirked in response.

She couldn't really fault him, he was just doing his job. She undoubtedly should have dressed nicer rather than her skinny jeans and a black T-shirt. Not to mention the slight yellow sheen across her eye, her bruise just hanging on. She really hoped she didn't carry the sulphuric stench from the mansion, she wouldn't be able to explain what it was. Alice subtly tried to smell her arm, the cotton luckily smelling of nothing.

She really stuck out compared the well -dressed men and women who were making themselves busy. The atrium was a hive of activity, the three public lifts packed as everyone seemed to have a place to be. Alice eyed the private lift, the only lift that would take her to the floors high above where Riley's penthouse was situated. She still thought it was weird he lived in an office building, even if he owned the building, and all the businesses inside.

A woman spoke loudly into her phone, her ridiculously

high stilettos clicking obnoxiously across the wooden floor. Alice took a second to recognise her, the oversized glasses hiding the majority of her face while her gorgeous red hair had been cut to just above her shoulder blades with the tips dyed black.

You've got to be shitting me.

Alice moved from her seat, trying to hide behind one of the large potted palms. An old man who sat opposite noticed, his wrinkled face creased in amusement.

"Welcome to Storm Enterprise, which business are you looking for?" The clerk greeted her professionally.

"I need to see Riley Storm immediately," the woman said while she hung up her phone.

"Name ma'am?"

"Are you saying you don't know who I am?" she squeaked, throwing her sunglasses onto the desk. "I'm Mandy Marshall of the Marshall family estate."

"Sorry ma'am, you're not on the list."

"I don't need to be on the list you imbecile."

"Unfortunately Mr Storm has strict rules, if you're not on the list, I cannot allow you upstairs."

"This is ridiculous, call him immediately."

"He has asked us not to interrupt..."

"Let me speak to your manager." She looked around for someone else, the other clerks ignoring her existence as they answered questions for other people. "What is your name?"

"Calm down ma'am, or I'll be forced to call security."

Alice couldn't help but smile as she saw the back of Mandy's neck turn red in irritation.

"Tell Mr Storm he will be hearing from me," Mandy snapped, her movements agitated as her heels slapped across the floor in retreat.

Alice smiled, watching her leave before turning to the clerk, his face open with distaste. *What was his problem?*

"Hey, out of curiosity, when was the last time you saw Mr Storm?" she asked politely.

"Why, does he owe you money or something?"

Alice almost leapt across the counter to smack the annoying smirk off his face. She even looked down, making sure she wasn't going crazy. She looked reasonably respectable, the black T-shirt was simple with a regular round neck. It wasn't even one of her slogan shirts, and she clearly didn't have the breasts to make it provocative.

Does he think I'm a call- girl or something? Bloody bastard.

"Why would he owe me money?" she glared, making sure he saw how aggravated she was.

His smirk faltered, eyes slightly alarmed. "My mistake, ma'am."

Does he have many prostitutes over? Great, now all she could think about was if he paid for sex. It wasn't any of her business what a grown arse man did with his money, or time. Alice didn't want to think about it, instead she checked her phone.

Still no messages.

It was like he had disappeared off the face of the earth.

"You waiting for someone, young woman?" the old man opposite asked, his hands clenched around a mahogany walking stick. He looked just as odd sitting in the gold marble atrium as she did with his bright pink Hawaiian shirt. He even wore shorts though the sky outside threatened more snow.

"Waiting for my team," she said loud enough that the clerk could overhear. "Mr Storm's under investigation, he asked me to come to his penthouse for a private meeting to discuss it, but...." She gave an audible sigh. "As Mr Storm has gone back on his word, I have to call in the big boys." She had no idea what she was talking about but hoped everyone else believed her.

"Oh, that young lad surely can't be in trouble? He is always so polite every time I see him." He squinted at her through his round glasses. "What is he under investigation for?"

"Well..." *Shit, what could it be?* "It's very..."

"Ma'am, ah Miss." The clerk waved for her attention. "What was your name again?"

Alice approached the desk with a full swing in her hips.

"It's Agent Skye, thank you..." she tried to search around for his name, but he wasn't wearing a tag. "Clerk man." She leant across the desk as far as she could to encroach on his personal space. He was already slightly nervous, she hoped it would push him over the edge.

"Do you have any credentials?"

"Of course," she replied, showing him her Paladin license.

"Did you say Mr Storm was expecting you?" He visibly swallowed, his eyes darting around in panic.

Alice smiled in victory. "I'm expected immediately. Can you call the lift for me please?"

"Yes ma'am, err, I mean, Agent Skye."

"Brilliant." She began to turn towards the private lift just as she thought of something. "Have you at least seen him in the last few days?"

"No, ma'am, I cannot say I have."

"Doe's he usually go off for days at a time with no contact?"

"Not usually." He licked his lips nervously. "Is he really in trouble? Mr Storm is a great guy."

Alice didn't reply, instead she smiled pleasantly as she made her way to the key coded lift.

Riley's penthouse was the only place on what she assumed was the top of the building, the lift not following the numbers designated to the floors. It had three identical buttons with no apparent marks. She clicked the top one, wondering where the second and third button led to.

Knocking loudly on the door she waited, hoping he would simply be in. Of course he wasn't, even after she banged louder and called through the door.

"Okay then," she mumbled to herself. "Plan B." She produced a small knife and a pin, unlocking the door quickly and slipping inside. "Oh, bloody Hell."

She didn't have a good memory of his living space from her previous visit, the room had been too dark, but she would have remembered if it was in such a state. The open plan living room looked like it had been ransacked, the sofa ripped to shreds, stuffing and fabric making it to every square inch. The TV was smashed, a black hole in the centre with shards of glass glittering on the scratched wooden floor. A shelf had been toppled over, some books strewn underneath while others had been torn apart, flung around in a rage. It looked like a storm had passed through.

Alice made her way to the gym, wondering if his selection of weight machines had made it out alive. As she was about to open the slide doors separating the gym to the kitchen she heard a hoarse voice.

"He's lost it. Look at the place."

Alice could barely see through the small gap, the lights inside dimmed as Xander stood with Sythe.

Fuck. Fuck. Fuck. Of course they would look here too.

Three punching bags had been destroyed, the sand that was supposed to fill them decorating the floor along with some glass shards from the mirrored wall. The room smelt of old smoke, as if one of the running machines had been run into the ground.

It shocked her, the violent display of rage that didn't match Riley's usual humorous attitude. Even when he was angry he didn't feel like he was capable of such a destructive streak. It was as if he had come home in such a craze that he didn't know how to react, his living room getting the brunt of force before he decided on physically exerting his fury.

"Can we bring him back?" Sythe asked his friend, his posture hunched. "I've never seen him rage like this. Axel yes, but not the Sire."

Alice tried to get closer to the gap without casting a shadow against the opaque glass.

"He hasn't turned beast," Sythe replied confidently to his own question. "We can bring him back."

"We don't know that yet," Xander declared.

"We would know Xee."

"We haven't been able to get contact."

"He will," Sythe said, confident. "It's his father..."

"Fucking arsehole," Xander snarled. "I haven't even been able to contact him. Complete silence from the Archdruid." He laughed, but it was hollow. "The Order isn't responding to my summons either."

"Fuck them, we don't need them. It's not like they've helped us before." Sythe studied one of the punching bags, kicking it with his boot. "You want us all to go in?"

"Maybe," Xander replied. "I haven't decided yet."

"Who said you get to decide?" Sythe laughed. "Wait, don't say Riley..."

"He's our Sire..."

"No need to get pissy Xee, I know who's the boss."

Sythe paced away, his hands fisting. "We need to find him, the boys are getting anxious."

"Do you think I don't know that?"

Alice had heard enough, there wasn't anything here that could help her find him. She tried to move back, her boot slipping on something as she crashed to the ground. Alice clenched her jaw, glaring at the bit of sofa cushion that had somehow found its way into the kitchen. She had been concentrating so hard on moving away quietly from the door that she hadn't looked beneath her feet.

"WHO'S THERE?!" Xander barked as he smashed through the door quickly followed by Sythe.

"Oh, hello," she tried to wave from her sprawl on the floor, ignoring the fact two swords were pointed towards her. "So, how are you?" Red dripped down her arm as she tried ungracefully to stand up. She had fallen onto glass, a shard cutting into her flesh just above her elbow.

"Alice?" Sythe mumbled as he put away his blade.

"I warned you to stay away," Xander said as he helped her up.

"I'm not really good with orders," she shrugged before pulling the shard of glass out and placing it onto the kitchen counter. It was deeper than she initially thought, the cut oozing blood. Alice caught the tea towel thrown at her head, holding it against her elbow.

"For fuck sake, sit down," Xander growled as he started banging through cupboards.

Alice sat on one of the two barstools beside the kitchen island, Sythe was on the other. She hadn't really had a good look at the kitchen, the room darker than she thought was comfortable, but Xander seemed to see perfectly, his sunglasses nowhere to be seen.

"What are you doing here?" he asked, his voice weirdly soft, not reflecting the anger clearly etched onto his face.

"Thought I left something here last time... ow," she scowled as Xander pulled the tea towel away to look at her wound. "Fine. I was here to see if I can find Riley."

"You not think we would check?" Sythe said around a mouthful of nuts.

Where the hell did he get nuts?

"I don't know."

"Stay still." Xander held her arm as he stuck three butterfly stitches onto her elbow, wrapping it up in a bandage. "Bloody liability."

She ignored him. "So you guys going to tell me more about Riley missing?"

Both the men looked at each other before Xander replied.

"How much do you know?"

"I know Mason is the Archdruid, who happens to be a major bastard and head of The Order." She watched their expressions remain closed. "I also know Riley is a Guardian, as you have been calling him 'boss' I assume all you guys are too." She wasn't going to mention 'Sire,' not until she knew more.

Sythe stopped mid crunch, looking slightly alarmed.

"Your father was Jackson Skye," Xander stated as if it explained everything.

"What aren't you telling me?"

"The Order is in shambles, Mason has gone AWOL since his arrest and isn't answering anybody." Xander looked towards Sythe, his eyes flashing silver before nodding. "Riley disappeared around the same time."

"Is that normal?"

"No. He tolerated his father more than we did, but..."

Sythe seemed to struggle to find the right words. "Riley always felt a responsibility."

"But you didn't?"

Sythe let out a laugh. "You have no idea."

"Riley wouldn't leave without an explanation," Xander said, matter-of-factly. "We're a team."

"Then we have to find him."

"Yes, we. Not you." Xander narrowed his eyes. "I can feel you, your energy electric even as you pretend otherwise."

"No, it isn't," she argued. She felt fine, her power under control.

"You need to stay away, you're unpredictable, like a live wire."

"It's not my fault I've been forced to have a Warden. I never asked for this."

"Neither did Riley," Xander stepped away, anger vibrating his shoulders. "You need to learn control, discipline. You're like a child, barely able to stop yourself from killing everyone around you."

"What do you think I've been doing?"

"Learn faster. Before it destroys you."

"Fuck you Xander. You're so far up your own arse you can taste your own breath."

"Like I said, childish." He turned away, placing his sunglasses onto the bridge of his nose. "Sythe, we need to go."

Sythe moved, heading through the house towards the lift. She followed them out.

"Wait, I have more questions..."

"The world doesn't revolve around you."

Alice stepped into the lift with them, a bad decision considering they looked like they wanted to kill her, their faces far from friendly. She had obviously overstayed her visit. Well, Xander's was unfriendly, Sythe just looked at her like she was crazy, which was debatable.

"Look, I just want to know if he's okay."

"Why do you care?"

She paused, she didn't know why.

"I just do." She tried to keep eye contact, although it was harder through Xander's glasses. "Neither of us asked for this, yet we're stuck together."

She could feel it then, her chi charged as it reacted to her anger. A violent surge of energy she couldn't control. Both Xander and Sythe could feel it too, their faces shocked as they tried to step further away into the small space. She wanted to smirk but decided it wasn't a good time. Tinkerbell appeared with a pop, bobbing around her head in a flurry of sparkles.

Xander stood still, barely moving as if he were a statue. When the lift opened at the atrium he pushed past, his long legs carrying him across the floor much faster than Alice could chase while Sythe stayed behind.

"Please," she called as they left the building. "Whether I like it or not, I need him. Now, where do you think he is?"

Xander stopped, his face turned up into the sun, his sunglasses protecting his sensitive eyes. He no longer looked angry, more lost.

"We don't know." With that admission he walked away, leaving her behind.

Alice just stood there in the street. It was then the sky decided to open, snowflakes gently floating down to start covering the ground in white. Cleansing. It was fitting really.

"Go away Roman," she murmured. She had spotted the black wolf as soon as she left the building. If he kept casually walking around in his animal form he was going to get fined, or maybe even put in the pound. "I've already helped you, what more do you want?"

Roman crept from behind the bench, his tongue rolled out on one side in a wolfish grin.

"This would be easier if you would shift and talk."

He responded with a chuff.

"Why you talking to a stray?" Sythe appeared silently behind her.

"Fuck me, why did you sneak up on me?" She tried to control her panicked heart.

"I didn't. You need to learn to listen better."

Sythe approached Roman, his long fingers brushing along his dark fur before snapping his hand back. Roman had tried to bite him, but Sythe moved faster, you wouldn't have been able to see his movement if you weren't watching directly. Even then it was hard.

Fuck. It was safe to assume that Sythe moved as fast as both Riley and Xander. Which meant the other four did too.

"Is there something you want?" she asked. She didn't mean for it to sound so pissy, but she was busy having a one-sided conversation.

"Where's your ball gone?" he frowned.

"It likes to come and go as it pleases," she shrugged. She wasn't going to admit her Tinkerbell was a physical reaction to her strong emotions. It was embarrassing enough already.

"I can see why he likes you."

"Huh?" She looked at Roman who just shrugged, one of his shoulders lifting as he tilted his head.

"Riley. He's fascinated. We're not allowed to be..." Sythe reached forward as if he was going to stroke her face.

Roman snarled, launching himself between them.

Sythe just studied Roman with his caramel brown eyes.

"Guess I'll see you soon, Alice." He winked as he turned back towards the building.

"What was that about?" she asked the wind because it had a higher chance of responding.

Roman didn't move until Sythe was out of sight.

She flicked his ear.

"Hey, you could have warned me he was there you know." He was standing in front of her, he would have been able to see him or even smell his approach. "It would have been better if you were human."

He just stared at her. It was getting harder to believe there was a man in there.

"If you shift, I'll buy you a nice juicy burger," she bribed him, hoping something would work. Surely it wasn't healthy for the amount of time he spent as a wolf.

One problem at a time.

Her stomach started to rumble. *Great.* Now all she could think about was a big juicy burger. Her stomach rumbled again, the vibration violent.

"Oh." She grabbed her phone from her pocket, answering the call.

"Agent Skye."

"It's O'Neil. How fast can you get down to the station?"

CHAPTER 29

Alice stood and watched through the two-way mirror as O'Neil and Brady tried to interview Gordon Potts. He sat there relaxed with his arms loosely folded, ignoring them as he stared past at his own reflection.

"Has he said anything yet?" Alice asked, frowning. She had gotten to the station as quickly as she could in rush hour traffic.

"Nothing," Peyton answered, his voice dark. "He's mocking us."

"What about a solicitor? Or even his wife?"

"He's made no phone calls." Peyton shrugged, not caring that he didn't have legal representation. "He also hasn't got a wife."

"What? Then who was the woman at the church?" He had said she was his wife, why lie?

"No idea, but he isn't legally married. The last thing on record was his previous marriage, which has been legally dissolved due to the presumption of death."

That's strange.

Alice shook her head, studying Potts as he just sat there freakishly calm. He didn't look like a man being threatened as a co-conspirator to mass genocide.

And that worried her.

She could make out O'Neil's mouth moving, but couldn't hear his words as Brady remained silent, his arms mirroring Potts. She assumed they were doing good cop, bad cop. O'Neil was probably trying to reason with him before Brady took over, using his six foot plus, wrestler frame to intimidate instead. Clearly the good cop routine wasn't working.

"Why was I called?" She had no experience in an interrogation. At least, not one where she couldn't threaten to stab or burn someone. Strangely enough, she didn't think that would go down too well in this particular situation.

"It was my idea," Peyton mumbled as he gave her a quick look, his attention returning to Mr Potts a few seconds later. "Since The Leader disappeared into thin air while inside his cell, I thought it would make sense to have an expert on magic close by."

"I'm not an expert..." she began before she realised what he said, "did you just say he disappeared?"

"No one called you? John Smith, also known as The Leader vanished into thin air. CCTV showed him sitting there one second and the next he had gone. There was no break in the time stamp." Peyton frowned, thinking. "In your experience, what could make a human disappear like that?"

"It's impossible..."

Humans had no connection to their auras, so was unable to harness them into a chi.

"Maybe it was a charm?" Just one she had never heard of.

Teleportation wasn't a common gift, only a small select amount of Fae could travel that way. Even then, they couldn't share it. It has been a power coveted by the many, yet no witch, mage or even other Fae had been able to replicate it.

"I suggested a boggart," Peyton shrugged.

"What have you been reading?" She eyed Peyton, trying to hide her smile. "Boggarts haven't been seen in over two centuries."

They were a type of faerie that liked to cause mischief in the marshes and make things disappear. They were also behind many child abductions which helped a rumour escalate that all faeries feasted on children. While the High Lords never admitted it, they never denied it either. Although, it was probably one of the reasons boggarts had been forced to disappear themselves.

"You could say the same about Daemons."

Fuck. He had her there.

"From my limited knowledge, Daemons can't disappear at will. But they can be forced from one location to another by calling their given name."

"But John Smith isn't a Daemon. His DNA comes back as one hundred per cent human."

"Which leads us back to square one."

Gordon started to move his arms slowly, one hand reaching up to his eyepatch which he flicked up, revealing his blind eye. Alice instinctively took a step back, the movement making Potts smile.

"This isn't a window, right?" she asked.

"No," Peyton confirmed even though he noticed Gordon Pott's response.

"Then how can he see us?" She moved forward, noticing his eye track her movement.

"He can't." He didn't seem convinced.

Alice couldn't stop herself from staring at his right eye, the one he had hidden behind the patch. The eye beneath was shrivelled like a prune, the colour a sickly grey surrounded by the darkness of the socket. It was disconcerting, something you would see in a bad zombie movie with terrible special effects. It didn't look real.

"What the fuck is wrong with his eye?"

Alice thought about it for a moment. "Black magic."

Every spell required a sacrifice in various levels of severity, especially potions, charms and physical circle enchantments. The majority of witches used plants or their own blood to quicken the spell, Gordon was sacrificing his own eye. It was a step before turning to the true dark, where the only cost that was sufficient would be death.

She wanted to feel his chi, understand how he could perform this sort of magic yet remain undetected. It made sense when she thought about it, someone had to be creating the deterrent around the church, yet Gordon didn't have the Breed vibe, never mind a witch.

Gordon remained silent, a knowing smile on his lips as he stared past the detectives towards Alice and Peyton. Brady stood up suddenly, causing his chair to crash behind him before he stormed out of the small room, quickly followed by O'Neil.

"He isn't talking," Brady growled as they approached. "The bastard is just sitting here."

"You guys have any ideas?" O'Neil asked, his eyes pinched as he reached into a pocket for a cigarette. "We can only keep him for another twenty hours before we either charge or release him."

Everyone stepped away from the mirror, whispering even though they knew they couldn't be overheard.

"Hit him?" Alice suggested, laughing at their less than impressed reactions.

"Something legal," Brady replied dryly.

"Why are you time restricted? We know he did it..."

"We can't charge him on an accusation. At the moment, we have no physical evidence against any of the suspects for the genocide. Without evidence, we don't have a case."

"We have the letters..."

"Which aren't concrete. It's known that a court can strike evidence that lacks a proper foundation. That means we need to prove he physically wrote it."

"And not some random person," Brady added. "Those letters don't mention Potts, so without a confession or any evidence we're going to struggle."

"If we don't charge him we're allowed to lawfully keep him for up to twenty-four hours. As it's a suspected serious crime we could apply for an extra seventy-two hours, but we still need something solid to get him on."

"The church is still sealed off from when we checked it over. The tech guys found nothing other than bovine blood."

"Bovine blood?" Alice asked. "That's..."

She sucked in a breath as something oily rubbed across her aura, the sensation similar to pins and needles. She turned the same time as Peyton towards the two-way mirror which had been smeared with blood, hiding Potts from view. Alice beat the men to the interrogation room, kicking the door down and drawing her sword at the same time.

She had never felt anything like it once she stepped inside, the air thick, coating her aura in a sticky substance she itched to remove. The room was washed in red as blood smeared the walls with hand- drawn symbols painted around his chair and partially across the desk.

"STOP, OR WE WILL SHOOT!" One of the men yelled as Alice's head buzzed as if she was underwater. Shaking, she tried to clear her ears, only realising the abhorrent blare was actually Potts chanting in a language she didn't recognise.

"NO!" she shouted, holding her arm out as O'Neil and Brady cocked their guns.

"He's in a circle!" Bullets can't penetrate an aura, they would simply bounce back.

Gordon grinned as he finished his chant, blood dripping down from his eye socket and onto the white floor. Alice took a second to realise the eye that was once in his head was presented to them on the table. He had ripped it clean out of his socket, using the resulting blood to draw the crude spell. Alice studied his circle, his aura a pale grey with flecks of green. It looked sick but strong.

"You mock our religion," Gordon sneered as he clenched his blood -soaked fists. "You don't understand what we need to do."

"How are you doing this?" Peyton asked as Gordon chuckled in response.

Alice shook her head again, the feeling of water still there. She flexed out her chi, wanting to touch his to help understand. She stretched it out for a fleeting second before she heard a snap, it resonating back like an elastic band.

"FUCK!" she yelled as she jumped. It had hurt, her whole body feeling as if she had been stung.

"I wouldn't do that if I were you."

"You do realise you're not human." Alice snapped, the sudden pain fuelling her anger. "Nobody human can do this." Not that she truly knew what he was.

"My Breed status means nothing. It doesn't mean the world isn't corrupt," he growled.

Alice noticed his arm move, almost touching his circle by accident. She needed to aggravate him, force him to pop it.

"We never said it wasn't, but people like you are the reason behind the corruption..."

"It's people like me who have the courage to try to stop it!" Gordon screeched before he started to snigger that turned into a deep belly laugh. "I have my job to do, as you have yours."

Gordon reached for the circle, a toothy grin on his face as he touched the bubble for it to pop. Alice jumped forward, her arm instinctively covering her eyes as smoke erupted around her, choking.

"ALICE DON'T!"

"SKYE?"

"FUCK!"

Eyes watering, she tried to blink through the cloud, unable to see anything. The floor vibrated beneath her feet, the shapes on the ground glowing red before disappearing altogether.

"Nice of you to join us," a voice sniggered.

Spinning she gasped, staring at Mason Storm through a silvery veil. The rest of the smoke dissipated, allowing her to see clearly that she was no longer at the station.

CHAPTER 30

Mason, The Leader and Gordon stood just beyond the silvery veil, a look of smug satisfaction painted on their faces.

Fuck. Fuck. Fuck.

"How did I get here?" she asked, looking around.

Where is here?

"By standing in my circle you followed the pathway," Gordon said as he held his hand to his eye, stemming the blood that continued to flow.

"Just like I knew you would," Mason added, smiling. "Stupid girl."

"My Leader, what are we to do with her?" Gordon asked, seemingly ignoring Mason as he looked expectantly to his right.

"This is not to do with us, my child. Our mission is to continue as we were."

The Leader looked at Alice inquisitively before turning to Mason.

"Mr Storm, I'm sure we will continue with our business shortly. I would appreciate it if you fixed this... loose end."

"Ah, we both know how you deal with loose ends, my friend."

Mason grinned at Alice, dismissing the others. Half his face was bandaged while his nose had a horizontal cut across the bridge and bruising around both of his eyes. At least she'd caught him good. If she weren't in such a highly stressful situation, she would have probably smiled.

"I bet you didn't think you would be seeing me again so soon?"

Alice remained silent, concentrating on her surroundings. She could feel the power vibrating through the concrete beneath her feet as the dark magic oozed from the silver circle surrounding her on all sides. The blood that had painted the floor sizzled, the overwhelming smell of death and bleach assaulting her nose. She wasn't in a pentagram, she was in two circles, one bigger than the other with runes painted in-between. Five smaller circles were equally spaced around touching the outer edge, each with an element smeared inside.

Cold seeped into her bones through her thin jacket as a low beat thumped.

Thump.

Thump. Thump. Thump.

Thump.

"No comment? How unusual for you."

"I have nothing to say," she replied, edging away until she touched the dome, causing pain to sear down her spine. She was trapped.

"Careful," Gordon smirked as he watched her wince. "You're in my circle. Only I can break it."

"I'm sure you're very proud," she said dryly.

Thump.

Thump. Thump. Thump.

Thump.

"This is very tiresome. If you do not mind, Mr Storm, but I will be taking my leave," The Leader said as he held up his hand. "I have no interest in seeing the main show. I will allow Gordon to stay to help you with your... project."

He gave her a last uninterested look before opening a door towards the back, besides two cells. One seemed empty other than a mop and bucket, the other she noticed a topless man kneeling, his face distorted by this dark hair. The cell door was open, the man seemingly stuck by the chains attached to his wrists.

I'm under the church.

She finally noticed the police tape that had been tossed carelessly onto the floor. She licked her dry lips, remaining calm.

Thump.

Thump. Thump. Thump.

Thump.

"You going to explain to me what he meant by 'main show?'" she asked, keeping them in her sight. She had to think of a way out and fast.

What the fuck is that noise?

Mason grinned. "Other than it being good business? I'm sure you would agree with me when I say Valentina needs to be removed from power," Mason continued without pause. "She has become so overwhelmed with her role that she is no longer impartial."

"And I suppose you should take over?"

"Of course. I should sit at the top of The Council, not that child." His face curled up in disgust. "The vampires have too much control under her power, even with their restrictions. Alas, all I needed was to nudge the church in the right direction."

"I thought all members of The Council were equal?"

Mason laughed. "Your ignorance is amusing. How could you possibly compare me to the likes of those animals? Or even a common witch?"

Alice heard a growl, wasn't sure where it was coming from. Her eyes landed on the chained man again, but he remained unmoving. Lights danced across his skin as his whole body tensed, the chains screeching as they were pulled with force. The pattern of the lights she recognised.

"Riley?" she called.

A growl in response.

"RILEY?!" she shouted this time, panic an acid on her tongue.

"My son made an ill-advised mistake," Mason snarled as he hit his hand on the outside of the cell. "I brought him up to trust no one, it's why I was able to chain him. Incompetent. His mother would be so disappointed."

Riley finally looked up, looking towards his father with hate in his eyes. His whole body tensed again, his muscles rigid as the lights flared up across his exposed skin.

Mason struck out once more, hitting Riley across the cheek even as he sagged against the chains. He knelt down, carefully holding his son's face in his hands.

"You were the strongest amongst them all, the leader. You were trained specifically to protect our race, our secrets. Yet your disobedience shames you. It was I who planned The Guardians, it is I who can destroy them."

Riley launched himself forward, making Mason scramble back out of his reach. The chains screeched as they began to stretch, the chain links warping under pressure.

Thump.

Thump. Thump. Thump.

Thump.

"Reckless boy," Mason snarled as he came to his feet. "You shouldn't have questioned me, my son. I have worked my whole life to be where I am, I will not let your conscience ruin it."

He was scared of Riley, she could see it in the way his hands shook, the way his eyes were wide, cautious.

"What have you done?" she asked, wanting to reach Riley as he tensed again, like an electric current was forced through his veins. She watched as a spark crackled through the air, knew it was from the silver cuffs that encircled his wrists.

She needed to get them off him.

Thump.

Thump. Thump. Thump.

Thump. Thump.

"My son still needs to be trained, he must become the Archdruid after me. He will learn. He will sacrifice, as I have."

"Sacrifice what exactly? Your empathy?"

"He will do what is right for our people." Mason turned to Gordon, who had stood there and watched the exchange. "And what is right for our people is to remove you. Permanently."

Gordon smirked, his hand patting against his thigh for another beat.

Thump.

Thump. Thump. Thump.

Thump. Thump.

He was beating her heartbeat.

Alice went to react when she felt the pressure in the

bubble change. Gordon mumbled beneath his breath as the blood runes painted onto the floor glowed with an eerie light. A pop of air behind her made her turn, even as the hair on her arms stood on edge.

"*ARMA!*" Alice screamed as a six foot plus man exploded behind her, his face contorted in rage as his red eyes scanned the room before settling on her. She watched him appraise her aegis shield, his expression turning confused as the horns on his head curled towards his brows. He stepped towards her as the wings behind him folded away, disguising themselves in the black Metallica T-shirt that suddenly appeared over his naked chest. His horns disappeared beneath his dark hair and his skin became pinker, less grey. The only thing that didn't change was his eyes, red and slit like a snake.

"What is this?" The Daemon disguised as a man asked in a smoky voice. "Why have I been called again?"

Alice tried to move back, realising if she went any further she would destroy the only thing protecting her. He gave her a last curious look before dismissing her, his attention on Mason and Gordon.

"This is not part of our agreement," he snarled, his fists clenching as dark veins appeared beneath his skin. Alice clenched her own fists, trying to stop the pulsating ache of her crescent scar. She tried clumsily to reach her harness strapped to her back before realising her blade wasn't there. A glint from the corner of her eye, her weapon laying a few feet away at the edge of the outer circle.

She was trapped in her own aegis inside another circle, without her sword.

Fuck.

"It isn't an agreement if we know your name, slave." Gordon grinned.

"I await the time where I tear your flesh from your bones you snivelling little cu..."

"Xahenort," Mason demanded, forcing the Daemons attention towards him. "We have called you to offer you payment."

"Payment?" Xahenort chuffed. "I have just feasted on four females." He moved towards Alice, his gaze evaluating her. "Why would I want this one?"

Alice hurled herself towards her sword, gritting her teeth as her aura rebounded back when her circle dropped. Kicking the blade up she gripped the hilt.

"ARMA!" She shouted just in time. "Back the fuck off small horns," she snarled, pointing the blade towards him as he loomed.

"That," Mason began," is Alice Draco."

"Draco?" Xahenort looked over her again.

It was weird considering he looked normal with the band T-shirt, ripped skinny jeans and Converse. Except for the eyes.

"I have no interest in this."

"Do you not know who this is? She was being used in a sacrifice..."

"I know who she is. I'm not interested, I have no such wish as my brethren to create an army."

Xahenort looked at her again, his face frowning as he tested her aegis shield with the palm of his hand.

"Is this the reason you called me?" he angrily asked.

"We are running out of blood, use the girl to refuel."

The Daemon caught Alice's eye, talking in a language she didn't recognise. She held the sword out, the runes dancing across the steel. His red eyes flicked to the sword, then back again before repeating the same phrase.

"Le'meloa nirha shilia."

She had no idea what he was asking.

"Stop talking to her!" Gordon shouted.

"Dricania polir shilia?"

"I don't know what you're saying," she explained, stepping back as Xahenort let out an exasperated sigh.

"How can you not speak the tongue of the ancients?" His red eyes narrowed. "Only those of blood can use Fae artefacts such as the blade of Aurora."

"STOP TALKING TO HER!" Gordon shouted once again before turning it into a chant.

"Daemon," Mason demanded its attention. "I will not ask again. Refuel with the girl. We need the blood samples immediately in the lab if we are to continue with our agreement."

"You can only call me because you have my name. That doesn't *control* me." Xahenort returned his attention to Mason before he pressed his palm to the floor, smearing the blood runes with his fingertips then licking the excess. "If I was to replace the blood of the caster with someone else's, this shield will fall." He shot her a look.

This shield will fall?

Alice considered the five points, able to touch part of them that were under the dome.

Replace the blood of the caster.

Alice sliced her hand, letting the blood drip through her fingertips.

Please let him not kill me.

She dropped her defence.

CHAPTER 31

Smoke sizzled as her blood mixed with the rune, creating a crack along the veil. Gordon turned white, Latin tumbling out of his mouth as he tried to keep his circle from falling.

She ran to the next one, smearing her hand across the floor before moving onto the next.

"It's almost time..." Xahenort goaded as his horns pierced through his hair. "I'm coming for you." His wings uncurled from his back, taking up most of the space inside the circle. His hands clawed, nails elongating as his T-shirt and jeans ripped. "You're mine."

Ducking beneath the leathery wings Alice moved to the last rune, her fingertips brushing it as the circle collapsed around her in a burst of sparkle. As Xahenort bounded through his wing caught her, forcing her to the ground as her sword clattered out of her palm.

"Riley!" she called as she scrambled to get back up, her hand reaching for her hilt before it was kicked further away by a black boot, closer to the cages.

"You have done nothing but get in the way," Mason snarled as he kicked her in the ribs, causing her to flip onto her back. He held a dark green ball of aura in his right hand, the energy growing as he pushed it towards her.

Alice rolled at the last second, trying to keep from screaming as the energy began to eat into her aura. She grit her teeth through the pain as she kicked out, hitting Mason in the knee hard enough to cause him to stumble. She searched for her own chi, coating her arms in just enough time to dissipate another ball of energy thrown.

"RILEY!" she shouted, trying to find him through the chaos. He was still in the corner, his face contorted in pain as he rode the electrical current forced through his body.

"He isn't going to help you." Mason reached down to grip her by the throat, pulling her up onto her knees. He seemed to ignore the flames on her arms as she tried to push him away, his eyes on the edge of sanity as he bared his teeth. "I'm really going to enjoy this."

He tightened his fist.

A crash as metal rattled, the noise shattering as it brought Mason's face around. In his distraction she pushed with all her weight, breaking free from his hold as fire ate away at his suit. She lifted a fist, punching him square in the nose with an audible crack. Mason's eyes went wide as blood poured down his face, his hands lifting up as Gordon clattered into him, taking them both down into a heap.

"I'm not finished with you, yet," Xahenort growled, his red eyes glowing as he jumped towards the two fallen men.

Alice moved quickly towards Riley, his dark hair covering his face with his body slumped forward. Her hands shook as she tried to touch the cuffs, her skin burning on contact.

"FUCK!" she cried, shaking her hands before trying again.

His chains had warped, no longer attached to the floor with the lock damaged. His tattoos glowed faintly across his skin, moving gently with each shallow breath.

"Please, wake up!"

She picked up a small chunk of concrete, bringing it down on the lock with all her strength. It shattered into pieces, allowing her to tug at the cuff once more, the metal pulsating beneath her fingertips as an electrical current shot through. She snapped her hands back, waiting for the current to pass before she started on the left cuff, her hands began to blister before it finally came free, falling from his wrist to spark against the floor.

Riley's breathing became less shallow, colour returning to his skin as she started to remove the right one. It moved a centimetre, her skin protesting...

A hand wrapped in her hair, pulling her back.

"I've had enough of this!" Mason screeched. "The Council should be thanking me for getting rid of you."

Heat seared her chest as he pushed his green arcane down, aiming for her heart.

Screaming through the pain she released her chi, the tumultuous energy flowing out of her in blue tendrils that surrounded them. Her blue fire scorched the concrete, aiming for Mason as he stumbled back. The blue devoured his green, absorbing the excess as Mason stared, mouth open in a gasp.

"Impossible!" He flicked out his hand, his chi trying to syphon hers. Control.

She felt her power hesitate, fighting the pressure before becoming stronger, the intense burning evaporating as she felt something caress her aura, adding to the torrential energy already flowing out of her. Silver sparked through her blue, pushing through Mason as if he was nothing.

She could feel something warm drip down her face, the copper settling on her lip as her vision blurred, the edges turning dark. She screamed, pulling the energy back inside before she became overwhelmed. Her power stopped like a faucet, leaving her empty, the absence of everything disconcerting as she fell to her knees.

She blinked, struggling to make out the fight in front of her, the Daemon's wing curled around his great body to act as a blade, the spike at the end of his wing arch sharp. She could no longer feel the pain, her whole body numb as she shook her head, unable to make out any of the noise other than the beat of her own heart that rushed through her head.

Sound came back in a brain- searing rush as she heard the screams of Gordon falling to Xahenort. A movement at the corner of her eye drew her attention to Mason who scrambled to his feet, half his suit burned away to reveal pink scorched flesh.

She pushed with her last bout of energy towards her sword, rolling to her feet with the blade turned to where Mason once stood.

But he was gone.

Taking a deep breath her bruised ribs protested, her vision struggling for clarity as she heard something scrape behind her. Spinning, she held the edge of her sword out, her arm wavering as the last of her strength vanished.

"You know my name," Xahenort said as he approached. He was covered head to toe in blood, the liquid soaking every inch of his large frame. His wings curled behind him, the bottom claw scraping against the concrete as it twitched.

He had ripped Gordon to shreds, pulled him apart with his sheer strength.

She used both her hands to hold her blade, making sure Riley was behind her as she steadied her pulse. Tinkerbell popped around the edge, gliding along the steel in what she hoped was a threatening way.

"I don't want your name."

"Yet, you know it." He tilted his head, his eyes moving to Riley before returning to her. "I am Xahenort, the original, the master of mistakes. In my thousands of years, I have never quite witnessed something like you, Draco." His attention shot to her sword. "Such power, yet you do not understand."

He started to edge towards her, his gaze fascinated as she stepped back, almost collapsing into Riley.

"I have taken my payment. Therefore I will let you be." He took a last look around the carnage, a private smile on his lips. "Until we meet again, War."

Smoke erupted around him, shrouding the room until he was gone.

Sheathing her sword she returned to Riley, his silver mirrored eyes wide open but blank. She ignored the burning sensation as she to pulled the final cuff off, the metal falling off his wrist just as he exploded into a burst of colour.

"Well, you seem to have been busy." A woman's voice laughed.

Alice stood there, unsure whether to concentrate on Valentina who had walked into the room, The Leader's head in her grasp or the wolf-like creature that suddenly stood before her. The beast nudged her out the way, placing himself between them.

"How, lovely." Valentina eyed the gore before settling on the beast, her expression turning to stone.

"Riley?" Alice croaked, her hand shaking as she reached for the pure white fur of the beasts back. Her hand touched silk, the strands soft but heavy. Black patterns decorated across his spine and legs, glyphs that matched the tattoos of the man. "What are you?"

The beast moved closer, his attention on Valentina as he snapped his long jaws in a warning. His head was the shape of a wolf – larger than a shifter with his shoulder hitting her sternum, but his legs were bigger, closer to a lion. Claws uncurled from his paws, as long as his fangs but serrated.

Alice kept her hand in his fur, using him to centre herself.

"How did you find us?" she asked Valentina as the beast growled, the sound smoky.

"I was coming to burn the place down," she said warily, holding The Leaders head up to show them. "Saw this pathetic excuse running away and thought I would bring him back to watch his beloved church fall to cinders." She glanced at the head, his face in permanent terror before she threw it away in disgust. "Pity."

Alice tried to hide her horror at the noise it made when it landed. Valentina carefully moved forward, never taking her eyes off the beast as she floated to observe the markings on the floor.

"Daemons again?" She sniffed as if disgusted. "Councilman Storm has failed again. Whatever should I do with him? Hmm."

Her eyes were completely black when she turned, her dark dress mopping up the blood as she approached. She was ethereal as she slowly reached up, hesitant to the beast as her pale hand touched the blood along Alice's face before gently licking it.

Riley went rigid as he growled again, his jaws opened to show his impressive fangs. His tattoos seemed to pulsate, almost moving across his fur as his long tail separated into several distinct furry whips. He launched at Valentina, his jaws wide but Valentina had already moved.

"Riley?" Alice reached for him, trying to calm him down.

"He isn't there right now," Valentina said as she sucked at her fingers again. "You should ask him one day to explain exactly what his father did to him. What he forced on his own son."

She cackled, even though she stepped back when Riley moved into a crouch.

She was afraid.

"I seem to have taken care of the situation. Thank you for your help Alice, I'll be keeping an eye on you." Valentina backed out, her gaze never leaving Riley's.

"Riley?" Alice bent down to his level, pulling at his fur. "Are you okay? We need to get out of here."

The stench of blood, death and sulphur was overwhelming. She desperately needed to repair her aura, could feel the ache of its loss.

He erupted into light, multi-colours bursting from beneath her palm. Gasping she wrenched her hand back, watching in awe as fur became skin. The coloured lights dimmed, settling into the black and red tattoos across his flesh.

"Riley?" Her voice quivered as she spoke, her legs wobbling before she fell to her knees. "What the actual fuck?"

"We need to get out of here!" Riley shouted as he gripped her arms, pulling her up.

"What the fuck?" She smacked at his naked chest. "You're a... what the? Fuck."

Riley gave her a gentle smile, the emotion not reaching his eyes. "The church is on fire."

"WHAT THE FU..." She smelt it then.

Riley grabbed her arm, pulling her through the church as fire crackled dangerously around them. A black plume of smoke threatened to cut them off before Riley crashed through a window, landing gently on his feet beside a grave. Helping her through Alice turned to watch the church, fire burning from within, fighting its way through the wood and brick.

Riley began to move away, pulling her with him.

"Wait."

He stopped, but he didn't face her. The marks on his arms were already fading, the burns from the cuffs disappearing before her eyes. His tattoos no longer glowed, no longer pulsated.

"We need to talk."

"Here?" He finally turned, his grey irises edging towards silver. "I need to deal with my father."

"We are not to be blamed for our parent's choices."

Or mistakes.

She needed him to understand that.

She couldn't read the emotion etched across his face. He opened his mouth to speak, but didn't.

She collapsed onto the grass, her legs unable to carry her weight, exhausted. Letting out a sigh she moved onto her back so she could watch the church burn.

It would have been beautiful if Xander wasn't blocking the view.

"You look like shit," he said as he began to pull her up before Riley's smoky growl stopped him. He released her hand, letting her drop back onto the wet grass.

Alice sucked in a pained breath, all her cuts and bruises starting to protest.

"Yeah, well, almost dying can do that to you." She shot a look at Riley, his eyes more silver than grey. He seemed fine, even for a man standing butt naked in the snow.

Groaning, she came to her feet, checking over her injuries.

Nothing broken, just a couple scratches and bruises. She couldn't help her grin, or the fist she pumped in the air for victory. Xander looked at her like she was crazy, but she didn't care.

"I need to call this in," she said.

"You need to leave, your aura is fractured and your energy is leaking," Riley said, his voice hoarse.

He was right, she knew that. Instead, she stood there, Riley to her left and Xander to her right and watched as the church crumbled into itself, the fire dancing against the wind as smoke billowed into the sky.

EPILOGUE

Alice played with the handwritten note that had been left on the edge of her bed late one night.

To wear if you ever come to Paris – Valentina.

The ribbon wrapped black package sat untouched in front of her, as it had been for the past week. It felt weird to receive something from Valentina, even weirder that she had left it for her to find inside her home. Was it a threat that she could get in without being discovered? Even Sam hadn't sensed her, and she had broken in when they were both asleep.

"That's a pretty box. You going to open it?" Michelle, Brady's wife asked gently. Alice had just met the woman and instantly knew why Brady had married her, a tender person compared to his great force.

"I suppose so," Alice replied quietly. It had been Jones' idea to throw a party to celebrate closing their first case. Nobody wanted to other than him, but he persuaded them otherwise. They all eventually compromised on a winter BBQ, one at her house.

"Back away from the pit, this is my domain," Sam growled at Brady who kept trying to take over poking the meat.

"You're doing it wrong," Brady grumbled back.

O'Neil watched them with a smile on his face, a bottle of open beer in his hand while Jones chatted beside him excitedly.

A light sprinkling of snow covered the garden, bringing the darkness of the box out in stark contrast. Black wasn't a welcoming colour. Alice pulled at the silk ribbon, letting the fabric drop onto the wooden table before she slid the lid off.

"Wow, that is beautiful," Michelle beamed, looking inside.

"Err, yeah," Alice mumbled. Inside on a velvet pillow sat a satin choker, the centre adorned by a Victorian style pearl cameo surrounded by white diamonds.

"Holy shit baby girl, that from fang face?" Sam whistled as he noticed. "You think that's real?"

Alice quickly shut the box, tying the ribbons back up and pushing it away. She didn't know why Valentina gave her such an extravagant gift. She didn't want it.

It had been several weeks since the last victim, all the contaminated blood in the city caught and destroyed. It was good that the contagion didn't keep, the carriers dying off before they had a chance to start an epidemic. The basement of the church held secret rooms that were only found once the building turned to ash. Rooms that held the personal belongings of around fifty sacrifices.

She felt better about Gordon's and The Leader's deaths more and more each day, especially when she thought about the innocent victims. Mason, on the other hand, had disappeared off the face of the earth. His office had released a statement that he would be unavailable for the foreseeable future. Which basically meant they had no fucking idea where he was. The Council only stated they were in the process of replacing the Councilman. Which also gave no information.

Xander or another one of the ninja wannabes had turned up at her house almost every night, just watching. She wasn't sure why but ignored them for the most part. She had invited them to the BBQ but they had all given her the same strange look.

'Why the fuck would you have a BBQ in December?' They had all asked, which she actually agreed with, but Jones didn't give her much of a choice. When Riley turned up she didn't invite him, his face cold when he asked her to continue their training.

She smiled, slamming the door in his face. She knew he had been busy trying to control the fallout of his family name being smeared across the media, all while negotiating with his father's business partners. But he didn't have to treat her like work.

She wasn't anybody's burden.

"What are you two doing up there?" Peyton called to Sam and Brady, who gave him a dark look in return. He sat beside her, quiet for the most part.

"So, you going to tell me what you are yet?" she asked, sipping her beer. It had become a game between them, she asked him questions that he sometimes answered. She knew for sure he wasn't human, at least, not one- hundred per cent as he claimed. He had turned at the same time as she did back at the station, had felt something as Gordon created his circle. Humans wouldn't have reacted as he did.

He gave her a sideways glance, his lips pressed into a thin line before she saw him smirk. "You want another beer?" he answered instead, standing up.

"Sure," she chuckled, "but be careful about those bloody boggarts." He didn't find it as funny as she did.

"Hey baby girl, can you get the door? I'm worried if I leave, big boy here will take over,' Sam called, scowling at Brady.

"Look, it's getting burnt!" Brady exclaimed as his wife handed him a glass of wine.

"It's probably just Dread," Alice shouted behind her as she made her way through the house. She gave a quick wave to Jordon, who was watching TV from the corner of the living room. Jordan hadn't really done much since Xander had explained he was haunted. The idea that something was moving him around gave Alice the chills, but it wasn't like she could do much about it. He just made his way back home regardless of where she left him.

"Hey, Drea ... oh..." she said as she opened the door.

"Alice," Theo said, nodding in greeting. "I'm glad you're home."

"Hi, can I help you?" She looked around for Roman, couldn't see him skulking around. "Where's your brother?"

"That's what I'm here about, actually," Theo said, sounding nervous. His hair was messy as if he hadn't brushed it in a while, and the shirt he wore was creased.

"Are you okay?"

He looked ill, his tone taking on a grey tinge that didn't look healthy. It brought the scar that sliced through his face out in contrast.

"No." He shook his head, anxiously reaching up to move his hair from his face. "We've found Rex."

Alice tried to hide her reaction at hearing his name. She didn't want anything to do with him, felt no guilt that he had run from his consequences. Especially since hearing what the bracelet he gave her did. For all she cared he could stay missing.

Yet, the look on Theo's face made her feel sick. "What's happened?"

"He's been arrested. They're going to execute him."

Alice stood there, unsure what to say.

Fuck.

The End of Book Two

This series continues with Rogue's Mercy: Buy here!

A personal note from Taylor

I hope you enjoyed Druid's Storm! If you want to show your support, I would really appreciate you leaving a review from the store you purchased. Reviews are super important and help other readers discover this series!

Check me out on Facebook, Instagram and TikTok!

Continue reading for an excerpt of Rogue's Mercy, Alice Skye book three.

ROGUE'S MERCY

Alice felt her nerves jump as she was patted down for the third time, her sword, gun and knife already removed and placed into a locked metal box at reception.

"Do you understand the rules?" the man who was getting too personal with her bra strap asked as he finished checking her for contraband. If he pinged it once more she wouldn't be responsible for her actions.

"Your colleague explained."

"Just so you understand, we have zero tolerance on rule breaking. This is a maximum security Breed prison."

No shit, Sherlock, she thought to herself as she tried to smile friendlily at him.

"There will be a maximum of five minutes with the inmate. He will remain in his cell, behind bars. There will be no touching."

"Does he know I'm coming?" She felt sick, panic rising as she fought her anxiety. The only reason Tinkerbell hadn't popped into existence to torment her was the anti-magic enchantments carved every few feet on the thick stone walls.

She didn't want to see him.

But knew she had to.

"He is aware he has a visitor. We do not give our inmates details as it sometimes riles them up."

Well, this is going to go well.

"Please, follow me."

Alice walked behind the guard as he accessed the locked door, the heavy metal bars swinging open with an audible groan as she was ushered through, the door quickly locked again behind her.

The stone walls continued throughout, creating a dark hallway with only flickers of candle light. Open archways opened out into slightly larger rooms that held four separate cells each. She could hear murmuring, crying as well as desperate spells muttered into the dark. Ones that were absorbed by all the anti-magic enchantments and totems that hung from the high ceilings.

The prison was erected inside a medieval castle. While the outside had been modernised, inside hadn't been touched Torches and small candles were the only source of light, the arched windows bricked in to the point they kept the stench of unwashed bodies thick at the back of your throat.

"Hello beautiful."

"Hey, whore."

"Oi, pretty lady. Come over here for a bit, I won't hurt ya. I got something thick and juicy you can..."

Inmates called at her, their faces appearing in the thin gaps between the thick metal bars as they blew kisses and gestured obscenely.

"GET BACK!" the guard shouted as he hit the bars

with his metal baton, the resonating noise a horrible high pitched twang that set her teeth on edge. "He's just through here."

They walked through one last archway, the torches closer together to allow more light to penetrate.

"This is the waiting wing," he said as an explanation. "Your guy is the furthest to the left. I'll be back in five minutes. There is nowhere for you to go, and every inmate is strictly behind bars. I would recommend you don't get too curious with the other cells without risking your face being ripped off."

"Duly noted," she replied dryly.

Alice took a deep breath, instantly regretting it before she stepped into the room, ignoring the curious looks from the few inmates who were to her right. As she walked she noticed most of the cells empty, the rooms looking reasonable with neatly made cot-beds and clean metal sinks. The exception was the blood smeared scratch marks that scored some of the floors and walls.

She felt her heart race as she approached his cell, hoped nobody had strong enough hearing to notice. It was weirdly tidy when she stopped, his bed made with military precision and his food bowl and tray washed up by the sink. His back was to her, his black T-shirt dusty and ripped, reminding her of when she had seen him in Dread's office what felt like a lifetime ago.

Alice fought her instant guilt at seeing him behind the thick bars. It was strange considering she knew why he was there, that he deserved it. Yet, after giving it much thought she understood his actions. She wasn't confident she wouldn't have done the same thing in his situation. It was then she knew she would stand with his brothers at the court, stand against Xavier who was the judge, jury and executioner.

She had never met The Councilman who stood on behalf of all shifters, a tiger with a vicious reputation for death.

He sensed her then, his back tensing as a growl resonated across the stone.

Buy Now!

ABOUT THE AUTHOR

Taylor Aston White loves to explore mythology and European faerie tales to create her own, modern magic world. She collects crystals, house plants and dark lipstick, and has two young children who like to 'help' with her writing by slamming their hands across the keyboard.

After working several uncreative jobs and one super creative one she decided to become a full-time author and now spends the majority of her time between her children and writing the weird and wonderful stories that pop into her head.

www.taylorastonwhite.com